Praise for Marta Perry

"Perry skillfully continues her chilling,
deceptively charming romantic suspense series with
a dark, puzzling mystery that features a sweet romance
and a nice sprinkling of Amish culture."
—*Library Journal* on *Vanish in Plain Sight*

"Marta Perry illuminates the differences between the
Amish community and the larger society with an obvious
care and respect for ways and beliefs…. She weaves these
differences into the story with a deft hand, drawing the
reader into a suspenseful, continually moving plot."
—*Fresh Fiction* on *Murder in Plain Sight*

"*Leah's Choice,* by Marta Perry, is a knowing
and careful look into Amish culture and faith.
A truly enjoyable reading experience."
—Angela Hunt, *New York Times* bestselling author
of *Let Darkness Come*

"*Leah's Choice* is a story of grace and servitude
as well as a story of difficult choices and
heartbreaking realities. It touched my heart. I think
the world of Amish fiction has found a new champion."
—Lenora Worth, author of *Code of Honor*

"Marta Perry delivers a strong story of tension, fear and
trepidation. *Season of Secrets* (4.5 stars) is an excellent
mystery that's certain to keep you in constant suspense.
While love is a powerful entity in this story,
danger is never too far behind."
—*RT Book Reviews*, Top Pick

MARTA PERRY

HOME
by
DARK

HARLEQUIN®
entertain, enrich, inspire™

Recycling programs
for this product may
not exist in your area.

ISBN-13: 978-0-373-77735-8

HOME BY DARK

Dear Reader,

Thank you for choosing to read the first book in my new Amish suspense series, which is set in a fictional community in my own part of Pennsylvania. I'm finding it a delicate balancing act but also great fun to combine the real places I know with my fictional community.

The Amish attitude toward nonviolence plays a large role in *Home by Dark*. It's sometimes difficult for people in the larger community to reconcile the very law-abiding nature of Amish life with the reluctance of the Amish to become involved with the law and its representatives. This attitude dates back to the earliest years of the Amish faith, when Amish were persecuted and killed by the law and government of the time. For the most part, an Amish person is more likely to forgive and/or ignore a crime against them by an outsider than to seek help from the police, and that attitude permeates the events of my story.

I hope you'll let me know how you felt about this story, and I'd love to send you a signed bookmark or my brochure of Pennsylvania Dutch recipes. You can write to me at Harlequin HQN, 233 Broadway, Suite 1001, New York, NY 10279, email me at marta@martaperry.com or visit me on the web at www.martaperry.com.

Blessings,

Marta Perry

This story is dedicated to my grandson, Bjoern Jacob.
And, as always, to Brian, with much love.

The gem cannot be polished without friction,
nor the person perfected without trials.
—Amish proverb

PROLOGUE

The DESERTED BARN loomed ahead of them, broken beams jutting up toward the darkening sky like menacing fingers. Benjamin Weaver shivered, and the gas cans Will had made him carry clanked together.

Will's head jerked around at the sound. "Keep it quiet." His voice was a low mutter of Pennsylvania Dutch. "You want to get us arrested?"

"Told you we shouldn't've brought him." Joseph Stoltz frowned at him. Both the older boys wore *Englisch* clothes, and they'd snickered at Benj for showing up dressed Amish.

All very well for them to put on jeans and T-shirts. They were both old enough to have started their *rumspringa,* and parents turned a blind eye to such clothes then. But he was only fourteen, and Daad would skin him if he found Benj in a getup like that. Daad had been upset enough lately with Benj's oldest sister, Rachel, coming back to town and not being Amish anymore.

He shivered again, half with cold, half with fear of where this adventure was taking him. It grew chilly at night this early in June, especially out here on the wooded hillside. He hadn't thought to bring a jacket when he'd crawled out his window and slid down the roof of the woodshed. He'd been too excited that Will and Joseph were letting him come along to think about that.

Now his mind was churning, and he didn't like what it was telling him. That it was a mistake for him to get involved, that he'd be shaming Daad and Mammi, that—

A loud creak sounded through the trees, and Benj didn't need Will Esch's gesture to drop to his knees behind the closest fallen log. Another sound from up ahead, one that he couldn't identify. Why would anyone be up here in the woods overlooking Deer Run at night? Nobody'd be interested in that falling-down old barn.

Nobody but Will, who figured it would make a fine blaze up there on top of the hill for the whole village to see. Benj eased his hands away from the gas cans and rubbed clammy palms on his pants. He'd thought they were just going to splash paint on the barn, not start a fire. He should have had better sense than to get involved in one of Will's schemes.

Will leaned over. "I'll go check it out," he whispered. "Wait for my signal, *ja?*"

With Will's eyes on him, Benj could only nod. Too late now for second thoughts.

Will slipped over the log and slithered through the trees toward the barn. Benj leaned against the rough bark, wishing he was home in his bed. Will was moving quickly—Benj could see him, a dark shadow weaving through the trees. He'd be at the barn in a minute.

Benj turned away, sliding down to sit on the ground. In no time they'd hear Will whistle. Benj would have no choice but to pick up the gas cans and go along. Will was right about one thing. That dry old wood would make a fine blaze. But if they got caught...

He'd never seen an Englisch jail, but it seemed a pretty fair guess he wouldn't like it.

"What's taking so long?" Joseph muttered, peering over the log. "I can't see him—"

He broke off at the sound of a motor. Lights swept through the trees, and Benj's heart stopped. A vehicle was coming up the old logging road toward the barn. If Will was seen—

A man's voice, shouting. Then, incredibly, a shotgun cracked through the woods, sending crows lifting in a noisy cloud from the trees. Benj was frozen, wits dazed by the sound.

And then Will vaulted over the log, shoving him with a hard hand. "Run," he ordered.

Benj scrambled to his feet, following Will, with Joseph a step behind him, bolting through the brush. Another report, a branch crashing to the ground, and he was running as hard and fast as he could, running as if the devil himself were at his heels, crashing through the undergrowth heading down the hill and toward the road, if they got to the road they'd be safe, no one would shoot there.

An eternity later they stumbled out onto the macadam of the two-lane road that wound through Deer Run. Across the way was Mason House, where his sister Rachel lived now. He could go to Rachel, he could tell her—

Will grabbed his arm, shook him. "Where's the cans?"

Benj blinked, then jerked his head toward the hillside. "Back there."

"Dummy." Will shoved him. "*Ach,* they can't tell who we were from that. All we've gotta do is keep quiet."

Joseph, always more cautious than Will, moved nervously. "But they were shooting. We should—"

"You should be quiet, like I tell you," Will snarled. "You didn't see anything, you don't say anything, not to anyone. Got that?"

He spun, grabbing Benj by the shirt. "Answer me. You got that?"

Benj nodded. He hadn't seen anything—that was for sure. Just a dark shape, wielding what had to be a shotgun. And right now he didn't know whether he was more afraid of Will or the man with the gun.

CHAPTER ONE

SOMETHING WAS WRONG WITH her little brother. Rachel Weaver Mason swept the paint roller along the wall of what would be the registration area for her bed-and-breakfast, darting a sideways glance at her brother Benjamin.

Benjamin knelt on the drop cloth, straw-colored hair hiding his eyes, as he carefully cut in the edge of cream paint next to the woodwork. Benj might be only fourteen, but like most Amish youth, he possessed a number of practical skills, along with a strong work ethic. He'd said he'd help her with the painting, and he'd turned up bright and early this morning for what he called a work frolic.

Rachel suppressed a faint twinge at the expression. With any ordinary Amish family, a dozen or more relatives would have shown up at the word she needed help with the house her mother-in-law had so surprisingly left her.

But she was not Amish any longer. Running away to marry Ronnie Mason at eighteen, leaving behind her home, her family and her faith, had put a period to that part of her life. Even though she'd come back to Deer Run in the end, a widow with a nine-year-old daughter to support, she couldn't expect to be treated as anything other than an outsider.

Only Benj, the little brother she'd hardly expected to remember her, looked at her as if she were family. The one time she'd seen her father since she'd returned, Daad had been as stiff and polite as if he'd never seen her before, and her heart still ached at the pain of that reception.

Was Daad hurting at the distance between them as well? Maybe so, but he'd never show it, and Mose, the brother who'd always been as close as a twin to her, copied Daad's attitude.

Maybe that was better than seeing the pain and longing in her mother's eyes. Mamm wanted her daughter back, wanted to be close to the granddaughter she barely knew, but Rachel's return couldn't wipe out the grief of her leaving. As for the two younger sisters who were little more than children when she'd left—well, Naomi and Lovina watched her as warily as a robin might eye a prowling cat.

"New paint makes it look better, for sure." Benj sat back on his heels, glancing up at her with eyes as blue as her own.

Innocent eyes, but holding an edge of worry that didn't belong there. Benj shouldn't be jumping at sudden sounds and glancing warily around corners. That wasn't normal.

"Was ist letz?" The question came out of her

without conscious thought in Pennsylvania Dutch, maybe because that was the language of her heart. "What's wrong, Benj? Are you worried about something?"

His hand jerked, depositing a drop of cream paint on the woodwork, and he bent to wipe it off with concentrated care. Benj was outgrowing the blue shirt he wore, his wrists sticking out of the sleeves, and the back of his neck was as vulnerable as her daughter Mandy's.

"Worried?" he said finally, not looking at her. "I got nothing to worry about, ain't so?" He tried to make it sound light, but his voice shook a little.

Rachel wanted to touch his shoulder, to draw him into her arms for comforting the way she would have when he was four. But she'd left then, abandoning him as she had the rest of the family. The fact that he seemed willing to start fresh with her didn't mean she could go back to the way things once were.

"I don't mean to pry," she said, choosing the words carefully. "But if you ever want to tell me anything at all, I can keep it to myself."

Benj seemed frozen, brush poised an inch from the wall. She held her breath, willing him to speak.

Then Mandy came clattering down the stairs, jumping the last few as if in too much of a hurry to take them one at a time, and the opportunity was gone.

"My room is all cleaned up," she announced. "Can I help paint now?"

Mandy had obviously fixed her own hair this morning. The honey-colored braids were loose enough that strands already worked their way free of the bands, and the part was slightly erratic.

"No pictures of puppies on the wall?" Benjamin grinned at Mandy, his troubles apparently forgotten for the moment.

"I'm way past that," she said loftily.

Rachel caught back a chuckle before Mandy could think she was being laughed at. Only nine, and Mandy sometimes sounded more like a teenager than Benjamin.

As for Benj, he treated Mandy like a little sister rather than the niece she actually was, to the obvious pleasure of both of them. He even had Mandy saying a few phrases in Pennsylvania Dutch.

"You can paint if you're careful." Rachel reminded herself that she'd wielded a pretty mean paintbrush at Mandy's age. Amish children learned to work alongside their parents almost from the time they could walk. "You can use this roller, and I'll go up the stepladder and do the top part."

"It's going to look so neat." Mandy grabbed the roller, and Rachel steadied her arm for the first few strokes. "It was nice of my grandmother to leave us her house, wasn't it? I wish we could have visited her."

Rachel used climbing the stepladder as a pretext for not answering the implied question. She certainly wasn't going to tell Mandy that the grandmother she'd been named after hadn't ever invited them to come, not even when Ronnie died.

Amanda Mason had known how to hold a grudge, and Ronnie had been just as bad. Well, he'd been hurt, and he'd tried to mask it by insisting he didn't care. His mother had always taken such pride in him that he hadn't expected her iron opposition to his marriage. He'd been so sure she'd come around, but she never did. Rachel's throat tightened, and she swallowed, trying to relax it.

Mandy swept the roller along the wall. "When it's all finished, then we'll start having guests, won't we, Mommy?"

"I hope so."

If they didn't... Well, she wouldn't go there. Ronnie had left nothing for his widow and child but a few debts, and his mother's gift of the house hadn't included an income to run it on. But Mrs. Mason had left a trust fund to cover Mandy's education, to Rachel's everlasting gratitude.

Mandy wouldn't be tossed out into an unforgiving world with an eighth-grade education, the way Rachel had been, per Amish custom. That was a little fact neither she nor Ronnie, wrapped in the glow of first love, had taken into consideration.

"That's not so bad." Benjamin was studying Mandy's efforts. "*Chust* don't go too close to the woodwork, *ja?* I'll do that with the brush."

"*Ja,*" Mandy echoed, her face serious and intent. Usually Rachel thought Mandy looked like her father, with that honey-colored hair and those changeable green eyes, but sometimes, as now, her expression was like looking into a mirror.

Benjamin moved over to paint next to Mandy, grinning at her, his face relaxed as he said something teasing to her about finishing first. His expression reassured Rachel. Surely there couldn't be anything seriously wrong, or he wouldn't be laughing with Mandy, would he?

She'd been jumping to conclusions, maybe putting her own worries and fears onto him. He was probably—

The front door rattled with a knock and opened. Rachel turned, brush in hand, and whatever she'd been about to think was forgotten when she looked at Benjamin. Eyes wide with fear or shock, body rigid, a muscle visibly twitching by his mouth.

She'd been right to begin with. Something was very wrong with her little brother.

Rachel forced herself to glance aside. Benj was at a sensitive age—he wouldn't like knowing he'd given himself away to her.

And she found her stomach jolting as she looked instead at Colin McDonald. He stood in her hallway, seeming as cool and relaxed as if he were in his own house. But then, nothing ever did ruffle Colin. Whether he'd been driving his truck far too fast up a mountain road or winning a bet by climbing to the top of steep slate roof on the Presbyterian church, he'd never betrayed a tremor. A challenge might bring a little added spark to his cool gray eyes, but that was all.

"Colin." Belatedly realizing she was on the step-ladder, paintbrush in hand, she climbed down, telling her nerves to unclench. "I didn't expect to see you today."

Or any other day, for that matter, but that was wishful thinking. Now that she was back in Deer Run, seeing Colin would be inevitable.

He arched an eyebrow, giving her the smile that had charmed most of the females in the township at one time or another. Even her, for a few brief moments, until she'd realized what he was really like.

"How could an old friend like me not come to welcome you back?" He glanced at the paint she'd managed to accumulate on her hands. "Don't think I'll offer to shake hands, though. Or give you a hug."

Same Colin, always just a bit superior. But she wasn't a shy little Amish girl any longer.

"Afraid of getting your hands dirty?" She let her gaze sweep over the spotless khaki pants and blue polo shirt he wore. Perfect as always. That strand of blue-black hair tumbling onto his forehead and the laughter in his eyes just added to the image of someone who had it all together.

It was that exterior, so Ronnie said, that had fooled adults into believing that whoever had caused a particular bit of mischief, it couldn't have been Colin.

His expression seemed to grant her a point. "Just

not dressed for painting, that's all." He let his gaze move on past her. "Hi, Benj. And here's Mandy, all grown up."

"Mandy, this is Mr. McDonald, an old friend of your daddy's. Benj…" But her brother was gone, sliding through the door to the kitchen with an unintelligible murmur.

Colin looked after him. "What's wrong with Benjamin? He and I are old friends, and he's looking at me as if I were a zombie."

"A zombie?" Mandy inquired. "What's that?"

"Like an ogre," Rachel said quickly, before Colin could attempt to explain. "From a fairy tale." She hadn't been able to give Mandy the safe, protected childhood she'd had, but she'd tried to guard her from the worst of current culture.

Mandy nodded, small face serious, and Rachel could practically see her storing that information away. Then Mandy pinned Colin with an assessing gaze.

"You don't look like an ogre," she observed.

"I'm not," he said quickly. "That was a joke, because Benj ran off when I came in."

"He didn't run off," Rachel said, exasperated at the turn the conversation had taken. "He's gone to the kitchen for some lemonade, that's all. Mandy, you can go and have a snack, too, while I talk to Mr. McDonald. Then we'll get back to work."

With a lingering glance at Colin, Mandy walked

toward the kitchen and disappeared from view. And, Rachel trusted, from earshot.

She turned back to Colin, hoping he'd take the hint and make this visit brief. She found him surveying her quizzically, making her uncomfortably aware of her frayed jeans and the oversize old shirt of Ronnie's she'd found in the closet. Why couldn't he have come when she was looking her best, not her worst? Not that she cared, she reminded herself.

"Trying to protect your daughter from my bad influence?" he asked.

Rachel felt her cheeks grow warm. "What makes you think that?"

He ignored the question, taking a casual step closer to her. She'd thought the past ten years hadn't changed him much, but she was suddenly aware that he was taller and broader than he used to be. The athletic boy had matured into a man.

Physically, maybe. Somehow she guessed that the teenage hell-raiser wasn't far under the civilized surface.

"You always did think I was a bad influence on Ronnie, didn't you?" Those cool gray eyes pinned her in place, and Rachel found her pulse fluttering erratically.

She'd had good reason to know it, but before she could attempt an answer, he stepped back with a rueful smile.

"Never mind. There's seldom any point in revisiting the past, is there?"

"I guess not." Too bad she did so much of it, especially now.

"Anyway, to business. You know I've taken over my dad's real estate firm, don't you?"

"No, I didn't." She hadn't been back long enough to get caught up on all the local news, and this particular item was a surprise. "What happened to the guy who said he'd never come back to this one-horse town?"

"He grew up." Colin clipped off the words, as if that might be a sore subject. "So Amanda Mason left this mausoleum to you, did she?" He sent a disparaging glance around the high-ceilinged hall, a few shreds of floral wallpaper still visible that Rachel had missed in her scraping. "Was that her way of punishing you for marrying her precious boy—to saddle you with this white elephant?"

"I don't know what was in her mind," Rachel said carefully. Colin didn't need to know how astonished she'd been to be contacted by her mother-in-law's attorney after all those years of pointed silence. "But it was very kind of her."

"Kind?" He looked at her as if she were crazy. "How would you like to list it with me?"

"List...?" Her mind went blank.

"Put it on the market." He said the words slowly, as if she were deficient in understanding. "You probably know it's a terrible time to be selling, but I think I can still get a decent price for you, as long as you're not expecting the moon and the stars." He paced toward the stairwell, as if mentally measuring the hallway.

Real estate market, of course. "That's kind of you, Colin, but I don't plan to sell."

Colin stopped in midstride, turning to give her an incredulous look. "You can't intend to live here."

That was a comment she'd made to herself a number of times in the past month, but hearing him say it made her bristle. "Why not? It's my house now."

"It's a wreck," he said bluntly. "I don't know what Amanda was thinking, but she let the place go in her final years. You'd have to sink a fortune in it to get it back the way it was, and I don't suppose she left you that."

"No." Just the house, a small yearly amount to pay the taxes and enough in a trust fund for Mandy's education.

"Well then, the only thing to do is sell the place." He made it sound as if she had no choice, but she did.

"I'm not going to sell. I'm going to run it as a bed-and-breakfast."

Colin stared at her, expressionless. "You've got to be kidding," he said finally. "Unless you've got an independent income, you can't expect to get by that way."

Rachel lifted her chin. Too bad she hadn't stayed on the ladder, so she could look down at him.

"Mandy and I will be fine, thank you. Mason House should go to my daughter, and I intend to keep it running until then."

"You'll be lucky if you don't starve, the pair of you. Jeannette Walker does okay at The Willows, but she's been at the B and B business a long time." He shook his head, turned away in frustration and then spun back.

"Look, did Ronnie leave you anything at all to fall back on?"

She stiffened. "I can't imagine why you think you have the right to inquire into my finances."

Colin's eyes narrowed. "I have the right to be concerned about my best friend's child."

"You saw Ronnie…what—once in ten years? I hardly think that qualifies you as a best friend." She stopped, took a breath, forced down the angry words that, once spoken, could never be taken back.

"That should put me in my place, right?" He gave her a crooked smile. "But I've never been very good at taking hints."

"Colin—" Should she apologize? But she hadn't said anything but the truth.

"Not very good at minding my own business, either." He walked to the door and then glanced back at her, hand on the knob. "I'll be around, Rachel. I promise."

The door closed behind him, leaving her wondering why that promise should sound remarkably like a threat.

COLIN HADN'T EVEN reached the steps of the wrap-around porch when the truth reared its head. He'd messed up badly, antagonizing Rachel instead of gaining her cooperation. The mixture of guilt and something he hesitated to call attraction had played havoc with his self-control.

Not that Rachel had controlled her temper very well, either. She'd come a long way, it seemed, from the shy, innocent little Amish girl she'd been. Her heart-shaped face and sky-blue eyes still had a slight hint of vulnerability, though, and even with her blond hair pulled back, no makeup and wearing a baggy shirt, he'd felt...well, something.

But this Rachel had given back as good as she'd gotten, with a quick flare of antagonism at what she undoubtedly saw as his interference. Small wonder. Marriage to Ronnie Mason would try the patience of a saint.

Colin went slowly down the steps to the walk, the carved wooden railing wobbling under his touch. If Rachel really intended to open this place as a bed-and-breakfast, she'd have to get that fixed before she had a lawsuit on her hands.

He stood back, glancing up at the house. A three-story Victorian, it towered over everything else in the village. Literally towered, since the whimsical Queen Anne design boasted an actual round tower at one corner, forming circular bays in the parlor and the room above it.

Deer Run hadn't changed all that much in the

hundred and some years since Mason House had gone up. Probably the best thing that could have happened to the village was the decision not to run a state route through the collection of homes and stores.

Deer Run had subsided into undisturbed rural slumber, eventually becoming a bedroom community for nearby Williamsport. The Mason place and, across the road, the Sitler place, a not-quite-so-imposing Victorian, formed the west end of the straggle of homes mixed with businesses that was Deer Run.

Colin had to admit that Mason House was considerably more appealing, even in its current state, than The Willows, the only other bed-and-breakfast in town. Even the weeping willow in the side yard was bigger than the one that gave Jeannette Walker's place its name.

Still, this was a crazy idea on Rachel's part. He didn't suppose Ronnie would have left her anything. Or have had life insurance. Ronnie had thought himself immortal—an excusable folly in an eighteen-year-old, but not in a grown man with a wife and child to support.

And now Rachel was about to compound the folly by sinking whatever little money she did have into this white elephant. She and the child would end up worse off than they'd started.

He reached the end of the walk and turned right. The sensible thing for Rachel to do was sell up. The antique furnishings would be worth a tidy sum, he'd think, even if he had trouble getting rid of the house for her. And she wouldn't need to know that he'd forego his commission on the sale.

She could start over someplace away from the memories this place had to evoke, away from the family that didn't seem ready to accept her.

With the exception of her little brother, apparently. Benj was a good kid, and he'd have been too small when Rachel left to know what a turmoil her decision had caused. At least she had him to give her a hand.

Colin's eyes narrowed. Rachel had been wrong about one other thing. Benj wasn't in the kitchen having lemonade. From where he stood now, Colin could see the boy slipping toward one of the dilapidated outbuildings behind the main house. *Sneaking* was actually the word that came to mind. Benj glanced around, the movement furtive, before disappearing into what had once been a stable.

What was the kid up to? He knew Benj pretty well, or as well as an Englischer was likely to know an Amish kid. The boy had been doing yard work for him for over a year. He'd have said Benj Weaver was the last person to have something to hide. It appeared he'd have been wrong.

Making a quick decision, Colin started across the lawn, skirting the willow tree. Benj hadn't come out yet. What could he find to interest him in the old stable? Maybe Rachel had asked the boy to check it out for some reason, in which case Colin was going to look like an interfering busybody.

He neared the stable and glanced toward the house, half-expecting to see Rachel's face at one of the windows, looking at him disapprovingly. But there was no sign of her. The stable door hung open, sagging on its hinges. Not touching it, he leaned over to look inside.

The interior had become the repository for everything that wasn't wanted in the main house—lumber piles, a couple of old bicycles, a massive chest of drawers, a miscellaneous collection of discarded furniture. A narrow passageway, almost roofed over with boxes, made its way through the chaos. Benj was on his knees, head poked into the opening.

"Looks like a good place to hide," Colin said, keeping his voice casual.

Benj jerked, banging his head on a crate. He edged out, rubbing his head, and sat back on his heels, eyeing Colin warily.

"I guess you could keep Mandy busy playing hide-and-seek out here," he suggested.

Benj's face cleared. "*Ja*. It would be a *gut* hide-out."

"Better be careful, though. Probably plenty of rusty nails mixed in with this junk. You don't want her to have to get a tetanus shot."

"I…I'll be careful." Benj swallowed, the muscles of his neck working, and shot another furtive glance around.

Colin leaned an elbow on the nearest crate and immediately regretted it. He'd have to change his shirt before he headed back to the office.

"I haven't seen you for a while, Benj. What have you been up to lately?"

There was no mistaking the flash of fear in the boy's face before he ducked his head. "Not much." He shrugged. "Helping Rachel is all."

Colin studied him thoughtfully. Something was clearly wrong, but like most adolescent males, Benj wasn't about to turn to a grown-up for help. Colin remembered that stage only too well. Still, how much trouble could an Amish kid get into in a place like Deer Run?

"Well, if you're helping your sister, maybe you'd better get back at it," he said.

Benj gave a quick nod, hopped to his feet and darted out the door without another word.

Colin watched him run across the lawn, then turned and glanced at the small opening in the piles of junk. He might, if he had to, be able to worm his way through there, but not today.

He stepped back out into the June sunshine, frowning thoughtfully at the back of the house. Whatever it was Benj thought he needed a hideout for, Colin doubted that it was an innocent game of hide-and-seek. But what on earth could a kid like Benjamin have to hide? And what was causing that spark of fear in his eyes?

CHAPTER TWO

BY MIDAFTERNOON, the early enthusiasm Mandy had shown for painting had predictably waned. Benj was quite willing to keep on working, but Rachel decided they'd all had enough for one day. The entrance hall painting was finished, and the prospect of starting another room seemed too daunting.

"Why don't you show Mandy the outbuildings?" she suggested. "She's wanted to explore, and I haven't had time to go with her."

"Sure thing." Benj wiped his hands on the edge of the old sheet she'd used to cover the marble-topped stand in the hall. He grinned at Mandy. "*Komm, schnell.* You remember what that means?"

"Come quick," Mandy said promptly. "Bet I can beat you to the back door." She darted toward the kitchen, with Benj letting her get a head start.

It was a relief to see her little brother acting normally again. "*Denke*, Benj. I know I can count on you to keep Mandy from trying anything too daring."

A shadow crossed his face at what had surely

been an innocent remark. Then he nodded, smiled and chased after Mandy.

Rachel frowned after him for a moment before going into the powder room that had taken the place of a large closet once Amanda Mason had decided she didn't care to go up and down the stairs too often. A quick washing got rid of most of the paint stains, but the face that stared back at Rachel from the mirror still wore the worried frown that had become almost a permanent fixture in recent months.

She forced a smile, trying to counteract the effect. With her hair pulled back from a center part and the lack of makeup, she looked…well, not like the Amish girl who had run away with Ronnie Mason. That girl had had rosy cheeks and stars in her eyes. With her hair pulled back and sans makeup, this was closer to the Amish woman she would have turned into had young love, in the shape of Ronnie, not intervened.

Splashing some cold water on her face, Rachel turned away from the mirror. Dwelling on the past was seldom a good idea, as Colin had said, and she'd been doing too much of that lately. She couldn't build a future on *what-ifs*.

Besides, she had Mandy. Fierce maternal love surged through her. Mandy was worth any sacrifice. The doubts Colin had voiced were the ones that kept her up at night, but she couldn't listen to them. She would make a success of her plans because Mandy's security and happiness depended upon them.

The house seemed empty with Benj and Mandy gone. She crossed the hallway and headed out the front door. She might as well check and see if any mail had found her at her new address yet.

The long porch across the front was one of the house's beauties. In her mind's eye, Rachel could see it the way she intended it to be, its gingerbread trim freshly painted, geraniums blooming in pots and hanging baskets, with comfortable rockers where her guests could relax.

She grasped the railing as she started down the steps, and it wobbled under her hand. Yet another thing she'd have to fix. She'd make up in hard work what she lacked in money.

The mailbox stood on a post next to the road, since Deer Run wasn't big enough to warrant a mail carrier who walked from house to house. She pulled it open, finding an electric bill that had apparently chased her from the rental apartment in Philadelphia and what appeared to be a complimentary copy of the *County Gazette*, a weekly newspaper that was primarily composed of advertisements.

Holding it conjured up an image of Daadi reading through it, word by word, after he'd finished reading *The Budget*, the Amish newspaper that kept far-flung Amish communities in touch. She could see him so vividly, sitting in the wooden rocker next to the gas stove, his drugstore reading glasses sliding down his nose.

"Rachel? It is Rachel Weaver, isn't it? I mean,

Rachel Mason, of course." The woman who'd hailed her hurried across the road after a cautious look in both directions.

Rachel waited, heart sinking. She'd been reasonably certain she could count on a call from Helen Blackwood, an elderly crony of her late mother-in-law, but she'd hoped to be a little better prepared for it. All the people in Deer Run she least wanted to see seemed determined to find her when she looked like a bag lady.

Not, she supposed, that Helen Blackwood would use those words. Having spent her entire life in Deer Run, Helen's knowledge of the wider world was probably limited to whatever she watched on television.

The woman had nearly reached her, and Rachel arranged what she hoped was a welcoming smile on her face. "Miss Blackwood, how nice to see you. I hope you're well."

"Right as rain." The woman's returning smile was somewhat guarded, as if she questioned her welcome. "But do call me Helen. After all, I was your mother-in-law's greatest friend."

"Helen," Rachel repeated, trying to infuse some warmth into the word. His mother's shadow—that was how Ronnie had referred to Helen in the light, contemptuous way he sometimes had of dismissing people.

Unlike Amanda Mason, who had never succumbed to the idea of women wearing pants, Helen had stuffed herself into a pair of navy stretch pants, worn with a three-quarter-sleeve blouse in a jaunty sailing print. Her sense of the fitness of things had apparently not extended to bare feet, because she wore what must be knee-length nylons with her sensible sandals. With her round pink cheeks and curly white hair, she looked like a china doll in improbable dress.

"I've been intending to come over and welcome you back to Deer Run, but I didn't want to intrude." Helen sent an inquiring glance toward the house, and Rachel realized she was expected to invite her visitor in.

"You caught me just finishing some painting," she said, indicating her paint-stained clothes. "Won't you come inside? I'm sure I can rustle up some lemonade, if my daughter and my brother haven't finished it."

"No lemonade for me, thanks, but I will come in for just a moment." Helen opened the wrought-iron gate, which squeaked in protest, and joined her on the flagstone walk. "I'm afraid you found the house in need of a great deal of work. I told Amanda and told her she should keep it up better, but she got rather..." Helen paused, as if selecting the word carefully. "Well...rather bitter toward the end, saying what difference did it make, since she had no one—"

Helen stopped, her already pink cheeks turning

a deeper hue. "Well, anyway, I'm sure that was just her illness talking."

"Most likely." Rachel was noncommittal. Maybe Colin had been right in his offhand comment about Amanda leaving her the house to punish her. No, she wouldn't let herself descend into that sort of cynicism.

This visit could be a blessing in disguise. If anyone knew why Amanda Mason had left her property the way she had, it would surely be Helen.

Rachel took a step to the left as they went up the stairs to the porch, making sure that Helen had the side where the railing was solid. Fixing the railing had better be promoted to the top of her to-do list.

Helen moved into the house and stopped, staring. "Oh. You've painted the hall. Amanda always insisted it be papered. I'm sure I don't know what she would say."

"I'm afraid wallpapering isn't among my skills." Rachel couldn't help the stiffness in her voice. She should have expected negative comments. Mason House was a landmark in the village, and people didn't like to see landmarks changed.

"I'm sorry, my dear." The sudden sympathy in Helen's voice caught her off guard. "Every time I open my mouth I put my foot in it, that's what Amanda used to say."

Maybe it hadn't been an easy task, being Amanda Mason's closest friend. Ronnie had come by his penchant for making cutting remarks from his mother, most likely.

"It's all right." Rachel led her guest into the front parlor, thankful that it was virtually untouched save for a vacuuming that had been desperately needed. Sunlight streamed through the windows in the circular bay, making patterns on the Oriental carpet. "It's natural that you hate to see the house changed after all these years."

"Well, change is inevitable, isn't it?" Helen sat down on the curving tapestry love seat, putting her feet together and glancing with apparent satisfaction at her slacks. "I tried to tell Amanda that once, but got my nose bitten off for my trouble."

"I suppose she preferred things the way they'd always been." Rachel darted a glance at the portrait of her mother-in-law that hung over the mantel. Amanda, with her coronet of white hair, regal bearing and elegant bone structure, had been suited to the style of a century ago. It was impossible to imagine her wearing Helen's current outfit.

"True enough." Helen patted her soft white curls. "Why, she insisted on wearing a hat to church every single Sunday, even when she was the only woman in the entire congregation with a hat. So it just goes to show you, doesn't it?" she added, a bit obscurely.

Rachel wasn't sure what it was meant to show, other than that Amanda had the courage of her convictions. And Rachel already knew that, didn't she? Amanda had cut off her only son without apparent regret when he married Rachel. Not even the birth of the granddaughter Ronnie had optimistically insisted on naming after her had made a difference. And that made the legacy of the house all the more inexplicable.

"I'm going to risk putting my foot in my mouth again," Helen said, leaning toward her. "But I believe Amanda realized, once it was too late, that she'd been wrong in the way she'd treated her son."

Rachel studied her face, but Helen seemed genuine. "Perhaps. But she never tried to get in touch with him."

"She wouldn't have known how to say she was sorry. Amanda wasn't always so rigid, you know. She changed after her husband died. Dear Ronald." Helen sighed. "He was devoted to her, and his death was such a shock."

"He had a heart attack, didn't he?" Ronnie had rarely spoken of his father's death.

Helen nodded. "Right down there at the creek." She gestured toward the rear of the house. "And then a few years later that Amish boy drowned in practically the same spot. You probably don't remember that, do you? Anyway, I think Amanda blamed herself that she hadn't put up a fence. Not that that would necessarily have stopped anyone from reaching the creek if they were determined to get there...."

Helen's voice seemed to fade as she prattled on about the dangers of the small dam on the stream behind the house, while Rachel's memory slipped backward twenty summers. She might have forgotten the death of Ronnie's father, but the memory of Aaron Mast was clear as crystal even though she hadn't thought of him in years. He'd been eighteen when she was ten, and she'd had the sort of crush on him that girls now seemed to have on the latest teen pop star. His death had been devastating.

She realized Helen was eyeing her curiously and knew she'd been lost in memories too long. "I do remember Aaron, yes. I didn't realize his accident bothered Ronnie's mother so much though."

"She became so strict with Ronnie after that summer." Helen's tone was mournful. "She was overprotective, and no boy appreciates that sort of thing. And she seemed to pin all her hopes for the future on him."

She knew this part of the story too well. "Those hopes were ruined when he ran away with me," she said bluntly.

"Yes, well…" Again Helen seemed to search for words. "I always thought if she'd handled it better, and frankly, dear, if your parents had, as well, things might have ended differently."

They might not have married at all—that was what Helen meant, and Rachel was mature enough now to know that was true. If it hadn't been for so much outspoken opposition…again, that was the past. She had to concentrate on now and on the future, for her daughter.

"I knew how Amanda felt, of course. That's why it surprised me so much when she left Mason House to me." Rachel let the comment lie, hoping Helen would pick it up.

"I was sure she'd do the right thing in the end," Helen said. "She might talk of leaving everything to charity, but at bottom, she'd never consider letting Mason House go out of the family. I remember the day Jacob Evans came to have her sign her will. That's Jacob Senior, not the son who's in the firm now. She said she'd provided for little Amanda's education. And she was content knowing that she'd grow up in this house. 'There's been enough sorrow and anger in Mason House,' she said. 'Maybe Ronnie's child will bring the joy back.'"

Ronnie's child. Of course that was how Amanda would have seen it, leaving out the woman of whom she'd disapproved so completely. There would have been no thought of Rachel in her final dispositions, except as the necessary guardian of Ronnie's child.

Well, she'd wanted to know why Amanda had left the place to her, and now she did. She could hardly complain if the answer wasn't to her liking.

"I'M HOME." Colin figured the announcement was hardly needed, since Duke, Dad's elderly black lab, had given his customary woof of welcome and padded over to receive a thump on the back.

But there was no answering call from the kitchen or the study. "Where is he, Duke?" Colin walked

back the hall toward the kitchen, poking his head
into the study and laundry room en route, his pulse
accelerating as each place he looked turned up
empty. Duke padded after him, head down, as if
accepting blame for his master's absence.

Colin opened the back door for a quick look at the
yard, but his father wasn't dusting the rose bushes or
checking out the young tomato plants in the garden.
Colin stood for a moment, hand gripping the knob.

Okay, think. Don't panic. If his father had fallen
somewhere in the house, Duke wouldn't be trailing
along at Colin's heels. That meant Dad had gone out.

"Did he go for a walk without you?"

Colin must be losing track of his mental facili-
ties himself, standing here questioning the dog as if
expecting an answer. Dad was an inveterate walker,
but he ordinarily took the dog with him, and that
fact provided Colin with a minimal measure of assurance. If Dad forgot why he'd gone out or how to
get back home, something that happened at times,
Duke could be relied on to pilot him safely home.

"Stay, Duke." Leaving the dog sitting forlornly
in the living room, Colin headed out the front door.
He'd take the car and do a quick spin around town.
No doubt he'd find his father walking casually back
from the coffee shop. There was no need for the apprehension that prickled along his skin.

Rachel would hardly credit it if she could see him
now, he thought wryly. In her eyes, he was obviously
still the hell-raiser who'd turned his parents' hair

gray. She'd never believe he could be as panicked over his seventy-year-old father as she must sometimes be over her nine-year-old child.

He'd nearly reached the car he'd left in the driveway when another vehicle pulled in behind his. Jake Evans, driving the battered pickup he'd had since college, came to a stop. Dad sat next to him, frowning a little with that faintly lost look he'd worn so often since Mom's death.

"Hey, Colin." Jake slid out, going around and opening the passenger-side door before Colin could get there. "I ran into your dad down by the antique shop and gave him a lift home." The look he sent Colin suggested there had been more to it than that, but whatever it was would keep until his father was out of earshot.

Colin nodded, caught between gratitude and grief—gratitude that most people in Deer Run seemed to accept his father's mental lapses with kindness, and grief that his father, always so sharp and in control, had to rely on others just to find his way home.

"Why didn't you take Duke with you, Dad?" He attempted to take his father's arm, but Dad pulled free with a sudden spurt of independence.

"Didn't feel like it," he said shortly, his lean face showing irritation. "I don't need Duke to babysit me, you know."

Don't you? Colin suppressed the thought. "Maybe not, but you know how hurt he is to be left behind."

Colin turned to Jake. "You should have seen that dog when I came in, head hanging like he'd done something wrong and couldn't figure out what it was. Come on in. There's probably some cold beer in the fridge."

"Sounds good." Jake fell into step with him, his faded jeans and frayed Lafayette T-shirt an ironic comment on having been recently named one of the area's most eligible bachelors by a regional magazine.

"So, you have to beat the ladies off with a stick since that article came out?" Colin couldn't resist needling Jake just a little.

"I should have known better than to speak to that reporter." Jake pulled the brim of his ball cap down as if hiding his identity. "I wouldn't have, but the senior partner insisted it was good publicity for the law firm."

Colin grinned, appreciating the comment for the joke it was, since the senior partner in question was Jake's father. "You sure he's not just trying to get you married off?"

Jake shuddered elaborately. "Please, don't say that. He reminds me every other week that I'm not getting any younger, and my mother sighs and says that all her friends are becoming grandmothers, and why can't she?"

Why indeed? Colin's heart cramped at the thought of his own mother. If she'd cherished dreams of grandchildren, he'd never known it.

In a few minutes they were settled in chairs on the back porch, cold cans in hand. His father, having apologized to Duke for leaving him, walked down to inspect the garden with the dog at his heels.

"He can't hear us. What happened?" Colin focused on the beads of moisture that formed on the can, not wanting to see the sympathy in Jake's brown eyes.

"Nothing too bad," Jake said easily. "I happened to be passing the antique shop when I spotted him. I figured you didn't know where he was, so I offered to drive him home."

He gave Jake a level glance. "There's more, right?"

Jake shrugged. "Your dad thought he recognized a bureau as belonging to his mother. Wanted it sent home right away. If Phil Nastrom had been there, he'd have known just how to handle it, but he wasn't. The clerk was a spotty teenager who wouldn't know a bow-front dresser from the kitchen sink, and he was getting a bit riled. I had a word with him. That's all."

It took an effort to unclench his teeth. "Right. Thanks, Jake. I'll speak to Phil."

"No problem. And you don't need to worry about Phil. Or any of the other old-timers in town, for that matter. They know and respect your dad."

"Yeah." He wasn't sure whether that made it better or worse. "Look at him." He gestured to his father, who was tying up a tomato plant that had sagged away from its stake. "Much of the time he's fine. It's bad enough that he had to give up the business. I can't take away his freedom, and he won't hear of having anyone else in the house to look after him." It kept Colin awake at nights, wondering what he was going to do when his father got worse, as he inevitably would.

"It's rough." Jake's voice was rough, too, with the slight embarrassment guys felt when sympathy was required. "Guess it's part of life, reaching the point that we have to take care of the parents. It just hit you earlier than most of us."

Colin nodded. There wasn't much else to say, and he'd do what he had to do. Right now he'd better change the conversation. It was getting downright maudlin.

"I stopped by to visit Rachel Mason today. Have you seen her since she got back?" he asked.

"No, we did most of our business in winding up the estate via emails and phone calls." Jake set the can down on the porch floor. "I guess either Dad or I should stop to see her, since we represented old Mrs. Mason. How is Rachel doing?"

"Okay, I guess." Actually, he doubted it, but it seemed disloyal to say too much negative. "She's trying to fix the house up to run it as a bed-and-breakfast. Seems to me she'd be better off selling for whatever she could get. What possessed Amanda Mason to leave her that white elephant?"

"If Amanda heard you she'd be turning over in

her grave." Jake grimaced. "There's a gruesome thought. The woman scared me to death, I don't mind telling you. Dad did most of the dealing with her, thank goodness. The one time he took me along to introduce me, she looked at me as if I'd crawled out from under a rock."

"She probably remembered you as one of Ronnie's cronies, leading her lily-white boy into trouble."

"She saved that for you, Colin, my boy. She just generally disapproved of the younger generation, which to her was anybody born after about 1950, I figure. Rachel was probably lucky Mrs. Mason cut her and Ronnie out of her life."

"I'm not sure Rachel sees it that way." He studied the beer can again before taking a final gulp. "So what exactly did old Amanda leave her?"

Jake squirmed in his lawn chair. "Come on, man. You're asking me to betray a client's confidence."

"The client is dead, and the will is on file in the county offices. Anybody who goes in there and pays the fee can get a look at it. You're just saving me a trip."

"True." It was Jake's turn to pick up his beer and gaze at it. "The will wasn't very complicated. Amanda wanted to put in some harsh language about her son marrying against her wishes, yada, yada, as if anybody cared, but Dad talked her out of that as undignified. In the end, she left the house and a small sum for upkeep to Rachel, not wanting Mason House to go out of the family and be cut up for offices or torn down and turned into a mini-mart."

"Hardly likely," Colin commented.

"No, but that was the argument Dad used to try to get her to be fair to Rachel. Even so, the amount of money she's to receive each year will just about cover the taxes on the place. At least the old woman listened to him about the little girl and left a tidy sum in trust for her college education. The rest went to various charities, I understand."

"Big deal. So Mandy gets to go to college, but in the meantime she and her mother can barely scrape by. Not what I call fair."

"Hey, don't blame me. It's the best Dad could do, and believe me, he had to fight for that much." Jake looked defensive. "Why do you care so much, anyway? I know you and Ronnie were good buds in high school, but a lot of water has gone over the dam since then."

He shrugged, having no desire to look too closely into his feelings. "No big deal. Like you said, Ronnie was a friend. I figure I owe Rachel a little support."

He'd failed to do the right thing when he was eighteen. If he hadn't been so intent on following that mysterious code by which teenagers lived, he might have prevented Ronnie and Rachel from a decision that had messed up several lives, as far as he could tell.

That wasn't his only failure, of course. He was doing his best to make amends for not being here when his parents needed him. Now he had a chance to make amends to Rachel, as well, if he could figure out how. And if she would let him.

CHAPTER THREE

THE WOMAN COMING out of the market stared at Rachel with such curiosity that Rachel almost felt compelled to explain her presence. She'd forgotten that open curiosity about one's neighbors wasn't just tolerated in a small community like Deer Run, it was also expected. Ushering Mandy ahead of her, she slipped into the store and let the door close behind her with a jingle of its bell.

"Wow. What a cool store. Did you used to come here when you were a little girl, Mommy?" Mandy stared with fascination at a case labeled Live Bait, and Rachel suspected a question about that was coming up next.

"I did, yes. But it's bigger now than it used to be."

It looked as if Anna and Jacob Miller had expanded their modest grocery into the next storefront, with a whole section devoted to crafts and trinkets of the sort beloved of tourists. In a few steps Mandy, forgetting live bait, had become absorbed by a display of small wooden Amish dolls.

"Rachel Mason!" The voice boomed from the

counter at the rear of the shop. "It wondered me when you'd get in here to say hello to old friends."

"Anna." A trickle of thankfulness ran through her at the warmth in Anna Miller's voice. "It is wonderful *gut* to see you."

She lapsed automatically into Pennsylvania Dutch and then caught herself. She'd told herself she would speak English in front of Mandy when they came back here, but she hadn't realized how difficult it would be.

Catching Mandy's hand, she led her daughter to the counter. "This is my little girl, Mandy. Mandy, this is Mrs. Miller."

"*Ach*, I would know her for yours in a minute." Anna beamed with satisfaction. "Mandy, do you know you look just like your *mammi* did at your age?"

Mandy blinked, looking at her mother as if assessing the truth of the claim. "Do I? I haven't ever seen any pictures of Mommy when she was nine, so I didn't know."

"*Ach*, no, you wouldn't." Anna had the trick of talking to a child as if they were contemporaries, which had always made her a favorite with the young ones. "Your *mammi* was brought up Amish, like me. We don't hold with taking photographs of people."

A gesture indicated Anna's blue dress and matching apron. There were more strands of gray in the brown hair smoothed back under Anna's *kapp*, and she'd added another chin or two to her round face, but otherwise she was much as Rachel remembered her.

"Why?" Mandy was being curious, that was all, but had such a blunt question of an adult come from an Amish child, it would have earned a quick reprimand from a parent.

"I'll tell you all about it later," Rachel said quickly. "You can go and look at the dolls while Mrs. Miller and I talk."

The flash in Mandy's intelligent eyes said she knew when she was being gotten rid of, but she returned to the display counter.

"You've expanded the shop, I see," Rachel said quickly. "Business must be good."

"So-so." Anna waggled her hand. "We get more tourists through Deer Run than we used to, so I told Jacob we had to take advantage of the trade. And there's talk that the gas drilling they're doing north of here will come to this area, too. That will bring in new people, I should think."

"Do folks want to see that happen here?" From the little she'd read, it sounded as if the new methods of gas drilling caused considerable controversy.

"Some do, some don't." Anna's face clouded. "The bishop fears the effect of easy money on the Leit."

The Leit. The Amish. She hadn't heard that expression in years. And the bishop had a typically Amish attitude, which ran exactly counter to contemporary culture, in a case like this. Making money too easily, or becoming what the world would call a success, could have a bad effect on humility, that typically Amish virtue.

"I'd think it safer to count on the tourists," she said.

"*Ja*, we do. As you will, too. I hear you are going to open Mason House as a bed-and-breakfast, ain't so?"

She nodded. News spread fast in a place like Deer Run. She'd only mentioned her plans to Colin yesterday. Of course, Anna would probably have heard through Rachel's family, not Colin.

"I hope so. I don't know what else to do with a house that size. It's way too big for the two of us." Something Amanda Mason had certainly known when she'd left her property as she had.

Anna nodded. "It's a *gut* plan, I think. And it will keep you here, where you belong."

"I'm afraid not everyone thinks I belong here." The words slipped out before she could caution herself that they were unwise.

"Don't you think such a thing. Your *daadi* will come around, you wait and see." Anna didn't bother pretending she didn't know what Rachel meant. "He is being as stubborn as old Mrs. Mason, and she accepted you in the end, *ja?*"

Rachel wasn't sure *accepted* was the right word, but she nodded. "I hope. So far Benj is the only one acting normal around me. And now you."

"Not *chust* me," Anna responded quickly. "You have plenty of friends here who will be glad to see you. And when you're ready to open, I will be mentioning your B and B to every tourist who comes in here. Folks will want to stay at a place run by somebody raised Amish. You'll see."

That comment stirred up more concerns. "I wouldn't want anyone to think I'm trying to make money out of having been Amish."

Anna spread plump hands, palms up. "Why not? Everyone else does, it seems. Folks say the tourists are going to *komm* anyway. We might as well make some money off them."

Anna had a point. It seemed she would have to get rid of any squeamish scruples if she intended to make a go of the business.

The bell jingled, and Anna glanced automatically toward the door. "Remember what I was saying about your friends? Here is one, I see. You remember Meredith King, *ja?*" She raised her voice. "Meredith, look who is here. You and Rachel were great friends when you were little girls, I remember."

Rachel turned, surveying the woman who stood giving her the once-over in return. Meredith King. Meredith lived just two houses down from Mason House, so she was practically a neighbor now.

The friendship Anna mentioned hadn't actually lasted very long, but Rachel's memories of her Englisch friend were oddly distinct. Meredith might no longer wear torn-at-the-knees jeans and faded

T-shirts, but her glossy dark brown hair was the same, worn sleekly straight to curve around a fine-boned face.

Meredith's chocolate-colored eyes seemed to warm when they rested on her. "Rachel, is it really you? I could hardly believe it when I heard you were coming back to Deer Run."

Rachel felt herself stiffen. "Brave of me, do you think?"

A delicate pink bloomed in Meredith's cheeks. "I didn't mean it that way. But if I managed to escape Deer Run, I wouldn't be coming back in a hurry."

Before Rachel could think of a proper response, Meredith had turned to Anna. "A quart of the goat's milk for my mother, please. And if Rachel has time, a couple of coffees and sweet rolls."

She glanced at Rachel. "Please? I can't let you get away without a talk after all this time. And Anna has the best coffee and sweet rolls in town." She gestured toward an area beyond the counter, which Rachel now realized was fitted with a few round tables and chairs, another addition since her time.

"Sounds great. But I have my daughter with me. Let me see if she's ready for something to drink." She went quickly to Mandy with the question, but her daughter was busy fitting the pieces of a min-iature wooden train together.

"Not now, Mommy." Mandy didn't bother to do more than glance up.

"I'll be over at the table if you change your mind."

It seldom worked well to try to distract Mandy from her single-minded absorption in the fascination of the moment.

The coffee and rolls were already on the table by the time Rachel joined Meredith, the rolls the traditional spirals oozing with so much brown sugar and cinnamon that her hands would need a thorough scrubbing afterward.

"She reminds me of you at that age." Meredith watched Mandy, smiling slightly. "Sweet and serious."

"Mandy has a mischievous side, as well." Rachel put a spoonful of sugar in her coffee and stirred. "But then I guess I did, too."

"As I recall, you were the one who talked us into catching minnows in the creek when I had a good dress on," Meredith said. "Not that I wasn't just as happy to get rid of that ruffled number my mother had picked out."

"I think you fell in the mud on purpose." Amazing, how easy it was to slip back to that relationship they'd had twenty summers ago. "I see you're picking your own clothes now." She nodded at Meredith's softly tailored shirt, worn with a single gold chain and a neat pair of tan slacks.

"Eventually even my mother had to admit that I wasn't the frilly sort." Meredith raised an eyebrow. "But your change in dress is more serious. How is your family adjusting to having you back again?"

Rachel shrugged. True, her denim skirt and plain

cotton shirt were modest, but they were a far cry from Amish clothing. "Mixed reception, I guess. Mammi is glad to see Mandy, I'm sure, but Daad and my brother Mose gave me a distant nod the one time I saw them."

She made an effort not to let the hurt show in her voice, but she had a feeling Meredith saw through it. Her face warmed with sympathy.

"What about your sisters? And the little brother... Benjamin, is it?"

Rachel nodded. "Benj, yes. He's the only one who acts normally around me." Except for those odd moments of fear and tension that still worried her. "The girls are like Mamm. Cautious."

"I'm sorry," Meredith said softly. "I know what it's like to turn to a parent who's not there."

"I heard about your father's death. I'm so sorry for your loss. You were still in college then, weren't you?" Meredith had always been her father's girl. She must have taken his passing hard.

Meredith nodded, staring absently down at her cup. "I still miss him. And my mother...well, she relies on me. So I'm still here."

Something about her tone explained Meredith's odd phrasing when she'd spoken of escaping Deer Run. She'd been talking about herself, not Rachel.

"Do you have a job here?" Jobs in Deer Run were few and far between, she'd think, it not being exactly a thriving metropolis.

"I'm an accountant. I have an office at the house,

although sometimes I work on site at some of the small businesses I deal with." Meredith's voice was carefully expressionless, but Rachel suspected she knew whose idea it was that Meredith's office should be at home, and she wasn't sure how to respond. Mrs. King had always been the clinging sort.

Fortunately, Meredith didn't seem to expect a response. She was watching Mandy again, amusement in her gaze. "Is she as imaginative as we were at that age?"

"I guess so. Although I don't think she could possibly be as imaginative as we were that summer we were ten." Rachel smiled, too, remembering.

"That was mainly Lainey Colton's fault," Meredith said. "She was the only kid I ever met who could create a fantasy world as real as that one was. We basically lived in Lainey's world that whole summer."

"Knights and fairies and dragons…trust me, that's not the usual imaginative fare for Amish children. Maybe that was why it enthralled me so much."

And it was equally unusual for an Amish child to spend so much time with two Englisch friends, but Mamm had been preoccupied in helping to care for Aunt Hannah, who'd been ordered bed rest during a difficult pregnancy, and she'd just been happy to have her children out from underfoot. Besides, Mamm had considered she had a duty to Lainey's

Amish great-aunt to provide a suitable companion for her visitor.

"It seems strange now, not seeing Lainey at all since that summer," Meredith said. "We wrote for a while after she moved back with her mother, but then we lost touch."

Rachel nodded. "The same with me. That whole summer was just…different."

"Different," Meredith echoed. "Remember how Lainey insisted Aaron Mast was an enchanted prince? And we followed him around for weeks, looking for a way to break the spell?"

"I remember." Aaron Mast, with his golden hair, even features, kind blue eyes—he'd been the perfect Prince Charming for three imaginative young girls. He'd probably never known, from the lofty heights of his eighteen years, how they'd felt about him.

Rachel drew in a long breath and blew it out in something that was almost a sigh. She hadn't thought of Aaron in years, and now he'd come up twice in two days.

"And then he drowned." Meredith shook her head. "When I look back at it, it seems to me the summer ended then. Our prince was dead, the parents clamped down on where we were as if we might fall into the dam as well and Lainey was sent back to her mother. The magic was over."

Over and forgotten, Rachel thought. And there was no reason at all for the odd foreboding at the back of her mind.

COLIN GLANCED INTO the window of Millers' store and stopped dead. Duke, strolling at his side, gave him a reproachful look and then sat down, leaning heavily against his leg.

Rachel Mason and Meredith King sat at one of the small round tables, heads together, talking. Something teased at his memory—an image of them as little girls, busily building a tree house in the massive oak tree in the side yard of the King house. It looked as if Rachel had found an old friend.

They were getting up now, obviously saying goodbye. With a sudden decision, he moved to the door and stood waiting for Rachel to come out.

She and Mandy emerged a few minutes later. Rachel's eyes narrowed a bit at the sight of him, but all of Mandy's attention was for Duke.

"What a nice dog. Is he yours? What's his name? Can I pet him?" Mandy pelted him with questions, not bothering with pleasantries.

"Yes. Duke. And yes, he'd like to be petted," he said, smiling at the child's enthusiasm.

"Nice dog," Mandy crooned, dropping to her knees beside the dog and stroking his glossy black fur. "You're such a good boy, Duke."

Duke, a sucker for compliments, obliged with a gentle nuzzling of Mandy's neck.

"Look, Mommy, he likes me." Mandy shot a glance at her mother. "See, I'm really good with dogs. If I had a puppy—"

"We'll talk about it later." Rachel sounded as if

that conversation was one they'd already had several times. "Say goodbye to Duke now. We need to get home." She shifted a bag of groceries to her other arm to reach for her daughter's hand.

He forestalled her by giving Mandy the leash. "We'll walk along with you, and you can lead Duke. He needs a walk."

"Can I really? Wow, thank you." The warmth in Mandy's little face made her response more than just the polite words of a well-brought-up child.

"Sure. And I'll carry your mom's package." He reached for Rachel's bag. She pulled away from him, but he didn't drop his hand. "Come on, now," he said softly. "You know perfectly well I can't walk you home with you carrying the groceries and my hands free. What would people think of me?"

"You don't need to be walking me…us…home at all." Rachel's pointed chin set stubbornly.

"Sure I do." He nodded to Mandy, already ten yards ahead of them on the sidewalk. "Mandy has my dog."

"You know perfectly well—" She stopped, maybe realizing how silly it sounded. "Oh, all right." She surrendered the bag. "If you must."

Satisfied, he fell into step with her. "You know, I'll start thinking you don't like me if you keep going on this way."

"I—" She stopped, seeming to change her mind about what she was going to say. "I wouldn't want people to start talking. That's all."

"Because I walked beside you and carried your groceries?" He raised an eyebrow. "We're not ten, and I'm not carrying your books home from school."

The warm peach of her skin seemed to deepen. "No. But you know how people talk in Deer Run. You just said it yourself, remember?"

"True." He could hardly deny it. "But you can't stop meeting old friends because of what people might say. I saw you and Meredith getting reacquainted," he added quickly, before she could remind him that they'd never exactly been friends.

"It was nice to see Meredith again." She took the diversion with a slight frown. "I was a little surprised she's still living at home."

"Are you kidding? With that mother of hers? Margo King has been a professional hypochondriac all her life. She used that to keep poor old John dancing attendance on her, and now that he's gone, she's guilted Meredith into taking his place."

Rachel darted a glance his way. "Cynical, aren't you?"

He shrugged. "I call 'em as I see 'em. If you're around them very long, you'll see for yourself. Everyone in town knows what Meredith's mother is like except Meredith."

"I doubt that everyone in town is as cynical as you are."

There was that word again. Was he cynical? He didn't think so. At least, not about Rachel and her daughter.

"Just wait and see," he said. "By the way, what's going on with that little brother of yours?"

"Benj?" Rachel's deep blue eyes widened. "Why? What have you heard?" The questions had a sharp edge of emotion. Was it fear? Surely not.

"Take it easy." He lifted his free hand in a gesture of surrender. "I just meant that I expected him to stop around and mow the grass today, but he didn't show up. Why are you worried about him?" He turned the question back on her.

"I'm not." She made an unsuccessful attempt to mask the anxiety in her face.

"You know, you're really not very good at telling fibs. You ought to practice a bit more."

"I'm not interested in telling fibs." The color came up in her cheeks again. "I don't know why Benj didn't show up. I'll speak to him about it. He shouldn't slack off on his work."

"Spoken like a true big sister," he said. "You don't need to bug the boy about it. But you *are* worried about him, aren't you?"

He waited, wondering if she'd try to lie again.

Rachel was silent for a moment, her gaze seeming fixed on her daughter. Mandy had stopped on the walk in front of Jeannette Walker's B and B, and she seemed to be telling Duke something to which he listened intently, his head cocked to one side.

Finally Rachel shook her head, sighing a little. "Maybe I'm imagining things. After all, I don't know Benj very well." The words contained a wealth of regret. "But he seems to be frightened of something. And he's keeping it secret, whatever it is."

He nodded, unable to dismiss her concern. "I've noticed it, as well. He's not in trouble with your dad, is he?"

"Not that I know of. I just wish he'd talk to me about it. Or somebody else, if not me."

"Don't start blaming yourself. Teenage boys don't confide readily in anyone older. Probably teenage girls are the same, but I can only speak for the boys." He tried a smile, hoping to lighten the moment.

"You were never an Amish teenager."

"Boys are boys, Amish or Englisch," he retorted. Maybe he didn't want to start talking about being a teenager with Rachel. There were too many minefields in that topic, like what had happened between them one summer afternoon. "Looks like Duke's making himself right at home."

He nodded toward Mason House, looming ahead of them like a monster ready to consume anyone foolish enough to count on it. Duke had flopped to his side on the porch floor, with Mandy sitting next to him. His head rested on her leg, and he wore a blissful expression as she petted him.

"Mandy loves dogs. She'll be pretending he's hers in no time at all."

"She ought to have a puppy," he said, hardly thinking of what he was saying because he was so lost in Rachel's expression when she looked at her child. "You had plenty of animals to take care of at that age."

"I lived on a farm," she reminded him. "If we got a dog I'd have to be certain it wouldn't disturb the guests. Or frighten them."

"You could keep a dog away from the guests, I'd think. And it would be a little added security for you and Mandy, if you're determined to stay here alone."

"There's nothing to be frightened of in Deer Run. I don't need a dog for security."

He held the gate open for her. "Times have changed. Even Deer Run is affected by the modern world, whether it looks like it or not."

Rachel seemed to shrug that off. She stopped at the porch steps and held out her hands for the grocery bag. "Thank you. I'll take that now."

"I'll carry it in for you." He went up the steps. "Maybe you'd be kind enough to give Duke a drink before we finish our walk," he suggested, aiming the words more at Mandy than her mother.

"I'll do it." Mandy leaped to her feet. "Hurry and open the door, Mommy. I have to get Duke a pan of water."

Rachel sent him a glance that mingled reproach with giving in. "All right. Let me get my keys."

He had his hand on the knob while she was fumbling in her bag for the keys. It turned under the pressure of his fingers, and the stained-glass paneled door swung open.

"Looks as if you forgot to lock it," he commented, pushing the door the rest of the way.

Rachel stood where she was, blue eyes darkening. "I'm sure I locked the door before we left. How can it be open?"

CHAPTER FOUR

COLIN GRASPED THE doorknob, holding the door ajar while he studied Rachel's face. She obviously believed what she was saying, but was that realistic? Wasn't it far more likely that she'd just forgotten to lock the door?

"Maybe the lock didn't catch when you went out," he said, trying for diplomacy.

Rachel's expression said she knew exactly what he was thinking. "I did not forget to lock the door, and I double-checked it when I left. You learn that much, living in the city."

Before he could answer, Mandy wedged herself between them, reaching for the door. "Let me go in, please, Mommy. I want to get a drink for Duke."

Rachel grasped her daughter's shoulders in a quick, protective movement. Obviously his idea was backfiring.

"I'll bet there's an outside faucet somewhere near the flower beds," he suggested. "Why don't you use that one? You don't want Duke's muddy paws in your house."

Duke's paws weren't really muddy, but maybe

that would distract the child from getting in before he'd had a chance to check the house.

"That's a good idea," Rachel said, seconding him before Mandy could object. "Remember the faucet and bucket where Benj washed the brushes? You can use that one."

"I remember." Mandy darted off the porch with Duke lumbering after her. Poor old boy was getting more exercise than he'd expected, but at least it got Mandy out of the way.

"I suppose Benj might have come over." Rachel reached for the door, obviously intending to see for herself.

Colin grasped her hand to forestall her and felt an almost visceral jolt at the brief contact. Rachel's gaze met his, her blue eyes seeming to widen before she dropped her gaze.

"Let me," he said. Before she could argue the point, he pushed open the door and stepped inside the entrance hall. He stood for a moment, listening, effectively blocking the door so that Rachel couldn't rush in behind him.

Nothing. The staircase, with its mahogany railing, wound upward in silence; the rooms to either side of the hallway stood empty and still. The house seemed to be holding its breath, waiting.

He shook off the fancy. "Doesn't look like anything's disturbed." He moved to the console table, letting Rachel come in behind him. "Except this." He gestured to the table, where a paper-wrapped sheaf of pink roses lay next to a basket of fruit, their fragrance perfuming the air.

Rachel stared at the roses as if they hid a snake. "Someone's been in here."

She still seemed upset out of proportion to the cause, and he reminded himself to proceed cautiously. The little he knew of her life in recent years didn't encourage him to think it had been free of trouble. Experience had probably convinced her that surprises were usually unpleasant.

"Maybe one of the other doors was unlocked," he suggested. "Anyway, people bearing fruit and flowers rarely have malicious intent, ain't so?"

His use of the familiar Pennsylvania Dutch tag was intended to break the tension, and it seemed to. Rachel's lips softened a bit, even if she didn't manage a smile.

"I guess you're right. *Denke*, Colin. I'm being silly. I—"

The sound of a footstep in the kitchen cut off whatever she'd been going to say. With a quick, instinctive movement he closed the space between them.

And then felt foolish when the swinging door to the back of the house opened to reveal Jeannette Walker, holding a milk-glass vase in one hand.

"Rachel, there you are. Hello, Colin." Jeannette came toward them quickly, apparently oblivious of having caused any alarm. "I stopped by to say welcome." She gestured with the vase. "Just looking for something to put the roses in. A bed-and-breakfast doesn't look welcoming without flowers, I find."

"They're beautiful, Ms. Walker." Rachel recovered her powers of speech. "It's so kind of you to bring them."

"Not at all. I know Amanda let the flower beds go terribly in recent years." Jeannette was at her most gracious—the successful innkeeper welcoming a newcomer who would be no competition at all.

While the women fussed over the arrangement of roses in the vase Colin scrutinized Jeannette, wondering what her agenda was. Prior experience of Jeannette Walker told him she always had an agenda. Whether it was a question of the right Christmas decorations for the village stores or the advisability of allowing a billboard at the edge of town, Jeannette rammed her wishes through with such subtlety that few people even realized they'd been manipulated.

The iron fist in the velvet glove—that was Jeannette. She wore her usual uniform of tailored slacks and sweater set with pearls—apparently what she considered proper attire for her position, winter or summer. She was only in her mid-forties, probably, but her tightly permed curls and carefully outlined lips made her look older.

Jeannette turned toward him as if she'd read his thoughts. "Colin, I'm surprised you're not working today. But then, I suppose the real estate business is rather slow at the moment."

He just smiled, inured to Jeannette's petty barbs. "Or I might be so busy that I needed a day off. Hard to tell, isn't it?"

Jeannette gave a slight sniff, dismissing him, and turned to Rachel. "Now, I want you to feel free to call on me anytime for advice. It's so complicated to set up a B and B—all those tax rules and safety regulations, the advertising, the record-keeping. And there's the difficulty of maintaining a web presence, because of course that's how everyone shops these days, even for vacations. And setting up online reservations can be such a nightmare. Believe me, I know how overwhelming it can be for someone with little experience."

If Rachel hadn't been overwhelmed before, she looked it now after Jeannette's recital of the tasks ahead of her.

"Just ask me for advice anytime," Jeannette reiterated on her way to the door. "I'm here to help."

Rachel stammered out a goodbye, and the door closed behind Jeannette.

"Help herself, more likely," he commented, his tone caustic.

"She was being nice," Rachel said. "Do you always have to be so cynical?"

That wasn't the first time she'd accused of that particular fault. "Didn't you see what Jeannette was doing? You…"

He stopped, seeming to hear an echo of Ronnie's voice in his words. Ronnie, berating Rachel for something left undone on that one occasion he'd visited them after they'd married. Ronnie, turning his caustic wit against the woman who was working a menial job to help support their little family.

"Sorry." He really did have to watch what he said. "I guess you got enough cynicism from Ronnie to last you a lifetime."

Rachel's chin lifted. "You can keep your sympathy to yourself. You don't know anything at all about our marriage."

"Don't I?" His temper flared at that. "I know what I saw. You working like a slave to keep food on the table and Ronnie using that sharp tongue of his to cut you to ribbons, blaming you..."

He stopped, knowing he'd gone too far.

Pain and embarrassment chased each other across Rachel's face, but then her shoulders squared. "If that's what you thought of us, I'm not surprised you never came back for another visit."

He reached out and grasped her wrist, feeling her pulse beating hard against his palm. "I didn't come back because if I had, I wouldn't have been able to resist the urge to knock Ronnie's block off. And maybe a little healthy cynicism would be good for you."

For a moment they stared at each other, and it seemed to him that the very air echoed with the beat of her pulse. Then she wrenched her hand free, the color coming up in her cheeks.

"You—"

The front door swung open to admit child and dog. "Duke had his drink. And I wiped his paws off, honest I did, Mommy."

With a fulminating look at him, Rachel turned to her daughter. "That's fine, dear. I don't mind Duke coming in, but give the leash to Mr. McDonald now. He has to go."

Mandy handed it over with a slight pout. "Come again soon, okay?"

"Sure thing, Mandy." He glanced at Rachel. Her lips were pressed tightly together. "Hard not to say what you think, isn't it?" he asked.

She unclenched her jaw. "Goodbye, Colin."

Mandy chattered about Colin's dog all through supper, making it impossible for Rachel to stop thinking about him. Colin, that is. Not the dog. Of course Duke was the only thing on her daughter's mind. Mandy had been asking for a puppy since she learned to talk, it sometimes seemed.

When they lived in the city, Rachel had found that a reasonable excuse not to burden herself with a dog. Now that they were ensconced in Deer Run, that reason no longer applied. She'd either have to come up with another one or give in.

Colin's suggestion that a dog would provide protection for her and Mandy might have some validity, although she hated to admit that since it came from him. She'd been frightened, almost irrationally so, to find the door unlocked and someone in the house, even so benign a visitor as Jeannette. Maybe Benj's fears were rubbing off on her.

Rachel carried dishes to the sink and turned on the hot water. They were eating in the kitchen, since it seemed silly for the two of them to sit in that formal dining room. Besides, it was the most cheerful room in the house, with its white walls and blue-and-white checked curtains at the many-paned south-facing windows. Some geraniums would probably do well on the two sills, distracting the eye from the faded linoleum on the floor and a gas range so elderly that it made her nervous every time she turned it on. Benj had lit it for her the first time, laughing at her fears.

Benj hadn't come over today, unless he'd been here while she and Mandy were out. That was unusual. He'd stopped by every day since she'd moved in.

Mandy carried her plate carefully to the sink and handed it to Rachel. "I'll clear the table, Mommy. Okay?"

"Okay. Thanks, sweetheart." She loved it when Mandy helped without waiting to be asked, although a slight suspicion lurked at the back of her mind that Mandy might be intent on showing that she was mature enough for a puppy.

"Is Duke an old dog?" Mandy set her milk glass on the counter with a slight clink.

"I don't know. What makes you ask that?"

"He has some gray hair on his face. I thought maybe that meant he was old."

"You're very observant." She tugged at one of the ponytails Mandy wore today. "You can ask—"

A knock at the back door interrupted her. Maybe Benj, although he usually just opened the door and shouted. She hurried to the door, wiping her hands on a dish towel, and pulled it open. A cheerful greeting died on her lips. It wasn't Benj. It was her father.

"Daadi." The word came out as something of a croak. "I didn't expect…come in, please." She stepped back, gesturing toward the kitchen, trying to talk naturally around the lump in her throat. If her father was ready to accept her…

But he was already shaking his head at the invitation, his dark blue eyes distant. Ten years hadn't really changed him much, save for a few gray hairs in the brown beard that reached his chest and a few more wrinkles around his eyes. His summer straw hat sat squarely on his head, looking exactly like the straw hats he'd worn since she could remember, and his suspenders crossed shoulders that were still strong.

"I am looking for Benjamin." He clipped off the words. "He is here, *ja?*"

Rachel blinked a little, shaking her head. "We haven't seen him today. Is something wrong?" She felt a small hand slip into hers. Mandy had come to stand next to her. She didn't speak, but she studied her grandfather curiously.

"Nothing." His expression belied the word, but it was clear that he wasn't going to confide in her. Still, the very fact that he'd come to her door made it clear that he was worried about Benj. "He missed his supper, and his *mamm* is fretting about it."

"Is Benj in trouble for missing supper?" Mandy asked.

Her father stared at Mandy for a moment, and Rachel had a sense that his expression was softening. "Not in trouble. But he should tell his *mammi* if he is going to be late, *ja?*"

"Ja," she echoed.

Daad raised his hand in a slight gesture, as if about to touch Mandy's face. Then he let it drop to his side and turned away.

Rachel's heart cramped. *Daadi, I know I broke your heart when I ran away. But I'm back now. Can't we be friends, at least, for Mandy's sake?*

She wouldn't say it, because she was afraid to hear his response.

"If I see Benj…" she began.

"If you see him, send him home. He has missed his supper."

"I'll tell him." But she was talking to her father's back as he walked away.

Rachel closed the door. She had known it wouldn't be easy, coming back. She just hadn't thought it would cause so much pain.

"Mommy, why doesn't he like us?" Mandy didn't sound hurt so much as curious.

"He doesn't dislike us, sweetheart." She picked her way through the thicket of explaining incomprehensible adult behavior to a child. "You see, he and my mother were really hurt when I ran away from them to marry your daddy. I think it's hard for him to forget that."

"Well, but you're back now." Mandy's tone was practical. "I wish we could make up and be friends. Then I'd have a grandpa and grandma like everybody else."

"I wish that, too." She couldn't let Mandy see her pain, because it was important that Mandy know she could count on her mother to be strong. "Maybe it will happen. We just have to be patient."

Mandy stared at her for a long moment in much the same way she'd studied Daadi. "I'll try," she said finally, as if being patient was the hardest thing in the world. Well, maybe it was to a nine-year-old.

Rachel managed a smile. "Now, why don't you find something to do while I finish up the dishes? Maybe we'll have time for a game afterward."

Mandy nodded. "I know just what to do. I'm going to make a picture of Duke. I'll show you when I'm done." She darted off, the kitchen door swinging behind her.

Rachel stared at the sink. She ought to get moving on the dishes. She ought to do a lot of things, but right now all she could think about was Benj. Her parents had to be very worried indeed for her father to come to her door.

The back window looked out over the outbuildings and beyond them to the creek and the covered bridge that crossed it, delineating Amish farms from the village proper. Daad had already appeared on the other side of the covered bridge. He paused for a moment, looking downstream, and fear curled inside her. Twenty yards or so beyond the bridge the stream tumbled over the small dam that had been there as long as anyone could remember. Pearson's Dam, it was called, but she had no idea who Pearson had been. The dam wasn't more than three feet high, but the force of water was such that a person could be swept under by it as if caught in a riptide. That was what had happened to Aaron Mast.

But Daad was walking on, heading for the stretch of woods along the south pasture. Obviously there had been no one at the dam.

Still, the fear was admitted, wasn't easily dismissed. She ought to do something, but what?

A memory slid into her mind as if it had been waiting for the chance. Colin had said he'd expected Benj to show up to work on the lawn. Maybe that was the answer.

Without giving herself time to think about it, she went quickly to the telephone in the hallway. It was the work of a moment to look up Colin's number and punch the buttons. If Colin thought she was making an excuse to call him—

She nearly hung up at that thought, but she already heard his voice in her ear.

"Colin, it's Rachel Mason. I'm sorry to bother you, but is Benj at your place, by any chance? My father is looking for him."

"He's not here now. Let me ask my father if he came over earlier."

She heard the sound of muffled voices and could tell that the answer was negative even before Colin came back on the line.

"Dad hasn't seen him today. Is something wrong?" His voice deepened on the question, and she knew he was revisiting their earlier conversation about Benj.

"No…no, nothing." That wasn't quite true, but it also wasn't Colin's business.

"Come on, Rachel. You wouldn't be calling me if nothing was wrong, now would you?" Something that might have been amusement threaded the concern in his tone. "What is it?"

"My *daad* stopped by to see if Benj was here, that's all. He didn't come home for supper. It's not exactly earthshaking." She tried to sound as if she were taking Benj's absence lightly and was afraid she didn't succeed.

"I'll come over," Colin said instantly, proving that she hadn't deceived him.

"No, don't do that. He's probably turned up by now." She rushed the words, regretting that she had called. "Thanks." She hung up quickly, before Colin could say anything else.

Walking to the rear window, Rachel peered out.

She couldn't see her father now. Had he gone back to the house? Or had he walked into the woods beyond the pasture?

Standing here worrying wasn't helping. She went quickly to the bottom of the stairs. "Mandy, I'm going outside for a minute. I'll be right back." Her voice seemed to bounce around the turn in the stairs.

"Okay, Mommy."

Judging by the sound, Mandy was in her room, probably hard at work on the promised picture. Since that room overlooked the willow on the side of the house, Mandy would be unlikely to see her in the backyard, looking…well, she wasn't sure where she was going to look. She just knew that doing nothing wasn't an option.

Pulling on the navy windbreaker that hung in the back hall, Rachel slipped out the back door. The sun was just beginning to disappear behind the ridge, and she knew how quickly darkness could claim the valley after sunset. The air was already cooling, and she was glad of the jacket.

The garage, the old stable, other outbuildings she hadn't yet identified—there were plenty of places for a skinny teenager to hide, even without going into the woods. But why was she thinking about hiding? Logically speaking, Benj had no reason to hide, but fear wasn't logical, and she had seen fear in her little brother's eyes lately, no matter how he tried to hide it.

She walked past the outbuildings toward the

covered bridge. Daad had already looked there, of course. She'd seen him. But that didn't stop her from wanting to have a quick glance herself.

The inside of the one-lane bridge was already dark, with the arched opening at the other showing an empty stretch of lane. The covered bridge had only one window cut into the side that looked downstream. It was a simple, utilitarian structure, built over a century ago to provide both access to the village from the farms and to give farmers a place to shelter a loaded wagon in case of a storm.

Rachel put one hand against a rough-hewn timber and shivered. When she was young, she'd seen the bridge as her gateway to the world. Now it seemed a barrier, cutting her off from what had once been so familiar.

Shaking away the thought, she turned back the way she'd come. She stepped out of the bridge and found herself face-to-face with Colin. Her breath caught.

"What are you doing here?" That came out more sharply than it should have, probably.

"Has Benj turned up yet?" He answered with a question of his own.

She shook her head. Surely Daad would let her know if Benj had been found. He'd know she was worried.

"I'm sure he's fine. Goodness, he's fourteen, not four." But she couldn't prevent a sideways glance down toward the dam, spilling over into its pool.

"You're imagining him falling over the dam. Not very likely."

Colin was quick as a cat, and it annoyed her that he read her so easily.

"No, of course not. Someone mentioned the deaths that have happened there, and I guess it was in my mind, that's all."

"Deaths?" Colin frowned for a moment. "Aaron Mast, I remember his drowning. And there was a story before that of an Amish girl who'd drowned—I think the grown-ups just used that to scare us away."

"I didn't hear about that one. Maybe my parents didn't think I needed scaring. But what about Ronnie's dad?"

Colin just stared at her for a moment, and then he frowned. "He didn't drown. He was fishing in the pond, I think, and he had a heart attack."

"I don't know why we're talking about that, anyway." She took a step toward the house, rubbing her arms. The sun had completed its descent, taking the warmth of the day with it. "Benj isn't there, and wherever he is…" She let that trail off. Where was he?

"I know where he might be," Colin said.

She whirled on him. "If you know, why didn't you say so, instead of upsetting me with talk about people drowning? Where is he?"

"I said might." Colin nodded toward the stable. "I happened to see him in there yesterday. Let's have a look."

He led the way, moving so quickly that she had to hurry to keep up. "I don't see why—" she began, but he gestured her to be quiet.

The door was partially open. Why hadn't she noticed that before? Colin stepped inside, and she followed him.

The dusty windows let in very little light. She blinked, trying to get her eyes to adjust to the dimness. Castoff furniture and boxes containing who knows what were stacked so high that they loomed like creatures preparing to attack.

A click, and then light blossomed, turning the lurking shadows into a pathetic collection of junk. Colin had obviously brought a flashlight. He aimed the beam on a narrow passageway between the crates.

"Come on out, Benj," he said. "I know you're in here."

Nothing. Silence, save for some vague creaks. She shook her head. "This isn't doing any good."

Colin ignored her, bending to focus the flashlight beam into the hole. "Don't make me come in there after you. It wouldn't be a pretty sight."

She started to turn away and then swung back at a scuffling noise, her breath catching. Benj came crawling slowly out into the light, blinking as if he were a mole hauled into the daylight.

"*Ja*, all right. I am here."

Rachel grabbed him, pulling him to his feet, not sure whether she wanted to hug him or shake him.

"Benj, what on earth are you playing at? Do you know Daadi was here looking for you? What do you mean by scaring everyone that way?"

He looked up at her, his expression so strained and miserable that she wanted the scolding words back.

She touched his cheek gently. "What is it, Benj? Please, tell me what's wrong."

"I can't." It came out as a whisper, and his head dropped so that he wasn't meeting her eyes. "I promised."

"A promise that makes you scared to death and upsets your family? What kind of a promise is that? Benj—" She ran out of words, not sure what to say in the face of his stubborn silence.

"Wake up, Benj." Colin's voice was so stern that her brother's head jerked back, his eyes going wide. "Okay, you made a promise. Trust me, I remember promises like that—stupid ones that you knew when you made them weren't worth it." Colin sounded as if he really was talking about himself. "It's time to straighten up and act like a man, not a kid. Now tell your sister what this is all about before I pull your dad in to hear it."

"No, don't." Benj's face went even whiter, if that were possible. "I'm sorry. I didn't mean…" Tears welled in his eyes, and he knuckled them away, shamefaced. "I don't know what to do. Will made us promise not to tell. But now Will is gone, and I don't know what to do."

"Will Esch?" Colin rapped out the question.

Benj nodded, choking back a sob.

Will Esch. Rachel repeated the name silently. She knew the family. Will must be a couple of years older than Benj.

"What do you mean, he's gone?" Colin seemed to be having more success getting information out of Benj than she had, so Rachel forced herself to keep silent.

"He…he was gone when his mother went to call him today. They think he's run off. But what if he didn't? What if something happened—" He fell silent so suddenly it was like shutting off a tap. He shook his head. "After I heard, I couldn't go home. Daadi would know the minute he looked at me that something was wrong. I had to think on it a bit." He gestured toward the hiding place, as if to say that had been his haven for thinking through his troubles.

"Okay, so you and Will and somebody else were involved in something you shouldn't have been, and Will made you promise not to tell anyone for fear you'd get into trouble." Colin had put the story together more quickly than she had.

Benj gulped and nodded.

"That doesn't explain why you're so scared. Come on, out with the rest of it."

The command in Colin's tone would have convinced someone a lot more sophisticated than a fourteen-year-old Amish boy, and Rachel could only be thankful he was there. She'd never have gotten this much out of Benj on her own.

"We were…we were trespassing." The way Benj seemed to be editing his words made Rachel fear they'd been doing something worse than trespassing. "And there was a man—he yelled at us, and we ran. But he…he had a shotgun. We got away, and Will said it would be all right as long as we didn't tell anyone, that the man couldn't know who we were. Will said if I told I could end up in jail." He seemed to run out of steam, his voice trembling.

Colin exchanged glances with her. "Look, first of all, nobody is going to put you in jail for trespassing. Secondly, if Will got a good scare over this, maybe he did decide to scoot out of town for a while."

"Maybe. Maybe he's hiding, but then maybe the man will come after me."

It sounded absurd, but obviously her brother took the possibility seriously. "Benj, this isn't something you can handle on your own. You need to tell Daadi—"

"No!" Benj took a step back, his eyes widening. He looked more afraid of telling Daad than of the man with the shotgun. "Please, Rachel, I can't. He would be so…so…"

"Disappointed." She finished the sentence for him. Of all people, she knew what it was like to disappoint Daad.

"*Ja*. Please…I—I know I should tell him, but not yet."

"Your dad's going to want to know where you've been," Colin said. "Are you going to lie to him?"

Benj shook his head. "I'll tell him I was over at Joseph's and forgot the time. That's the truth. Just not all of it."

Rachel could only hope he hadn't picked up that rationalization from her, back when she'd been hiding her meetings with Ronnie. "But if Will is hiding, Daad ought to know, so he can talk to Will's folks."

"I can't. If I told Will's folks, he would…" Benj let that trail off, as if he couldn't imagine what Will might do. A tear trickled down his cheek, and he didn't even attempt to wipe it away. "Rachel, promise me. Promise me you won't tell Daadi. Please." He caught her hand, clinging to it, and her heart seemed to jolt.

She couldn't speak for a moment, and the silence seemed alive with crosscurrents—Benj's desperation, Colin's determination, her own indecision.

If she told Daad, she would ruin the relationship she'd begun to build with her brother. If she didn't tell him, and Daad found out, he would never forgive her. Either way, she stood to lose.

But she didn't really have a choice, not with her brother looking at her with such despair in his eyes. "I will not tell Daad," she said slowly.

She wouldn't. Which meant she had to find a way of dealing with the situation Benj had gotten himself into on her own.

CHAPTER FIVE

COLIN WALKED WITH Benjamin as far as the covered bridge, half-thinking the boy might make a bolt for it rather than go home. But Benj walked, if reluctantly, up the lane, and his father came out to meet him.

Colin turned back, emerging from the darkness of the covered bridge into the gentle haze of twilight in the valley. He couldn't help a sideways glance down toward the dam. It looked so peaceful, the water tumbling over the edge to form a quiet pool beneath the trees. But local people knew that peacefulness was deceptive, and kids had always been warned away, even before Aaron Mast's death.

He headed for the stable where he'd left Rachel, only to see her disappearing into the back entrance of the house. The door closed with a somewhat determined thud.

So Rachel didn't want to have a conversation with him about her brother's story. That was a shame, because he had no intention of letting it slide.

When he reached the door he found that Rachel might have closed it, but she hadn't locked it. He tapped on the frame while opening the door. This was not a talk he wanted to have through the door.

Rachel spun to face him, annoyance clear in her expression. But he could see past the annoyance to the very real worry that dwelled beneath.

"I don't want to be rude, but I really wish—"

"Be as rude as you like," he invited. "I'm sure you don't want to discuss your brother with me. But it's too late. I heard, and I'm not going to walk away and conveniently forget."

"Why not?" She didn't say it angrily. She actually looked as if she needed an answer to that question.

Because I have something to make up to you, Rachel. "Because Benj is a friend, and he's in trouble. And because you're a friend, I hope, and you've just agreed to keep quiet about that trouble."

"I suppose you think I should have told on Benj." Her voice snapped with irritation.

"You sound like your little brother. Isn't that what Benj did? Making a stupid promise got him into this grief." Resisting the impulse to touch her arm, he gestured toward the kitchen table. "Come on, Rachel. You know I'm not going away that easily, and *I* didn't make any promises. So let's sit down and talk this over."

Her temper hung in the balance for an instant, but then she nodded, capitulating so suddenly it took him by surprise.

"You're right, of course. I'm sorry for snapping. Sit down. I'd better check on Mandy."

He'd like to think she'd given in because she trusted him, but he wasn't that naive. He pulled out one of the ladder-back chairs and sat. No, she'd agreed to talk because of his implied threat. Trust had nothing to do with it.

He glanced around the kitchen. He'd never been in it, that he recalled. Mrs. Mason hadn't encouraged Ronnie to entertain his friends there. And they certainly hadn't wanted to sit in that formal parlor, so the result had been that they'd gathered elsewhere. It looked more welcoming than he would have imagined, but maybe that was Rachel's touch.

Rachel was back in a moment, letting the kitchen door swing shut behind her. "She's up in her room, so she won't hear us. I don't want Mandy knowing anything about Benj's situation." On the subject of her daughter, Rachel was uncompromising.

"She won't hear anything from me," Colin said. "But that story of Benj's—you don't imagine he was telling us the whole thing, do you?"

"No." Rachel rubbed the back of her neck tiredly. "I'm sure he knows more than that—where they were, and what they were up to, for instance. As for the man with the shotgun…" She let that trail off and sank into the chair opposite him. "Do you think that was real?"

He frowned, picturing Benj's face when he'd said those words. "I think he believed the man had a shotgun, but whether he really did or not is another question. That might have been Benj's guilty conscience imagining things."

"He does feel guilty, doesn't he?" She grasped on that part of his words. "That's good, I think. Maybe it will discourage him from doing anything so foolish again."

"Maybe." Knowing teenage boys he doubted it, but let her hold on to her illusions. "And the man could have had a gun. It would be a rare house around here that didn't have a hunting weapon of some sort. And someone hearing prowlers on his property might well carry one to investigate."

Rachel nodded, a shudder going through her. "Benj should have realized that sort of thing might be dangerous. Why on earth would he sneak out like that?"

"Because the older kid asked him, or maybe dared him, and he had to show what a man he was." He could remember more than a few instances when he'd fallen for similar temptation. "Somebody once dared me to raid Franklin Sitler's apple trees, and I was stupid enough to do it. That old man can move faster than you'd think. He took off after me with a BB gun, and I was lucky to escape a peppering. Not so lucky when my dad found out, though."

Dad hadn't been one to spare the rod and spoil the child in those days, but hearing his father accuse him of stealing had hurt worse than any physical punishment.

Rachel actually smiled at that, but then she sobered just as quickly. "Mr. Sitler has that reputation." Rachel glanced toward the front of the house, as if she could see through the walls to the house across the street. "If they trespassed on his property—"

Colin snorted. "Trespassed? They were planning more than that, believe me. Some sort of vandalism, or I miss my guess."

Rachel's eyes widened. "I can't believe Benj would be involved in vandalism. He knows that's wrong."

"Of course he does. There'd be no fun in doing it otherwise." The expression on her face made him dial it back. Now was not the time to tell her about the things he and Ronnie used to get into. "Look, this business about Will Esch disappearing—that's what bothers me. Benj didn't seem to know what to really think about it, just that it scares him."

"Running off is all part of *rumspringa* for some boys. They think they have to see a little of the Englisch world before they settle down. At least, with him out of the way, Benj won't be getting into any more trouble."

He hated to burst her bubble, but he had to. "Benj doesn't see it that way. He's acting even jumpier than he did before. And that's why you ought to let your dad handle it."

"I know. I know." Rachel's eyes were filled with misery. "But you heard Benj. He's more frightened of disappointing Daad than of whatever it is he's gotten involved in. Believe me, I know that feeling."

He reached out, clasping her hand where it lay on the table. "I'm sorry. He still hasn't forgiven you?"

Rachel shook her head, looking down at the maple surface of the table, probably to hide the fact that there were tears in her eyes. She took a breath so deep he could see her chest rise and fall. "I promised Benj. I know it wasn't a smart promise to make, but I can't let him down. If I tell Daad, Benj will never forgive me."

"Right. And if you keep his secret and your father finds out, he'll never forgive you."

She nodded, not looking up. She seemed to have forgotten that he was holding her hand.

"Well, I guess there's just one thing for it, then." He forced some cheerfulness into his voice. "I guess we'll have to find out for ourselves how serious this business is."

She did look up at that, and she drew her hand away from his. "We?" The spark came back into her voice and her face. "I don't recall asking for your help."

"You forget, Benj told me as well as you. That means I'm in."

She shook her head firmly. "I'll try to get Benj to tell me more, and I'll question my sisters and see if they have any notion of what he was up to. There's nothing you can do."

"Sure there is. I can find out if anyone's been complaining about vandalism, for one thing. If a homeowner chased off a bunch of kids, he'll be talking about it."

Alarm filled her face. "You won't let on that Benj is involved."

"What do you take me for? No, never mind, don't answer that." He already knew what she thought of him, and he didn't need to hear it again. "I'll be subtle. If we could find out where Will Esch went…"

He pondered, turning over possibilities in his mind. Trouble was, the Amish tended to stay off the grid. There was no easy way to trace an Amish kid who wanted to vanish.

"One of my sisters might know what the other kids are saying. They're more likely to know than the adults." Rachel was looking better for having a plan for what to do about Benj's trouble.

"Good idea." He hesitated, wanting to touch her reassuringly but thinking he'd better not push it. "We'll figure it out. Try not to worry."

She nodded, managing a faint smile. "Thank you, Colin. I'm not sure why you're taking so much trouble over this, but thank you."

He did touch her then, just a quick, feather-light brush of his knuckles against her hand. It was a tenuous truce between them, one that could collapse at a breath. But he'd take what he could get where Rachel was concerned, it seemed.

BY THE NEXT DAY, Rachel was planning her first approach to solving Benj's problem. She had to find out what, if anything, her mother knew about it. Benj seemed to think he was succeeding in keeping secrets from their parents, but Rachel doubted it, at least where Mamm was concerned.

The major issue in seeing her mother was catching Mamm at a time when Daad wasn't around. If Daad was there, the conversation would never get deeper than meaningless chatter.

Fortunately she'd glanced out the side window in midmorning and spotted Daad and Mose going up the lane from their farm in the wagon. They turned right at the road, headed in the direction of the feed mill.

If that was where they were headed, they'd be some time. Though the men would deny gossiping, the mill was the center for male exchange of news and views about anything and everything that went on in the valley and beyond.

Once the wagon had moved out of sight, she called to Mandy to join her, and soon they were headed back along the lane, Rachel carrying a couple of empty egg cartons that would serve as an excuse for her appearance at her parents' farm if one was needed.

Mandy skipped beside her, her sneakers making a hollow sound on the floor of the covered bridge. "Has the bridge been here a long time, Mommy?" She gave an extra jump to emphasize her question.

"Longer than I can remember, anyway." It had never occurred to Rachel to wonder, but she'd never been as curious and questioning as Mandy was. Was that because of the way she'd been brought up, or simply an innate difference between them? "There might be a date on one of the end posts. Let's look."

They emerged into sunlight, and Mandy darted to the right, clutching the end post to peer at it. "There's nothing here," she called. "Maybe the other one." She started for the other post, but Rachel caught her hand.

"We can look on the way back. Right now I want to get to the farmhouse before—"

Before her father got back. No, she didn't intend to say that, did she?

"Before what, Mommy?" Mandy always pitched on just the thing you wanted her to ignore.

"Before it gets too late to make those cookies you want to bake. We need to get eggs, remember?" She held up the egg cartons, as if they verified her intent.

"I remember. Chocolate chip or peanut butter?"

"Whichever you want." A full cookie jar had been a given in her childhood. *May a child never run out of your pantry with a tear in his eye.* Her mother had been a firm believer in that old Pennsylvania Dutch saying.

Mandy darted ahead of her as they walked up the lane to the farmhouse, blithely sure of her welcome. Something seemed to squeeze Rachel's heart. She never wanted her child to lose that bright self-confidence.

As they neared the house, Mandy started for the

front door, but Rachel shook her head. "We'll go to the back. In the country, people mostly go to the kitchen door."

Mandy fell into step with her, but her head tilted as she came out with the inevitable question. "Why?"

Rachel shrugged. "I don't know." Her daughter was making her question things she'd always taken for granted. "I guess the kitchen is the busiest place in the house, and people just naturally go there."

She stepped up onto the porch and came to a halt at the screen door. Knock, or just go in? It seemed ridiculous to knock on a door she'd run in and out of thousands of times.

Luckily it was decided for her. Lovina, her sixteen-year-old sister, spotted them and darted to hold the door open for them, her freckled face widening in a smile that seemed genuinely welcoming. "Rachel and Mandy. *Komm, komm.*" She shooed them inside. "Mammi, look who is here."

The farmhouse kitchen never changed, it seemed—the same faded linoleum on the floor, the same wooden cabinets, surely the same long pine table at which she'd shared family meals for so many years. The gas range contained several steaming kettles, and the air was filled with the sweet, rich scent of strawberries.

"You're making strawberry jam. I hope we haven't come at a bad time." Rachel stopped just inside the kitchen, her gaze on her mother's face—

still, even stern, with lines carved probably by Rachel's deeds. If Mammi didn't want her here…

"Daad and Mose went to the mill. They won't be back for ages," Lovina said quickly.

"*Ja*, that is so." Mamm looked at Mandy, her expression softening. She wiped her hands carefully on a dish towel and then held them out to Mandy. "Will you give your *grossmammi* a hug, then?"

Luckily Mandy didn't require any urging. She went willingly, wrapping her arms around Mamm's waist. They made a strange picture, the gray-haired figure in dark Amish garb holding tightly to the ponytailed child in jeans and a bright aqua T-shirt.

Mamm's gaze met Rachel's over her child's head. It was a look filled with a complex mix of emotions, mingling love, fear and worry. But not blame, Rachel thought, and gratitude filled her heart. This might not be easy, but at least she had a chance to mend fences with her mother.

Her other sister, Naomi, who must be twenty by now, gave a sudden exclamation and rushed to lift the kettle off the stove. "*Ach*, we will burn the jam for sure if we don't get it bottled."

"Let me help you." Rachel reached for the heavy kettle, but Naomi drew it back. Rachel's hands fell to her sides. Apparently she had presumed too much with Naomi.

"I'll help Naomi," Lovina said quickly. "You and Mamm sit and talk, *ja?* There's a jar of tea in the fridge."

Rachel looked to her mother for approval. There were unexpected pitfalls even in the familiar kitchen, it seemed.

"*Ja, ja*, I will get some tea." Mamm scurried to the gas-powered fridge. "And Mandy will like lemonade, ain't so?"

"That sounds good, Grossmammi." Mandy delivered the unfamiliar word with confidence. "Can I help?"

"*Ach, now, chust* sit here next to me." Mamm had glasses and drinks on the table in a moment, and from the familiar cookie jar emerged handfuls of snickerdoodles. "Now we can chat, *ja?* Benjamin has been helpful to you?" She made it a question.

"I don't know how I'd get along without him," Rachel said frankly. "There's a lot to be done to the house."

"I wish…" Mamm let that thought trail off, but Rachel thought she could fill in the rest. "Benj is a *gut* boy. Smart, too."

Lovina turned from ladling transparent ruby jam into jars. "Not smart enough to stay away from that Will Esch," she said.

Here was her opening, if she could take advantage of it. "What's wrong with Will?" she asked.

"Nothing," her mother said quickly. She sent a look toward Lovina that Rachel didn't have any trouble interpreting. *Don't talk about a member of the faith before an outsider.* "But he is older than Benj, that's all."

"Anyway, he's gone now." Lovina apparently wasn't easily squashed. "Went away in the night, I hear."

"Enjoying his *rumspringa*, is he?" Rachel ventured another question, aware of Mandy's bright eyes taking it all in.

"He is sixteen," Mamm said. "Sixteen-year-olds don't always have *gut* sense." Her tone was final.

Before Rachel could frame another question, the screen door banged. Benj stood there, his fair skin reddening as he seemed to feel himself the target of all those eyes.

"Benj, there you are." Mamm's voice was gently scolding. "Your sister is here," she added unnecessarily. "You will take Mandy out to get some eggs, *ja?*" Obviously Mamm had spotted the egg cartons Rachel had nearly forgotten about. "And then…"

Mamm glanced at the clock, and Rachel understood. She was meant to be gone by the time Daad and Mose got home.

"*Ja*, sure," Benj said with a quick grin for Mandy. "*Komm*. I'll show you how to snatch the eggs away from the hens."

Mandy jumped up, always ready for something new. "You mean we're going to get the eggs right from the chickens?"

"For sure. Where do you think eggs come from?"

"The store," Mandy said, following him out.

There was a little silence when the door closed behind them, and Rachel had a sense of time slipping away. If she was going to talk to her mother about Benj, she'd better do it.

She studied her mother's face, wondering how to begin. Maybe just plunge in.

"Have you noticed that Benj seems to be worried about something lately?"

Mamm's expression didn't change, but Rachel saw a flicker of something in Lovina's face. And maybe Naomi, also, but Naomi turned away quickly as if to deny it.

"He is…" Mamm hesitated. "Benjamin is fourteen. Most boys that age are moody. That's all it is."

It was a flat denial that anything could be wrong. Did her mother even believe her own words? Somehow Rachel doubted it. But clearly, whatever she thought, she wouldn't discuss Benj's problems with Rachel.

If Rachel had stayed here, married someone in the faith, had a family in the church, it would have been different. Rachel would have been the oldest married daughter, the one Mamm confided in. But she'd given up the position when she left.

Naomi moved suddenly, peering out the window. "It's Daad, back already."

Rachel's stomach tightened. The last thing she wanted was another uncomfortable exchange with her *daad*. But that was just what she was going to get.

She stood. "I'd better get home."

"Ja, ja." Mamm stood, too, wiping her palms on

her apron. She seemed about to hustle Rachel out the door, but then she stopped, touching Rachel's arm. "*Komm* again," she said softly.

Rachel nodded, unable to speak. She went outside quickly, but not fast enough. Daad was already getting down from the wagon, his gaze fixed on her, and then looking questioningly toward Mamm.

"Rachel." He said her name heavily. "Why are you here?"

Beyond him, Mose held the lines. He seemed to be looking toward her, but his hat brim shielded his eyes so that she couldn't be sure.

"She came to buy some eggs," Lovina said, her tone pert. "Nothing wrong with that." She gestured toward the chicken coop. Benj and Mandy were already on their way back, Benj hastening his stride at the sight of his father.

Rachel pulled a couple of dollars from the pocket of her denim skirt. If she had been under the *bann*, no Amish person would do business with her, but she wasn't. She had left the church before making baptismal vows, and there was no reason other than Daad's stubbornness for refusing her.

Daad gave a curt nod. "*Ja*. That's fine." He paused as Mandy came running up to them.

"Benj showed me how to take the eggs from the nesting boxes," Mandy said, obviously trying to get the terminology right. "It was fun, and I didn't get pecked."

"Gut, gut," Daad said. "You will have eggs for your supper?"

Mandy shook her head. "I'm going to bake cookies," she said. "I'll save some for you."

There was a little silence, as none of the adults seemed to know quite what to say in the face of Mandy's calm assumption of a relationship with her grandfather.

"That is *gut,*" Daad said finally. "I will like that." He went into the house without another word.

"ONE MORE chapter, Mommy. Please?" Mandy, fresh from her bath, snuggled against her pillows, giving Rachel the beguiling smile that was uncannily like Ronnie's.

"That's what you said at the end of the last chapter." Rachel put the dog-eared copy of *The Lion, the Witch and the Wardrobe* facedown on the bear-paw quilt that covered Mandy's bed. "I know stalling when I hear it."

"Not stalling, honest. I just love the story. I have to know what happens next."

Precious as the bedtime ritual was, Rachel was only too aware of the unfinished laundry downstairs, piling up just like everything else in her life. "You can read one more chapter on your own, all right? Then it's lights-out time."

Mandy pouted a little, but she quickly gave that up as unlikely to gain any further concessions. "Okay."

Rachel bent for one last hug and then retreated before Mandy could think of any other great reasons to put off bedtime. Stifling a yawn, she headed downstairs to the waiting laundry. She'd trade bedtimes with Mandy in a snap, but she didn't have that option.

The faint aroma of snickerdoodles lingered in the back of the house. After tasting her *grossmammi*'s cookies, Mandy had clamored to make those instead of her usual chocolate chip favorite. The aroma had somehow made the big house feel more like home.

Rachel had left a light burning in the kitchen, but the hall to the pantry and laundry room was dark. She groped for the switch, still not familiar with all the peculiarities of the old house.

The switch wasn't in the logical place to the right of the door. Of course not—this part of the house had probably been carved out of a larger room in one of the numerous renovations the place had seen.

She groped her way along the hall, feeling for the switch. Just as her fingers touched it, a sound came from the back door—a frantic scratching, as if something were trying to get in.

Rachel froze. Then she pressed the switch and the hallway was flooded with light. Something moved beyond the glass in the back door, and her stomach gave a visceral twinge before she realized it was Benj, his white face and palms pressed against the pane.

She reached the door in a few quick steps, flipped the lock and yanked it open. "Benj, what on earth—"

Her brother bolted inside. "Close it, *schnell*. Someone is after me."

The rational part of her mind insisted that was ridiculous, but the fear in Benj's voice couldn't be denied. Rachel shut the door and locked it before turning back to him.

"Now, what's going on? Why are you out so late? What are you afraid of?"

Benj sidled away from the door. "I had to talk to…to somebody. I couldn't get away 'til after chores, and then I couldn't find him right away, and…" He seemed to run out of words, sending another glance toward the door.

Rachel grasped Benj's arm and led him into the kitchen, well away from whatever it was that spooked him out in the dark. "Out with it. I suppose you were talking to the other boy who was in this mess with you and Will. Who is it?" It was the tone she used with Mandy when she didn't want any further argument.

"Joseph," Benj said. "Joseph Stoltz."

She registered the name, not sure which of the several Stoltz families had a teenager named Joseph. "Did you finally find him?"

"Ja." Benj looked down, obviously not eager to say more.

"What did Joseph have to say for himself?" Her sympathy for teenaged boys was unraveling rapidly.

Benj looked up, the whites of his eyes showing like those of a spooked horse. "He said Will didn't say anything to him about going away. He didn't want to talk—afraid his *daad* was going to hear. He kept telling me to go home."

She had the sense he was holding something back. "What else?"

Benj bit his lip, as if to keep from speaking. "He…he said maybe the man with the gun got Will. And I started to walk home, but it was getting dark, and I think someone was behind me, and I saw your light so I came to the door." The words spilled out, and Benj fixed his gaze on her face, pleading with her to believe him.

"Benj…" What could she say? She was caught between sympathy and exasperation. "For goodness sake, this is Deer Run. Nobody is following you around just because you were trespassing."

"But Will is gone." His voice rose, trembling on the verge of going back into the treble he'd probably shed fairly recently. "And there was someone behind me."

"Probably it was someone walking his dog." She hesitated, trying to think what was best to do. She couldn't send him out into the dark to walk home, scared as he was. But Mandy was already in bed….

Benj was welcome to stay here for the night, of course, but there was no way to tell Mamm and Daad. They shared a phone shanty with the next farm beyond theirs, a safe distance from the house to discourage idle chatter on the phone. In this case, they might as well not have one at all.

"Go up to Mandy's room and tell her to put on her robe and slippers and come down. I'll get the car out and drive you home. You'll have to explain to Mamm and Daad why I'm driving you home, though."

"*Denke*, Rachel." Benj looked as if even that was better than going out in the dark alone. He went quickly toward the stairs.

Shaking her head, Rachel grabbed her key ring and a flashlight. Benj's fear was getting out of hand. Sympathetic as she was, she simply couldn't believe in a shadowy figure following her little brother through the streets of Deer Run.

Maybe the necessity of telling Daad why she'd brought him home would lead into confessing the whole story. That would be the best solution.

Little though she wanted to admit it, Colin had been right. Her father was the proper person to handle this situation. She should never have made that promise.

Rachel went out the back, not bothering to switch on the flashlight. It wasn't really dark yet, though the shadows lengthened, spreading pools of blackness near the overgrown lilac hedge.

Obviously Joseph, whoever he might be, was just as spooked by this situation as Benj was. It sounded as if Will Esch had been the ringleader, guiding the other two boys into mischief they wouldn't have thought of on their own.

A breeze set the trailing branches of the weeping willow swaying, almost as if someone sheltered behind them, sending them moving in response to his presence.

Nonsense, her practical side asserted itself. Her imagination was getting as bad as Benj's.

Her feet found the gravel lane, and she moved toward the garage, the surface crunching under her feet. She took a few more steps and froze, her breath catching. Was that an echo of her steps, somewhere behind her? Or was it someone coming along the lane, matching his steps to hers?

Nonsense, she told herself again, but it wasn't quite so robust a response this time. Her fingers tightened on the metal cylinder of the flashlight, and she felt oddly reluctant to switch it on. If she did, she could see if anyone was there. But she'd be lighting up herself as well.

She mentally measured the distance to the garage. Twenty yards, probably. The doors yawned open like a black mouth, but there was a faint reflected glimmer from the back bumper.

In any event, the garage was closer than the house now. Somehow, with that sense of someone behind her, she couldn't retrace her steps. She moved forward, trying for an assurance she didn't feel, and again had that faint sensation of an echo to her steps.

That had to be it. Just an echo. Sound carried in the dark. There wasn't anyone there. There couldn't be.

Quickly, before she could lose her nerve, she covered the rest of the distance to the garage. She touched the trunk lid, cold under her fingertips, and her courage flowed back now that she'd made it. Benj and Mandy would be waiting—they'd wonder what was taking her so long.

Something rustled in the garage, bringing her heart into her throat. She pressed the button on the flashlight, sending its beam into the garage, but before she could even register what she was seeing, something swept toward her, a shape rushing right at her face.

With a stifled cry, she flung up her arms, ducking away, trying to protect her face—

A soft call, a flap of large wings, and the barn owl she'd disturbed swooped off through the night.

A shaky laugh escaped her, and she leaned against the car, the metal cold against her. She was as bad as Benj, letting herself be spooked that way.

She slid into the car, started it and backed out, her headlights reflecting nothing more startling than the glowing eyes of some night creature sheltering under a rosebush.

She pulled to the porch. Benj and Mandy came out and climbed into the car, Mandy chattering away, no doubt pleased at this interruption in her bedtime.

Rachel listened with half her attention, making

the sweeping turn onto the lane and heading toward the covered bridge. *Foolish,* she scolded herself. She wasn't a kid anymore. She was the adult in charge. She couldn't let herself be frightened by normal country night sounds.

She glanced into the rearview mirror as she entered the covered bridge, and her breath caught. From the dense shadow of the lilac bush, another shadow seemed to detach itself—a man-shaped shadow.

CHAPTER SIX

THE LIGHT ON top of the township police car revolved importantly, casting its glow over Mason House, then the street, then the Sitler house, the road and back again. Colin pulled in behind it, his heart lurching in his chest.

Meredith King had been right to call him. She'd have gone to Mason House herself, she'd said, but her mother was having palpitations at the sight of the police car just down the block, and Meredith couldn't leave her.

Colin jumped out, slamming the door, and headed for the house, his pulse racing. Rachel? Mandy? If something had happened to them—

Movement at the front window drew his eye. Rachel stood, hugging Mandy close to her, talking to Jim Burkhalter, the township chief of police. They were all right.

But something had happened, or the police wouldn't be here. Taking a breath, he composed himself. It wouldn't do any good to rush in there like an idiot. Rachel would think…well, he didn't know what she would think, but it would probably raise her hackles if he acted as if he had any right to be worried.

He sidestepped the young patrolman on the porch, who looked as if he couldn't decide whether to stop Colin or not, and moved quickly inside. Rachel's blue gaze touched him, and he thought he read relief there. Maybe he wasn't as unwelcome as he'd thought. Whatever had happened, at least she and Mandy looked fine.

"Hey, Jim. Rachel." He winked at Mandy, and she responded with a grin. Whatever was going on, she seemed to be treating it as entertainment. "What's going on? Jim, you know you're going to have the neighbors complaining about that light, don't you?"

Jim, bulky and balding, sent an annoyed glance out the front window. "Davis!" he bellowed. "Get out there and switch off the light before we have the whole town here."

He glanced at Rachel. "Sorry. Guess I shouldn't have shouted, but Colin's right." He gave Colin a mock glare. "Brought you, didn't it?"

Taking that as an invitation, Colin joined them. "Actually, it's not visible from our place. Meredith called and asked me to see if something is wrong." He raised an inquiring eyebrow.

"Ms. Mason reported a prowler," Jim said, in much the same tone he'd say that she'd reported a cat stuck in a tree. "We had a look around. Didn't see any sign of anyone."

"When did this happen?" Colin wasn't as sanguine as the police chief.

"About a half hour ago. I was..." She hesitated, seeming to edit her words. "I was driving my brother back to the farm, and I thought I caught a glimpse of someone in the bushes by the house. Maybe I overreacted, but I didn't want to come into the house. I called the police on my cell phone."

Driving her brother back to the farm, was she? So Benj had something to do with this. And why had she been driving him, anyway?

"Well, now, you did the right thing," Jim said. "A woman and a child alone in this big place—naturally you didn't want to come in until we'd made sure everything was all right. Don't you think a thing about it. That's what we're here for."

Jim did everything but call her "little lady" and pat her on the head. He was kindness itself, but he clearly thought Rachel's imagination was working overtime.

"That's what the township pays Jim for," Colin added. "No point in having police if we don't call them when we need them."

"Just what I was saying." Jim didn't look especially gratified at his interference. "You be sure to lock up at night, Ms. Mason, and you might think about having a few more outside lights put in. Maybe even get a dog. A pup would let you know for sure if anyone was prowling around outside." He headed for the door.

"You just call again if you need us." He went out, closing the door.

"Or if you need another dose of condescension," Colin added.

Rachel frowned at him. "I thought Chief Burkhalter was very nice. He came right away when I called."

He wanted to say she should have called him, but he didn't suppose she'd appreciate it. "Maybe you ought to give Meredith a ring. Just let her know everything's okay," he said instead.

"Yes, I should." She hurried to the phone.

Mandy tugged on his sleeve. "Did you hear what he said? The policeman? He said we should have a dog."

"I heard. He made a good point, too." He glanced at Rachel, who was obviously listening to them even as she reassured Meredith. Rachel frowned at him.

"But that's really up to your mom, you know," he added.

"I've been asking and asking for a puppy," Mandy said. "Ever since I was a little girl. I ask in my prayers every night, and when I make a wish, that's what it is." She gave an elaborate sigh. "Mommy always said a little apartment wasn't good for a dog, but now we have a whole big house, and a yard, too."

Somehow he had the feeling Rachel wasn't going to be able to hold out much longer. "Dogs can be a lot of work, you know. You have to feed them and brush them and walk them."

"I'd do it. Mommy wouldn't have to do anything." Her words were interrupted by a huge yawn.

Rachel hung up and came toward them. "We'll say good-night now. It's time Mandy was in bed."

He thought he'd ignore the dismissal. "Good night, Mandy." He smiled at Rachel. "I'll be taking a good look around outside while you put her to bed. Then we can talk."

She stiffened. "I don't think—"

"You're not content with the cursory inspection Jim Burkhalter did, are you? Besides, we need to talk about a few things that were omitted from the police report."

"What was omitted, Mommy?" Mandy's bright gaze went from her mother to him.

"Nothing." Rachel's tone was firm. "Off to bed now. Mr. McDonald is just going to check the yard for us."

Taking that as acquiescence, Colin headed out through the kitchen, pausing to grab the heavy flashlight he'd noticed Rachel kept by the back door. He wouldn't be leaving until he'd satisfied himself one way or the other.

But after a half hour's search, he had to admit that the chief had been right. No one was there now, which didn't mean someone hadn't been there earlier. Watching who? Rachel? Or Benjamin? Maybe Benj's fears had some basis in fact.

A few minutes later he'd rejoined Rachel in the front parlor. She'd drawn the ornate drapes and turned on all the lamps, a silent testimony to the fact that she was sure she'd seen something, whatever she might say. Rachel sat down in a bentwood rocker, and he took the chair opposite her.

"Okay," he said. "Now tell me all the things you left out when you talked to Chief Burkhalter."

"I couldn't tell him about Benj," she protested. "You know that."

"I know you're as white as the proverbial ghost," he said roughly. "Why were you driving Benj home?"

She sighed. "All right. He showed up just when I was putting Mandy to bed, scared half to death. He'd been talking to the other boy—Joseph Stoltz, it was. Anyway, Joseph had planted the idea that maybe the man with the gun had gotten to Will. So of course Benj thought someone was following him." She stopped, shaking her head. "He was imagining things. He must have been."

"Only you saw something, too," Colin reminded her.

She nodded, her forehead wrinkling. "I said I'd drive him home. So I went out to get the car. I was going to bring it to the porch, because I didn't want Mandy walking across the grass in her slippers. Anyway, I kept thinking I heard something. But it was just a barn owl." She was obviously trying to convince herself.

"But you saw something," he reminded her.

She nodded. "When I was pulling out toward

the bridge, I glanced in the rearview mirror. And I saw…I thought I saw…someone move by the big lilac bush."

He frowned. He'd like to come back in daylight and have a thorough search around that lilac bush for any sign someone had been there. "Anything distinguishing about him? Man or woman? Amish or Englisch?"

"It was impossible to tell." She looked down at her hands, clasped in her lap. "It was just a shadow, about the size or shape of a man. But it was so fast— it might have been anything. Including my imagination." She made an effort to smile, but it wasn't convincing. "Anyway, I probably shouldn't have called the police, but Mandy was with me."

And she wouldn't take chances where her daughter was concerned, that was clear.

She glanced at the mantel clock, a ponderous Victorian piece. "It's late. You should go."

He probably should. People would talk, of course. They always did. "Don't you want to know the results of my search into anyone complaining about vandals on their property?"

She blinked. "You really did that?"

"I really did," he assured her. "You'd be surprised what you can learn if you hang around the hardware store and the feed mill for a bit. Lots of interesting stuff. But nobody talking about vandalism, or chasing kids off their property."

She looked relieved. "That's good, isn't it?"

"It's odd, that's what it is. If Benj is telling the truth about the man chasing them, why isn't the story going around? It's just the kind of thing people talk about, but no one did."

Rachel rubbed her forehead. "I guess you're right, but I'm too tired to make any sense out of it. And you should go. People will see your car, and it's bad enough that the police were here."

He'd like to stay until he was sure that the last trace of apprehension was gone from Rachel's face, but she was right. He'd simply make things more difficult for her by staying.

"Okay, okay." He rose. "Guess I know when I'm not any more welcome than the police."

"You know that's not what I meant," she said, following him to the front door and grasping the knob.

"Try not to worry." He stepped onto the porch, and then held the door with one hand as she started to close it. "There is one place where I agree with Chief Burkhalter, though. He was right. You should get a dog."

That made her smile. "I guess I'll have to give in on that one, won't I?" She paused for the space of a breath. "Thanks for coming, Colin. I seem to keep saying that, don't I?"

"Anytime." The barriers between them might be crumbling, but he couldn't take anything for granted. "Good night, Rachel."

He went quickly across the porch and down the steps, listening as she closed and locked the door behind him. As he reached the car, he saw a flicker of movement at one of the windows in the Sitler house across the street. Someone watching? Or maybe just attracted by the noise on a quiet night?

He opened the car door, glancing down the street to see if anyone else had been disturbed. Several houses down from the Sitler place was The Willows. Jeannette Walker stood framed in the window, holding the curtain back with one hand as she stared down the street toward him. Did she realize how visible she was? Probably not.

Annoyed, he waved to her elaborately and had the satisfaction of seeing the curtain drop from her hand at once, masking the window. He'd been right. People were interested, and people would talk.

RACHEL FOUND HERSELF hesitating at the prospect of going out of the house the next day. Ridiculous, to suppose that everyone would be thinking ill of her because of the police car disturbing the quiet last night.

Wasn't it?

Well, maybe not. Deer Run was a small community, the sort of place where people knew all about their neighbors. At the very least, they'd be curious.

She wouldn't be a coward about it. Taking the toolbox she'd resurrected from the cellar, she headed out front. She really had to make an effort to fix that front railing before someone fell.

"Hi, Mommy. Look where I am!"

Mandy's voice came from above. She was perched on the limb of the large oak that anchored the corner of the lot.

"What are you doing up there?" Rachel repressed the urge to tell Mandy to get down at once. Climbing a tree was a natural challenge for a nine-year-old.

"There's a little seat up here, see?" Mandy patted the crosspiece of wood she sat on. "Who do you think put it here?"

She managed what she hoped was a natural smile. "Your daddy, I'd guess. I remember he had a tree fort up there when he was a little older than you are."

She'd been able to see the Mason place from the farm, and Ronnie's activities had always fascinated her. One of their first actual encounters had occurred when he'd caught her watching him while he was catching minnows in the creek just upstream from the bridge. She'd ended up joining him, splashing and laughing as if he'd been an old friend.

"Can I make one, too? I could bring up some boards to make a floor, and..." Rachel could almost see Mandy's wheels turning.

"Not without someone to help you." That came out too sharply, and she tried to smooth it over with a smile. "I have another project I have to do right now. Later I'll see if I can find some boards for you to use." Preferably ones that didn't have any protruding rusty nails. "In the meantime, why don't you figure out a plan for a fort? Decide which branches you're going to put it on, and how long the boards need to be."

"Cool." Mandy began scrambling down. "I'll get a ruler and some paper. And when Benj comes, I bet he'll help me." She raced into the house.

The mention of Benj sent Rachel's thoughts tumbling back to the previous night's events even as she checked the railing. Would Benj have told Daad the whole story once he got home? She could only hope he had.

Inevitably, thoughts of the previous night led to Colin. He'd come, thinking she was in trouble. He'd cared, accepting the responsibility that went with friendship, even though she hadn't been particularly nice to him. And when their hands had brushed lightly, her insides had leapt so that she couldn't pretend to herself that she was unaffected.

The problem was that when she let down her guard with Colin, things happened. She stared at the board in front of her, trying to concentrate and only succeeding in seeing Colin's face. She knew, only too well, what giving in to Colin could lead to. All those years ago, it had led to that kiss, and its aftermath had been particularly problematic.

She had to stop thinking about him.

The gate squeaked, announcing a visitor. Rachel looked up warily, but it was Meredith, possibly the one person she was happy to see at the moment.

"How are you?" Concern darkened Meredith's

brown eyes. "It looks as if you're none the worse for last night's excitement."

"I'm fine." She dusted her palms off on her jeans.

"Don't let me interrupt the work." Meredith sat down on the step, apparently not worried about getting her navy pants dirty. "We can talk while you do whatever it is you're doing. The police didn't find anyone lurking around?"

"Not a soul. I'm sure Chief Burkhalter is convinced I'm a hysterical female jumping at shadows."

"I never did think very highly of his intelligence," Meredith said. "Naturally a prowler isn't going to hang around if he hears a siren. Come on, Rachel, give. I can tell there's more to this than you thinking you spotted someone in the yard. Why were you driving Benj home anyway?"

Naturally Meredith would see how silly that was. They had run all over the place in the summer twilight when they were kids.

"Benj was spooked," she said, picking her words carefully. Of course, she'd only promised not to tell Daad, but she didn't want rumors of Benj's misadventures getting around. "He'd been to see a friend, and he started imagining someone was following him when he was walking home."

"If he weren't Amish, I'd say he'd seen too many horror movies," Meredith commented. "And that still might be it, depending on who his friends are."

Rachel nodded, knowing as well as Meredith that

Amish kids found ways of watching television, even going to movies, without their parents finding out.

"I did think he was imagining things, but I said I'd drive him home. When I pulled out, I glanced in the rearview mirror, and I was sure I saw someone step out of the shadow of the lilac bush." She glanced toward the overgrown hedge of lilacs that marked the border between Mason House and the next property. "So I called the police." She shrugged, sitting down next to Meredith. The railing could wait. She didn't have that many chances to renew an old friendship. "I probably overreacted."

"I don't think so." Twin lines appeared between Meredith's brows. "Deer Run may be a peaceful place, but bad things can happen anywhere these days, and maybe that's always been true. You have your daughter to consider."

"I won't take chances with Mandy." There were no qualifications to that statement.

"What did Benjamin think?"

"I didn't mention what I saw to him. I just drove him on home before I called. He was nervous enough without my adding to it." She clasped her hands in her lap. "Funny that no one came over from the farm to see what was going on, though."

Meredith shrugged, a graceful movement of her slim shoulders. She had always had that natural grace, moving like a dancer instead of a gawky kid.

"They probably didn't even notice. I should think

Mason House would block their view, and they might have already been in bed."

Something that might have been relief swept through Rachel. She hadn't realized that the family's disinterest bothered her until Meredith gave her a logical explanation. "You're probably right. I didn't think of that."

"I'm sure your family would come if you needed them." Meredith touched her hand lightly, clearly understanding what lay behind the words. "I just wish I could have, but my mother...well, I thought calling Colin was the next best thing."

"I appreciate it." She studied Meredith's face. "But why Colin?"

Fleeting embarrassment slid across her face and was gone. "Well, I knew that he'd been around to see you. I mean, he was Ronnie's friend, and it's natural..."

"People are talking, in other words." Rachel was beginning to be resigned to it.

"You know how Deer Run is." Meredith's voice had an unexpected edge. "They love to gossip about other people's business. It's perfectly natural for Colin to give you a helping hand. And if there's anything more—"

"There isn't," she said quickly. "There couldn't be."

Meredith's bright gaze seemed to indicate that Rachel was protesting too much. "Well, it would be nobody's business if there was. It isn't as if you're Amish any longer."

"No." The casual words were true enough, but they set up a lonely echo in her heart.

"That line between Amish and Englisch can be a bigger issue than people think. You know that better than anyone, but…" Meredith let her statement trail off.

"But what?"

"I know what it's like, as well. My dad was Amish. You knew that, didn't you?"

Rachel could only shake her head, surprised and a little shocked. John King had been Amish? Well, the name fit. There were plenty of Amish King families in Pennsylvania. "I didn't know. I don't know why no one ever mentioned it."

"Ancient history to them, I suppose." Sorrow shadowed Meredith's eyes. "My father gave up everything to marry my mother, just as you did for Ronnie. Sometimes I wonder if…" She didn't finish.

But Rachel thought she knew where the sentence was going. "If it was worth it?" She drew in a breath. "I don't know how your father felt. But I know that even if my marriage wasn't what I had hoped, it was worth it because it gave me Mandy. I'd guess that your dad felt the same way."

"I hope so." Meredith's voice was husky. "I—"

"Well, look at the two of you. Just like old times." The voice startled Rachel. She'd been so intent on their conversation that she hadn't noticed the woman who'd paused by the gate.

She stood, thoughts chasing through her mind. The woman seemed to know her, but her face rang no bells. Older than she and Meredith, certainly, probably near forty, with ash-blond hair grazing the shoulders of a silky blouse and a face so carefully made up she might be ready to step in front of a television camera instead of strolling through Deer Run.

"It's nice to see you, Laura," Meredith said, maybe guessing her dilemma. "I'm sure you remember Rachel Mason. Rachel Weaver, she used to be."

"Of course." Laura's smile was gracious but oddly distracted, as if she couldn't think why she'd started this conversation. "Nice to see you." She turned, drifting across the street with an aimless air.

"Laura Wells?" Rachel had finally put two and two together, but it was hard to reconcile the woman she'd just seen with the lively teenage beauty who'd had half the boys in the valley in love with her.

"Laura Hammond, now. She married Victor Hammond."

"Hammond Markets?"

Meredith nodded. "I can't imagine why. Victor is the most boring man on the face of the earth." She grinned. "Hammond Markets is one of my clients," she added in explanation.

"She's changed." It was all Rachel could find to say. Her gaze followed the slender figure moving without direction down the sidewalk. "She looks like a…a mannequin."

"Or a sleepwalker. Speaking of marriages not working out." Meredith grimaced. "I shouldn't say that. It might not even be what changed her. Aaron's death probably did that."

Rachel blinked, putting together the pieces. "I hadn't thought of the two of them in years. Aaron was the handsome prince, and Laura the beautiful princess who had him in her spell." She shook her head. "It's a wonder to me we got away with everything we did, slipping around spying on the two of them."

"We didn't do any harm." Meredith's tone was practical. "We never told anyone about their secret meetings."

"We thought it was romantic." Amish and Englisch, star-crossed lovers to their young eyes. For the first time it occurred to her to wonder if that childish dream had anything to do with her falling for Ronnie.

"It wouldn't have worked," Meredith said. "Laura never had the guts you did." She grinned. "Inelegant, but true."

"Still, she must have been devastated when Aaron died that way. I don't remember seeing much of Laura after that summer."

"I think her parents sent her away to school," Meredith said. "Anyway, the next thing anyone

heard about her was the big splashy wedding to
Victor."

"Why Victor?" Rachel did remember him, now
that she made an effort. Pudgy, awkward, pedantic, with an incipient paunch even when he was a
teenager.

Meredith shrugged. "All that money, I suppose.
Dennis Sitler and a couple of other guys were in the
running for a time, but she picked Victor. And as
far as one can tell, Victor wanted to marry her because she was the prettiest girl in the valley. Doesn't
exactly make one want to rush out and risk matri-
mony, does it?"

No, it didn't. But then, she was already well-
versed in the perils of that particular institution.
She and Ronnie had been in love, but would he have
been so eager to marry her if she hadn't seemed so
unattainable? Somehow she doubted it.

By late afternoon, four or five people had managed to drop by on one excuse or another, including
Helen Blackwood, obviously wanting to hear why
the police had been at Mason House the previous
night. Rachel shuddered to think how garbled the
story would be by the time it had been transmitted
a few dozen times.

At least she'd gotten a little work done between
interruptions. Hands on her hips, she stood in the
doorway of the largest bedroom and surveyed the results of her labors. The new curtains were hung, the

wide woodwork polished, the massive four-poster covered with a double-wedding-ring quilt. She'd put fresh cushions on the window seat that curved around the circular bay. This bedroom, with its attached bath, had been Mrs. Mason's and was in the best shape, and it was actually ready for visitors. That was cause to celebrate.

Rachel headed downstairs, realizing that it had been too long since she'd checked on Mandy. Voices from the front yard had her hurrying her steps.

She reached the porch to discover there was no reason for alarm. Mandy was on her way down the oak tree, while the cause for her descent stood at the bottom, looking up, his plumy tail waving.

Duke wasn't accompanied by Colin, though. It was his father, James McDonald. Rachel wasn't sure whether she was relieved or disappointed.

The older man was smiling at something Mandy had said, his eyes crinkling in his lean face. He turned at the sound of Rachel's step on the porch stair, smile faltering.

"It's nice to see you, Mr. McDonald. I'm Rachel. Rachel Mason," she added when she didn't see a spark of recognition in his face.

"Oh, of course. Rachel." He held out his hand to shake hers. "Sorry I didn't recognize you. I guess this nice girl is your daughter, then."

Mandy had reached the ground and thrown her arms around Duke's neck. The dog sat, patiently bearing her embrace.

"Yes, Mandy is mine." Rachel shook her head. "I'm afraid she's fallen in love with Duke."

"The feeling must be returned." His smile warmed his slightly austere face, giving Rachel a hint of where Colin had gotten his charm. "Duke insisted on coming right in. I hope you don't mind."

"He's always welcome, and you are, as well. May I get you something? Some lemonade or one of Mandy's snickerdoodle cookies?"

"No, no, not just now." He glanced at his watch, puzzlement in his eyes. "I guess…I think I should go home."

He seemed suddenly uncertain, as if he'd forgotten what he meant to do.

"Is something wrong?"

"No, I don't think…where's Duke?" His tone was querulous.

"Right here," Rachel said, masking her concern and trying to sound soothing. She patted her leg. "Here, Duke. Come here, boy."

Duke trotted to her obediently, followed by Mandy, protesting.

"But Mommy, we were going to play."

"Mr. McDonald wants him," she said. But Colin's father was looking down at the dog, still with that puzzled expression. It began to frighten her.

"Is something wrong, Mr. McDonald?" She touched his arm lightly. "Can I help?"

He shook his head, seeming somehow lost. "I

don't know. I think I should go home, but I don't seem to remember."

Alarm flickered like lightning. Should she do something? Call for help? This wasn't normal, was it?

She shouldn't overreact. Nobody would thank her for that. "Mandy and I are going to walk home with you. Is that all right?"

"Yes, yes. That's nice of you, my dear. What did you say your name was?"

"Rachel. Just let me get my keys and lock the door first." She gestured to Mandy to stay with him.

Mandy nodded, taking his hand and smiling up at him.

Rachel hurried into the house, grabbing keys and cell phone and rushed back out again. Was James ill? It seemed odd that Colin wouldn't have mentioned it, if so.

Or maybe not so odd. Colin had been doing his best to help her, whether she wanted that help or not. In return, she hadn't even inquired into his life. A wave of shame swept over her. Just how selfish was she?

CHAPTER SEVEN

COLIN BACKED OFF on the accelerator as he reached the outskirts of Deer Run. He'd probably broken a few speed limits on his way, but he was nearly home now. He'd better calm down before he reached Dad. And Rachel, for that matter.

Her phone call had shaken him. But then, she'd sounded a bit shaken, as well. Apparently she'd found his father in her yard, and he'd seemed confused about getting home. When he wasn't any better after they'd reached the house, she'd called Colin.

Obviously she hadn't heard any rumors about his father's condition yet. It was hard to believe the town gossips hadn't passed that on already.

Colin pulled into the driveway, parked and got out, trying not to look as if he were panicky. Rachel was waiting when he entered the front door, and her rueful smile eased the tension he felt.

"He's much better now," she said quickly. "I'm so sorry I brought you rushing home from work. I shouldn't have called, but—"

"You did the right thing," he said quickly. "Where is he?"

"On the back porch with Mandy and Duke. They're playing checkers." She smiled. "Well, not Duke. Your father seems fine now, really." A shadow of embarrassment crossed her face. "Maybe I over-reacted. Anyone might be a bit confused. Maybe he'd been out in the sun too long."

Colin moved into the dining room, where he could see the porch through the wide window that overlooked the garden. Dad and Mandy sat on either side of the small table that held the checkerboard. Duke's head was visible above the board, and his gaze moved back and forth as if he were watching a tennis match.

"It's not that. I'm just sorry it was you who found him." Realizing how that sounded, he shook his head, turning back to her. He really was clumsy where Rachel was concerned. "I didn't mean it that way. It's just that most people in Deer Run know about his condition, so they wouldn't have been as alarmed."

Rachel looked at him steadily, blue eyes very serious. "Why haven't you told me?"

He shrugged. There was no good answer to that question. "I don't like people pitying him."

Color came up in Rachel's cheeks, and her eyes snapped. "I don't feel pity. Just concern."

"Trust me, there are plenty who do." That came out with more bitterness than it should, and he shook his head. "Sorry. I suppose it's me, not other people. It's rough to see him so…lost."

The momentary annoyance disappeared from her face, leaving tenderness in its wake. "I know." Rachel's voice was soft. "I'm sorry. Is there nothing the doctors can do to help?"

"Not much, apparently. He's on medication. It's Alzheimer's." The word was still hard to say. "The effect on his short-term memory is showing. He gets confused easily."

A burst of laughter from the porch drew their gaze to the back window. Mandy was clapping her hands while Dad smiled indulgently.

"It hasn't affected his ability to play checkers," Rachel said. "That's the first game Mandy has won, and she's a demon checker player."

"Funny." He reached out, clasping the back of a dining-room chair, its smooth curve fitting his hand. "The way the mind works, I mean. He hasn't lost any of his skill in games, and he can still figure out the percentage on mortgage loans in his head. But he can't always remember how to get home. Although Duke would have gotten him here, if you hadn't found him," he added quickly.

"I'm sure he would."

He shot her a look. "You're thinking I should hire somebody to be with him. I would, if he'd agree. The doctor suggested a health aide, but Dad was outraged at the very idea." He stopped, realizing that a tantalizing aroma was coming from the kitchen. "Are you cooking something?"

Again that faint flush deepened the color in

Rachel's cheeks. "Well, I saw that you had some chicken in the refrigerator, so I thought I'd just start it for your supper. I hope that's all right."

He didn't know why he was surprised. Feeding people in times of trouble was a tradition in Deer Run. When Mom died, the refrigerator was so full of food they'd ended up giving most of it away.

"More than all right. I'm afraid my skill in cooking is limited to putting meat on the grill, and we're both getting tired of that."

"I can imagine." She looked at him as if considering something. "I don't want to offer unwelcome advice, but have you thought of getting one of the Amish girls to come in a few hours a day, just to clean and start supper for you? Your father wouldn't need to know she was keeping an eye on him, as well."

When she spoke, it seemed an obvious solution, and he didn't know why he hadn't thought of it himself. Maybe he'd been too busy concentrating on the problem instead of the solution.

"I don't suppose he would, especially if it gave him a break from my cooking." He raised an eyebrow. "Did you have a particular Amish girl in mind?"

"Well, I did think my sister Lovina might do." Rachel's cheeks flushed slightly, as if she thought she'd spoken out of turn in suggesting her sister. "Lovina would probably welcome some work away from the farm, if Mamm can spare her. She's just a teenager, but I'm sure she's responsible. And a good cook, since Mamm trained her."

He glanced again toward the window. His father's face was animated as he talked with Mandy across the checkerboard. What were they finding to say to each other? Obviously it would be good for Dad not to be alone all day when he was at the office.

"Will you sound out Lovina on the subject?"

"Of course." Rachel hesitated, and he sensed that there was something else she wanted to say.

He smiled at her. "Go ahead. Come out with it, whatever it is."

"I just…I guess I wondered if that was the reason you came home and took over the business. Because of your father's condition."

Now it was his turn to hesitate. He didn't go around talking to people about it. But Rachel wasn't just anyone.

"My mother had cancer and they didn't tell me," he said bluntly. "Mom didn't want anything to distract me from my big, successful career. That Christmas…I knew they hoped I'd come for a visit, but I went on a skiing trip instead. Figured there'd be plenty of time to spend Christmases with them. There wasn't. Mom died in the spring, and by the time I came home, it was too late to do anything but say goodbye. I didn't want it to be too late for my father, too."

"I'm sorry." Rachel put her hand over his, and he saw that her blue eyes were swimming with tears.

He was exposing all his vulnerabilities to her, and that was something he didn't care to do with anyone. Admitting to himself that he'd been wrong was bad enough. Admitting it to Rachel brought them too close, too soon. He cleared his throat, shaking his head.

"We all have to grow up and figure out what's important sometime," he said. "It just took me longer than most. And speaking of growing up, have you seen Benj today?"

It wasn't the most graceful change of subject, but Rachel accepted it. She shook her head. "He hasn't come over. I'm hoping he finally told Daad the whole story. If someone really was lurking around, watching him last night…well, Daad needs to know."

"Yes, he does. This person, assuming he was following Benj, was on your property. That means Benj has involved you in whatever's going on." He thought again of the panic he'd felt when he'd heard the police were at her door. "He's not being fair to you."

"He's my brother." Rachel's tone was soft but very firm. "If he is in trouble, then I am involved, and I wouldn't have it any other way."

He looked at her, unable to put words to his exasperation. The problem was that he understood, only too well, because he felt the same way about her. If she was in trouble, then he was involved, and he wouldn't have it any other way.

Starting supper for Colin and his father was an effective reminder to Rachel that she really had to stop at the market. Most people in Deer Run drove to Williamsport once a week for a major grocery run, then filled in at Millers' shop in between. She'd probably fall into that pattern, as well, but for the moment, she could pick up enough for the next few days from Anna Miller.

Mandy went immediately to the crafts section when they entered the store. Anna was busy ringing up another customer, so Rachel waved and began browsing the aisles, carrying one of the baskets that were provided near the door for shoppers. Unfortunately her comparisons of cereal boxes were disrupted by the image of Colin's face when he talked about his father.

Seeing a parent deteriorate would be hard for anyone, and Colin seemed to be bearing the burden alone. In an Amish community, that sort of mental decline would be accepted as part of the cycle of life, with family and church helping as a matter of course.

Colin was alone, and he was showing a depth of responsibility she wouldn't have expected from him. And he was being so attentive and helpful in her situation with Benj. It was past time she stopped looking at him as if he were still that reckless teenager he'd once been.

The bell on the door jingled. Rachel glanced over. Franklin Sitler, owner of the house across from

Mason House, had come in, seeming unchanged in
the years she'd been away. He'd always looked old
and rather fierce to her, with his hunched figure, his
beetling eyebrows and his hooked nose. He walked
as if he owned the whole town and the people in it,
and age apparently hadn't diminished his arrogance.

At least he didn't notice her. He was stamping toward the counter, followed by a younger man, mut-
tering something that sounded as if he were annoyed
about his order. Or maybe he just always sounded
that way.

Every kid in the village had been scared of him
at one point or another, including Colin, apparently.
She remembered the story of Colin and Sitler's apple
trees. If Benj and the other boys had been trespassing, or worse, committing vandalism on his property, Benj had good reason to be afraid. But Franklin
Sitler would hardly follow Benj around or lurk outside her house. If he had a problem with someone,
he'd confront them head on.

"Rachel Weaver." Her name came out in a hoarse
bark, and she nearly dropped the can of soup she'd
just picked up. Mr. Sitler had spotted her.

"Rachel Mason now, I think." The other man—
fortyish and tall, with a lean, well-bred face—smiled
at her, and she realized who he was. Dennis Sitler,
the old man's grandson. The recognition might not
have come so easily had Meredith not mentioned
him when they were talking about Laura Hammond.

She returned his smile. "It's nice to see you again, Dennis. And Mr. Sitler."

The older man just glowered at her, not speaking, making her wonder if he realized she now lived right across the road from him.

"I was married to Ronnie Mason," she said. "My daughter and I are living in Mason House now."

"I know who you are. And what you're doing." He clamped his teeth on the last word, as if he'd like to take a bite of it.

"Doing?" She was more confused than alarmed, and she found herself glancing at Dennis for guidance.

"Starting a business right across from me in a quiet residential area," the elder Sitler barked. "There'll be traffic at all hours, disturbing my rest, probably trying to park in my driveway, for all I know. I won't have it, you hear me?"

Dennis put a restraining hand on his grandfather's arm. "Don't excite yourself. The whole valley can hear you."

Sitler shook him off. "Don't care if they do."

She couldn't just stand here gaping at him, no matter how startled she was. "Mr. Sitler, I'm afraid there's been some misunderstanding. It's true I'm opening Mason House as a bed-and-breakfast, but I'm sure my visitors won't disturb you in any way."

"What about police cars at all hours of the night? You don't think that was disturbing?" He leaned toward her, and Rachel had to stiffen her legs to keep from backing away.

"I'm sorry if that bothered you." She'd find it easier to sound sincere if the man hadn't started bellowing at her. "I had to report a prowler. I'm sure you wouldn't want anyone prowling around your property."

Maybe she shouldn't have used that particular argument. If Benj had indeed been on Sitler's property...

"Don't believe a word of it. Nobody would dare." But he seemed to be running out of steam, for which she could only be grateful.

Anna came bustling toward them, having disposed of the previous customer, handing two filled shopping bags to Dennis.

"Your order is ready for you."

"That's right," Dennis said. "The car is waiting. Let's get on home now, all right?"

Sitler stood irresolute for a moment. Then, with a last baleful glare, he turned and stamped toward the door, thumping the floor with his silver-headed cane as he went.

Dennis turned an apologetic smile on Rachel. "I'm sorry about that. He gets fixated on a subject sometimes, and you can't get him off it."

"It never occurred to me that he'd be upset by my plans. After all, The Willows is right down the street from his house." Trouble with Mr. Sitler was the last thing she needed.

"Of course your business isn't going to cause problems, any more than Jeannette's does, but I've given up expecting him to be rational," Dennis said. "The police car last night riled him, apparently. I hope you were all right. If I'd been here, I'd have come over to check on you."

He looked so concerned that her stress ebbed. "I appreciate that, Dennis. We're fine. My imagination was probably working overtime."

"I'm glad you're all right. And don't worry about my grandfather. I'm sure that by the time you're ready to open, he'll have forgotten all about it."

"I hope so. I really want to be on good terms with my neighbors."

Dennis's lips quirked in amusement. "If you can stay on good terms with my grandfather, you're a miracle worker, isn't that right, Anna?"

Anna chuckled comfortably. "*Ach*, I don't mind the things he says about my food. He always comes back, ain't so?"

Dennis nodded. "He doesn't mean most of the things he says these days. It's good of you to take it that way."

The blare of a horn from the street made him tighten his grip on the bags. "I'd better get him home. Rachel, I'm glad to see you back in Deer Run. I wish you every success." He went quickly out the door, probably hoping to reach the car before his grandfather resorted to the horn again.

"He's right, you know." Anna patted Rachel's

shoulder comfortingly. "That old man's gotten sourer with age, and how Dennis puts up with him is more than I can say. But then, he's family."

Family. That said it all, as far as Anna was concerned.

"Sitler is lucky to have him close. Is Dennis still living in Deer Run?"

Anna shook her head. "Got a condo in Williamsport overlooking the river, so I hear. He's with one of the banks there. But he comes out at least once a week to help the old man. Doesn't like him living alone, he says, but there's a cousin of his staying there now, so maybe that takes some of the worry away."

She thought again of Colin and his father. Colin was showing far more responsibility than she'd have thought possible. She'd have to make an opportunity to speak to Lovina soon.

"Funny thing, Dennis never marrying," Anna went on. "Folks used to think he and Laura Wells would make a match of it. Goodness knows he was crazy about her when he was young. But there, most of us don't end up with our first loves, and maybe that's for the best." She stopped, as if realizing what she'd said.

Rachel would have to get over being sensitive about Ronnie if she expected to get along here, it seemed. "Are you saying Jacob wasn't your first love?" She kept her voice light with an effort.

"He wasn't, but you won't go telling him that,

ja?" Anna chuckled and headed back to the counter. "And don't you mind anything Sitler says, either. His bark is worse than his bite."

Rachel could only hope that was true, especially if her little brother had managed to run afoul of the man. Her worry, never far away, resurfaced. "Anna, have you heard anything about Will Esch being missing?"

Anna looked a little surprised at the change of subject, but she nodded. "*Ja*, there's been some buzzing about it. I hear the bishop went to see his *mamm* and *daad* to see if there was anything he could do. It's a shame for Will to worry his folks that way."

"So you think he ran off?" It was the logical explanation—far more logical than her brother's nightmares about someone taking him.

"*Ja*, what else?" Anna spread her hands. "You know how teenage boys are. They get to thinking there's more to life than working on the farm— think they're going to go out in the world and drive a fancy car and make a lot of money. They soon find out how wrong they are."

"His parents must be half out of their minds with worry." She could imagine how Mamm and Daad would feel if it were Benj.

"*Ach*, well, Will has always been a bit wild. I doubt it came as much of a shock to them. And word is they think he's gone to join a cousin who's working down at the shore, so that's not as bad as being off on his own. He'll come home, dragging his tail behind him, like the nursery rhyme says, ain't so?"

"I'm sure you're right." She'd like to be as confident of that as Anna seemed to be.

BY THE TIME she and Mandy reached home, Rachel had decided she'd had enough drama for one day. Unfortunately, it didn't improve her disposition any to find a stranger standing at the front door, knocking.

"Can I help you?" She went toward him with Mandy skipping along in front, carrying the lightest of the bags.

"Mrs. Mason?" He stepped out into the sunlight, giving her a better look at him. Middle-aged, balding, he carried a satchel that made her assume instantly that he was selling something.

Whatever it was, she couldn't afford it. "Yes, I'm Mrs. Mason." She went up the steps to the porch, eager to set down the grocery bags while she fished out her key. He drew a card from his shirt pocket and handed it over with something of a flourish. "Edward Evans. I represent the tricounty tourist bureau."

"I see." She took the card. "What can I do for the tourist bureau?"

"It's not what you can do for us, Mrs. Mason. It's what we can do for you. The tourist bureau puts out a seasonal booklet giving visitors information about businesses and places of interest in the area, as well as promoting special events. Anything to bring in those tourists, you know." He smiled broadly, making a gesture as if reeling in a fish.

"I'm afraid I can't afford an advertisement right now...." she began.

He shook his head. "No, no, that's not why I'm here. Not that we discourage advertisers, of course, but your name was given to us as someone starting a new bed-and-breakfast in Deer Run, and in order to consider listing it, it's necessary that it be inspected and approved. So, I'd like to come in and have a look around."

Appalled wasn't a strong enough word for her feelings. She had exactly one room ready to be seen by anyone at the moment.

"I'm nowhere near ready to open, Mr. Evans. Much as I'd like to be listed in your guide, it's too soon for that."

"Better too soon than too late," he said, propping one hand on the door frame.

Clearly she wasn't going to get rid of the man unless she let him come in. Rachel unlocked the door and pushed it wide.

"I'll be happy to show you what Mason House looks like so far, but please understand that we're still working on the house."

A half hour later she was showing him back out, reminding herself of those words. She wasn't ready to open. And judging by her visitor's reaction, he didn't think she ever would be.

He stopped on the walk, looking up at the house and then taking in the view on either side. "I will say you have a lovely setting here, but the condition of the house…" He didn't need to finish that sentence. "Well, I'm afraid I can't list you in the current issue. You can try again at the end of the summer, if you like."

It was on the tip of her tongue to say that she hadn't really tried to be included this time, but she repressed the words. She couldn't afford to make an enemy of the man.

"Thank you. I appreciate your time."

"Yes, well…" He looked as if he were searching for something encouraging to say. "Your proximity to an Amish farm is a plus, of course. You might want to feature that in your advertising."

She couldn't imagine what Daad might say to that. "It's actually my parents' farm."

"You're Amish?" His eyebrows rose so high she could see his scalp lifting.

"Not any longer." She wasn't sure what she was now.

"Even so, that gives you something the other local B and B owners don't have." He actually sounded excited. "People will be fascinated by the idea of staying at a place run by someone who was raised Amish. You might even consider offering your guests the chance to have a meal in an Amish home. There are plenty of places in Lancaster County doing that, but nobody around here that I know of."

"I don't know...." She couldn't imagine how her father would react to that suggestion.

He beamed at her, as if she were a dull student who'd unexpectedly scored well. "That puts a whole new face on things. You get in touch with me when you have the place ready, and I'll come out and take photos, help you write up your listing in the publication." He shook her hand briskly. "Pleasure to meet you, Mrs. Mason. A real pleasure." And he was off, leaving her staring after his car.

"Why are you standing there with your mouth open?" Meredith leaned against the fence, what appeared to be a large book tucked under her arm.

"I'm not." Rachel shook her head. "Well, maybe I am. It was the oddest thing. This man from the tourist bureau showed up without any warning. I certainly didn't get in touch with him. Anyway, he spent a half an hour telling me why I wasn't going to succeed in running a bed-and-breakfast. And then when he found out I'd been raised Amish, he did an about-face and talked about how great that was, as if I'd capitalize on being Amish to get customers."

"Well, why not?" Meredith was practical, as always. "If you're going to run a business, you have to take advantage of every edge you have."

"It seems...wrong, somehow." She wasn't quite sure how to explain it, especially in light of Anna Miller's encouragement on the same subject. "To take advantage of having been Amish to make money."

"Everyone else does it. I don't see why you shouldn't." Meredith's forehead crinkled. "But you said you didn't contact the tourist bureau, so how did he find you?"

"I don't know. That's why I said it was odd. I'm not exactly keeping my plans a secret, but it's hard to understand how he'd find out."

"Unless someone called him," Meredith said. "Someone who knew you weren't ready yet and wanted to discourage you." She sent a meaningful glance down the road toward the sign for The Willows.

"Jeannette wouldn't do that," Rachel protested. "Or at least not maliciously."

Meredith shook her head. "You are so naive when it comes to someone like Jeannette. Trust me, I've seen her in action. She's as nice as can be until you get in her way, and then you'd better watch out."

Rachel stared at The Willows for a moment, half-imagining she saw Jeannette at the window, watching them. But she had enough to worry about without thinking there were enemies where there weren't.

"Well, if she did intend to discourage me, she didn't succeed. I'm not giving up that easily."

"Good for you." Meredith's smile warmed her face. "Actually, I came over to bring you something." She took the book from under her arm, and Rachel realized it was a battered scrapbook, its gold lettering peeling off.

"Our journal," she said, taking it in her hands. They'd started the book that summer they were together, recording their ideas about their fantasy world, drawing pictures, pasting in bits of imagined souvenirs. "That's amazing. You've kept it all this time?"

"Not on purpose," Meredith said. "I was looking for something in the attic yesterday and found it, stuck under some old dolls. I glanced through it last night. I can't believe we went to such lengths to live in that fantasy we created. I thought you should see it. And your daughter might get a kick out of it."

"I'd like to show her." She held the book carefully against her.

Although she wasn't so sure she wanted Mandy emulating the things they'd done that summer. Or even sure she wanted to remind herself, now that she knew how the story ended.

"Does it still bother you, knowing what happened to Aaron?" she asked. Naturally everyone had been upset at the time, but she seemed to be reliving it too much since she'd come back to town.

"A little, I guess." Meredith glanced past her, in the direction of the creek. "I suppose we all have things in our past that we'd like to change, if we could."

Meredith sounded as if she were thinking of something in particular. Rachel waited, but Meredith didn't go on.

"I suppose you're right," she said finally. Things in the past. And sometimes, maybe, things in the present that she'd change, if she could.

CHAPTER EIGHT

COLIN LOOKED ACROSS Rachel's kitchen at Rachel and her sister Lovina chattering as they fixed iced tea and the sticky buns Lovina had brought. They were talking half in Pennsylvania Dutch, half in English, and he suspected Rachel didn't even notice when she switched from one to the other.

It had taken Rachel less than a day to set up this meeting with her sister. He wasn't sure whether that meant Rachel was concerned about his father or eager to see her sister get a job. Or both. Well, whatever her motives, he couldn't complain if it got him what he needed.

"Come, you must try Lovina's sticky buns. She's a good cook." Rachel set the gooey confection in front of him, seeming unaware that the cadence of her voice had slipped into the almost singsong tone of Pennsylvania Dutch. She sat down across from him, with Lovina taking the chair next to him.

"I'm sure she is," he replied. "So Lovina, has Rachel explained to you what the job would involve?"

"*Ja*, she has." Lovina was remarkably like Rachel had been at that age, with her wide blue eyes and corn-silk hair, but with a pert liveliness that he didn't remember from the younger Rachel. "You would want me to take care of the house, start the supper and watch out for your *daad*."

He nodded, unsure how to phrase what had to be said next. "My father is forgetful these days. He doesn't need nursing care or anything like that—just someone to be in the house and know where he's headed if he goes for a walk. But you would have to be tactful about it. He'd resent it if he thought you were there to take care of him."

"Like Onkel Simon, *ja*, Rachel?" Lovina darted a quick look at her sister. "He never wanted to think he couldn't do all he used to do, so we had to be careful not to hurt his feelings."

Colin nodded, liking her quick understanding, but before he could get in a comment, Rachel spoke.

"Have you talked to your father about this idea? What did he say?"

"He was saying how good that chicken was that you fixed yesterday, so it was easy to introduce the idea. Apparently he's as tired of my cooking as I am. Anyway, I put it that Lovina needed work, and we'd be helping her out, too." He smiled at Lovina. "I hope you don't mind."

She smiled back, dimples showing. "*Ach*, no. It is true. Most of my friends have jobs of one kind or another, but Daad is so cautious about what I do because…" She stopped with a glance at Rachel.

"Because I ran away," Rachel finished for her.

"It's okay, Lovina, you can say it. I'm just sorry it had such an impact on you."

Lovina clasped her hand in quick sympathy. "Don't worry about that. You're back now, and that's all that counts."

Colin discovered that he had a lump in his throat. He'd never had siblings, so he didn't know what it was like, but obviously these two had a bond that hadn't been broken by ten years apart.

"So we're settled? Can you come afternoons during the week from about one to five?"

"*Ja*, sure."

So it was as easy as that to take a big weight off his shoulders. A few more exchanges about pay, and it was a done deal. "Great, that's settled." He hesitated, but the opportunity to get Lovina's opinion was too good to miss. "So tell me, how's Benj doing?"

Lovina sent a questioning look at Rachel, who nodded. "It's all right. Mr. McDonald has been worried about Benjamin, too."

"Colin," he corrected gently. "I've gotten to know Benj pretty well since he's been doing yard work for us. I've never seen him like this."

"It's all that Will Esch's fault." Lovina's eyes snapped. "Mamm doesn't like me saying it, but it's true. All the teens know how wild he is."

"Drinking? Cars?" he questioned.

"No, not that." She grinned suddenly. "That'd be normal for some of those boys. But word is that he got into making a mess on folks' property, some-times even Englisch folks." She stopped abruptly, maybe afraid she'd said too much.

"You think he was leading Benj into trouble." He kept his voice calm. "Maybe that's what has Benj so upset lately."

"Maybe. Benj didn't tell me anything, but that's what I think. Seems like most of the older guys know better than to hang out with Will, but…"

"But Benj might have been excited that Will wanted to do something with him," Rachel finished for her.

Lovina nodded. "It's a *gut* thing Will went away," she said. "Only—" She stopped, looking down at the uneaten sticky bun on her plate.

"Only what, Lovina?" Rachel touched her sister's shoulder gently. "I just want to help Benj, you know that. And Colin wants that, as well. If you know anything else about Will, please tell us."

Lovina shrugged. "It doesn't have anything to do with Benj. It's just that one of the guys has a cell phone, and he called the cousin that Will's folks figured he's run off to. And the cousin said he hasn't heard a thing from Will, and why would anybody think he was there?" She pressed her lips together for a moment. "Not that I care, especially. But if Will isn't there, where is he? And why did he run away?"

"I can't begin to guess," he said. His gaze met

Rachel's, and he saw that she didn't like this development any better than he did.

Somehow, one way or another, they had to get the truth out of Benj.

"So did you want me to start this afternoon?" Lovina seemed eager to get away from the subject of Will Esch. "I would be happy to do that. I just have to go home and tell Mamm and finish my chores. I could be there by one o'clock easy."

He was about to say tomorrow would do, but Lovina was so eager that he nodded. "Great. I'll see you at one, then."

"*Denke*, thank you." Lovina swept her sister a quick hug and then she was out the door, moving as if she were jet-propelled.

"She seems excited about the job," he said into the sudden quiet once Lovina had left.

Rachel nodded, pushing a piece of sticky bun around on her plate. "I never thought about the effect my leaving would have on the younger ones. I didn't think at all."

The sadness in her voice touched his heart. "Most of us don't do much thinking at that age. We just act on feelings." He deliberately kept his voice from betraying the sympathy he felt. Rachel spent enough time regretting the past, it seemed to him.

She looked at him, and for an instant it seemed the same memory was in both their minds—that kiss they'd shared. Rachel blinked, seeming to push the subject away. "What did you think about what she said about Will?"

"It worried me, same as it did you. It's high time Benj told us the whole story. You can't keep hoping he'll confide in you. You'll have to push him."

Anger sparked in her face. "You think I don't know that? He's my brother, not yours."

"Well, then, what are you going to do?"

She sucked in a breath, her face firming. "He's supposed to stay the night tonight, in order to make an early start on some work we're doing tomorrow. Once Mandy is in bed, we'll have a talk."

"Good." He only hoped her need to keep her little brother's friendship didn't prevent her from pressing as hard as she needed to. He pushed his chair back. "Where's Mandy now?"

"Why?" She looked startled by the sudden change of subject.

"Because I have something in the car I want to show you," he said with exaggerated patience. "And you might not want Mandy to see what it is."

"She's up in the tree house she's been building." Rachel stood, a bit of foreboding in her expression. "What is it?"

"Come and see."

He led the way out the back door to where he'd parked in the gravel pull-off behind the house. As he grasped the handle of the car door, he was the victim of second thoughts. Just how angry might she be at what he'd done? Well, as long as Mandy didn't see, there was no harm done. He pulled open the door.

"Have a look."

The black Labrador puppy, roused from sleep by the door opening, stood up, tail wagging, eyes bright. Colin stood back, letting nature take its course. He suspected Rachel's soft heart wouldn't resist for long.

"He…or she is adorable. But I don't think…"

The puppy licked her hand, and Rachel seemed to lose track of what she was saying.

"She," he said quickly. "The owner has been calling her Princess, but she'd adjust to a new name fast enough, if Mandy wants to call her something else."

"Mandy…you got this dog for Mandy?" A variety of emotions chased across Rachel's face. "Colin, we can't possibly accept. I know how expensive a pure-bred dog can be, and that's just too much. Besides, you didn't even ask me if I was ready for Mandy to have a dog."

"I'm asking you now," he said promptly. "Mandy doesn't know, so if you refuse, the pup will go straight back to the breeder. And the breeder's an old friend who owed me a favor. He was happy to repay me with this little lady." Colin ruffled the pup's ears. "Come on, Rachel. You might not be ready, but Mandy is. And Labs are naturally protective of their families. She'll let you know if anyone is prowling around, believe me."

"You think you have an answer to everything,

don't you?" Rachel said it sternly, but he saw the smile lurking in her eyes.

"If I had the answer to everything, I wouldn't be so worried about Benj," he said. "And you. Please, Rachel. Take the puppy. Let me at least know you have an early-warning system if you're in trouble."

She was very close, so close the scent of her teased him, so close he could see her eyes darken, hear her breath catch. The moment lengthened, the very air between them seeming to vibrate. He imagined the feel of her lips under his, the softness of her skin...

Rachel took a careful step back. Her gaze still clung to his face, but she called to her daughter.

"Mandy? Mandy, I'm around back. Come here and see what Colin brought for you."

"Coming, Mommy." A second later Mandy raced around the corner of the house, and Rachel turned to her.

Too late, Rachel, he said silently. *It's too late now to pretend you don't feel anything.*

The question was what, if anything, they were doing to do about it.

"HELP! Help!" Benj was collapsed on the floor of the family room, laughing helplessly as the puppy licked his face and Mandy tickled him. Benj looked as if he were about eight, with all the worry and strain gone from his face.

Rachel watched them, smiling. She'd certainly

rather watch them than look at the spreadsheet of expenses she was attempting to put up on the computer. At moments like this, she began to wonder if Jeannette had been right when she talked about how complicated it was to start a business.

Meredith would probably say that Jeannette had just been trying to get rid of the competition. For that matter, Colin had implied the same. Maybe she should listen. They certainly knew Jeannette better than she did.

Benj rolled over, shedding both puppy and Mandy, and got on all fours, yipping at Princess. The pup responded with a wiggle of excitement, yipping back.

They'd all be too riled up to sleep at this rate. And much as she hated to spoil Benj's fun, once Mandy was in bed they had to have a serious talk. Colin was right—she'd let this go too long. Will was missing, and no one knew where he'd gone. Benj had to spill whatever he was keeping back about his involvement with the boy.

Giving up on the expenses, she closed the program. "All right, time to call it quits, you two. It's getting late. Mandy, run up and get ready for bed, okay? I'll take Princess out for a last walk."

Benj nodded, gathering up the mugs from their hot chocolate and the empty popcorn bowl. "I'll clean the dishes up." He went quickly to the kitchen.

Rachel suspected she knew why he was so eager. He didn't want to be the one to take the puppy out, now that it was dark. He still shied away from the windows once the shadows started to press against them.

Mandy, of course, didn't give up so easily. "Can't I have Princess sleep in my room tonight? Please, Mommy?"

"We already talked about this, remember? Princess will sleep in her own crate, where she'll feel safe, and I'll probably have to take her outside sometime in the night."

The portable crate had been a gift from Colin, as well as puppy food, a water bowl and even a collar and leash. He'd thought of everything.

Mandy opened her mouth as if to argue, and then she seemed to think the better of it. She bent to kiss the puppy's head. "See you first thing in the morning, Princess. I promise."

"I'll be up to tuck you in soon."

Rachel saw her daughter start up the stairs before fastening the leash onto Princess's collar. Mandy was generally good about going to bed when it was time, and Rachel could hardly blame her for being overexcited now that her dream had come true. If only it were that simple for all her dreams.

At first the pup was inclined to balk at being led, but when Princess realized they were going outside, she trotted along with Rachel happily enough. Snatching a flashlight, Rachel led her out the back door and across the porch to the lawn, eager not to have any accidents in the house.

The night was warm and clear, with a nearly full moon turning the grass to silver. Rachel tilted her head back. The stars splashed across the heavens with a generous hand where there were no competing lights to diminish their sparkle. The Milky Way was a faint, gauzy trail, and Rachel traced the invisible line through the end stars of the Big Dipper to find the bright star at the end of the Little Dipper's handle.

For a moment she was standing outside the barn with Daadi, pressing close against his side while he pointed out the constellations, naming the stars as if they were old friends. They were, to him. Farmers lived close to nature, appreciating what it had to give.

A hard tug on the leash brought her back to the present. Princess, apparently not content with any of the shrubs close to the house, wanted to go farther. Letting the puppy lead the way, Rachel walked across the lawn. She didn't bother turning on the flashlight she'd taken from its hook by the back door. The moonlight was so bright it really wasn't needed.

Princess, nose down and tail wagging, was intent on investigating every smell in the backyard. Probably it hadn't occurred to Colin that in presenting them with the puppy as a means of protection, he'd also given Rachel a reason to be outside in the dark. She'd have to point that out to him.

Thinking about Colin led her inevitably to those

moments when they'd stood so close, when she'd felt that overwhelming surge of attraction and known he felt it, too. And he'd sensed her reaction—he'd have to. She wasn't that good at hiding her feelings.

Her face warmed despite the slight breeze that stirred the leaves on the apple tree by the shed. He'd known, yes. But at least neither of them had acted on that attraction. As long as they didn't act, she was safe.

Safe from what? a small voice at the back of her mind inquired.

Safe from folly, she answered herself firmly. She'd made enough mistakes in her life, and she couldn't afford another one. She had Mandy now, and Mandy had to come first. She couldn't get involved with someone just because he had a charming smile or because he showed unexpected depths of character. The only way she could succeed in creating a home for Mandy was to be accepted here, and she wouldn't achieve that by getting involved with Colin or anyone else.

The breeze, growing stronger, lifted her hair, and a bank of clouds drifted over the moon, shielding its light. Rachel shivered. "Come on, Princess, time to take care of business."

Princess ignored her, staring at the shed, her small body a black shape in the shadows. The puppy went still, seeming to freeze, gaze intent on the dark oblong that was the half-open door to the shed.

Half-open. Rachel repeated the words silently.

Hadn't she closed that door and snapped the latch? She didn't like the idea of the outbuildings standing open, encouraging Mandy to explore them.

She took a step toward the shed and then stopped. She wasn't afraid. Of course not. But she couldn't help visualizing the man-shaped shadow she'd seen the night Benj was so frightened.

And now Benj was at her house again, and the dog was suddenly pressing against her leg, her small body quivering and tense. Rachel's grip tightened on the flashlight. Turn it on? If she did, what might she see? Or who? If she did, she'd be showing herself just as clearly.

Better, far better, to move away. Pretend she hadn't noticed anything, go back toward the house. If someone was in the shed, she was trapping him there by standing right in front of it, and cornered people, like cornered animals, could be dangerous.

"Come on, girl." She tried to keep her voice light. Casual. "Let's go back to the house."

But Princess planted all four feet firmly. *Come on*, Rachel demanded silently. She bent to pick up the puppy. She'd remove her bodily if she had to.

But before she could grab the dog, Princess started to bark. Feet planted, tail erect, every hair on her body seeming to stand up, she barked furiously at whatever it was she could see or sense or smell in the dense shadows of the building. The sound echoed, surprisingly loud for such a small dog, seeming to roll to the ridge and bounce back again.

"Princess, stop that!" Her thoughts raced furiously—the house, Benj and Mandy were there, she couldn't risk having them rush out to see what was wrong, she had to protect them. But Princess, far from being calmed, was barking even more fiercely, straining at the leash, trying to pull Rachel toward whatever it was that lurked in the shadows.

Rachel raised the flashlight, gripping the smooth metal cylinder. Before she could switch it on something huge and dark erupted from the shed, knocking the flashlight from her hand, sending her stumbling backward, feet sliding on the grass, going out from under her—

She was on her hands and knees in the grass, the ground cold and damp under her fingers, dazed at the sudden shock of being swept off her feet. Princess yanked at the leash, pulling it painfully around her fingers, barking and snarling in a furious effort to get at the intruder.

Hold on. Don't let her go. But with a final wrench Princess was free, chasing a figure that was no more than shadow across the lawn, behind the stable. He'd get to the line of trees by the creek and he'd be gone, but Princess—she couldn't lose the puppy, Mandy would be heartbroken—

"Princess, come, girl, come." She scrambled to her feet. "Princess!"

A rush of footsteps behind her sent her whirling,

raising the flashlight like a weapon as a man loomed out of the dark. A hand grabbed her arm even as recognition shot through her and she gasped.

"Colin. What you doing here?"

"What's wrong?" His voice was hard and urgent. He clasped her arms, running his fingers down to her hands, brushing at the grass and twigs that clung to them. "Did you fall? What happened?"

"Someone was in the shed. Princess knew, she chased him. If she's lost..." Rachel couldn't seem to help the panic in her voice.

Colin took the flashlight and switched it on, sending a strong circle of light piercing toward the shed. The door hung open drunkenly, one hinge broken, mute testimony to the force with which the figure had lurched out of the shed. "Never mind the dog. The man—which way did he go?"

"Around the back of the stable." She bent, hands on her knees, trying to get her breathing back to normal. "We've got to find Princess."

"Sounds like you're more worried about the dog than the intruder." Colin swept the flashlight beam towards the stable. "You can stop worrying about Princess. She's back."

The puppy came trotting toward them, ears perked, tail waving, looking pleased with herself. *I chased a stranger away from my people*, she seemed to be saying. *Aren't you proud of me?*

Rachel sank to her knees, gathering the puppy

into a hug. "Good girl, good girl. You chased him away."

"Looks like she did more than that." Colin squatted next to Rachel, so close she could feel the warmth that emanated from him. He reached out, removing something from the dog's mouth. "It looks as if Princess took a bite out of him."

He shone the light on what lay on his palm. It was a tiny scrap of denim.

"Jeans material." Gathering up the leash that Princess was trailing, Rachel stood. "It has to be."

Colin closed his hand over the scrap. "It's evidence, of a sort. Not even Burkhalter can say you imagined this. I'll call him—"

She grabbed his hand before he could pull his phone out. "No. No police."

"Are you crazy? Why on earth wouldn't we call the police?" He grabbed her wrists, and she could feel his urgency right through her skin, making her senses swim. "Make sense, Rachel."

"I am making sense." She took a breath, trying to marshal her arguments. "We can't call the police, not yet. Not until we hear the whole story from Benjamin."

We, she'd said, as if Colin was teamed with her. Never mind that now.

"Whatever he's involved in, I'm not bringing in the police until I know what it is. Besides, I tried calling the police before, and all that happened was

Jim Burkhalter patting me on the head and telling
me to go play with my dolls."

"Even so..." Colin began.

"Besides, just having the police car out here once
was enough to have all the neighbors talking and
Franklin Sitler furious with me," she continued. "I
can't risk making an enemy of the man."

His grasp eased, just a little. "I suppose you have
a point there. You can't identify the person?"

She shook her head, feeling her tension ebb as
they talked. "He was nothing more than a shadow.
A man. Taller than I am. That's about all I can say."

Colin let the silence stretch. In the glow of the
flashlight she could see his face, all angles and shadows, frowning and intent. Finally he jerked a nod.

"All right. Let's have a talk with Benj. But if we
don't get the whole story this time, I'm taking him
to the police myself."

CHAPTER NINE

COLIN KEPT HIS hand on Rachel's arm as they walked toward the house. He couldn't get rid of the protectiveness that had surged through him when he'd seen her on the ground. It had taken him by surprise, and he didn't know what to do with it.

They'd reached the steps to the porch when Rachel stopped, looking up at him. "You didn't answer my question. What are you doing here?"

It was inevitable that she'd nail him on that subject. He may as well tell the truth—part of it, at least.

"I started thinking about Benj staying here tonight. He was here the last night you saw a prowler, too." He shrugged. "I thought I'd better check in, that's all."

That wasn't all, of course. That wasn't mentioning the concern for her that had driven him to scout around Mason House in the dark.

But Rachel was nodding, satisfied. "I thought of that, too. It has to have something to do with Benjamin's story."

"That's why we have to know all the things he

left out the last time." Colin started up the steps, but Rachel stopped him with a hand on his arm.

"I'll talk to him. You don't need to stay."

"I don't?" He managed to tamp down the anger, replacing it with the sarcastic tone he knew she hated. "Sorry, Rachel. I'm too involved now for you to dismiss me. Like it or not, I'm in this to stay."

He went up to the porch and across it to the door, not waiting to see if she followed him. But she did, apparently realizing that argument was futile.

They went inside. Benj turned from the sink, his eyes widening at the sight of Colin.

"I'll go up and settle Mandy in bed." Rachel's tone had a touch of tartness, and she went quickly to the stairs and up them.

Benj looked after her and then fixed his gaze on Colin again. "*Was ist letz?* Why are you here? Did something happen?"

"Did you expect something to happen?" Colin planted his hands on the table and leaned toward him. "When Rachel went outside by herself tonight?"

And that was Colin's responsibility, wasn't it? It hadn't occurred to him, when he'd had that bright idea about the puppy, that Rachel would be the one taking the animal out at night.

"I…no, no. I mean, nobody would hurt Rachel." Benj swallowed, his Adam's apple working.

"Maybe nobody intended to," Colin conceded. "But when Rachel was out there alone, she surprised somebody hiding in the shed. He knocked her down, trying to get away. Princess chased him off."

Benj's face was ashen. He sank down to his knees, holding out his hand to the puppy. She came to him and he held her, murmuring something to her in Pennsylvania Dutch.

Rachel came back into the kitchen, her gaze going from him to her brother. "What did you do?"

"I told him the plain truth." Colin yanked out a chair. "And now we're going to sit down here together, and Benj is going to tell us just what is going on."

Rachel looked as if she would object. Then, with a little shake of her head, she pulled out another chair and sat. "*Komm*, Benj. You know Colin is right. You have to tell us the whole story."

"But I…I did." Not looking at them, Benj sat down, head hanging.

"No, you didn't." Colin let his frustration show in his tone. "Come on, Benj, out with it. You haven't told us the whole thing, not by a long shot. And that nearly got your sister hurt tonight."

"Colin, you don't need…" Rachel began.

"We can't sugarcoat it." He was beginning to feel as frustrated with Rachel as with Benj. "This situation could be serious, and we can't deal with it unless we know all of it." His hand shot across the table and grasped Benj's wrist. "Out with it, Benj."

"Ja. Ja." The boy sent an anguished look toward

his sister. "I'm sorry, Rachel. I did not want to cause trouble for you. It's all my fault."

"I know you didn't mean it," Rachel said softly. "Just start at the beginning and tell us everything that happened."

Benj gulped, nodding. "*Ja.* Everything. Will Esch...everybody knows how brave he is. He's not afraid to do anything. And when he asked me to go along with him and Joseph, I thought...well, I thought..."

"You figured the other kids would look at you the way they look at Will if you got to hang out with him," Colin suggested. It wasn't difficult to figure that one out. Guilt flickered. He'd once been the guy who wasn't afraid to do anything. How much trouble had he caused for other people?

"*Ja.* So he told me to sneak out of the house one night, and we'd do something that would have everybody talking—"

"When was this?" Colin interrupted. Just as well to nail this all down.

Benj thought for a minute. "It was Tuesday night, a week ago."

Colin nodded. "Go on. How did you get out?"

"I waited until I heard Daadi snoring. Then I climbed out my window onto the roof of the porch and slid down the post to the ground." There was a certain shamefaced pride in Benj's face at his exploit.

Colin managed not to comment on that. "Where did you meet Will and Joseph?"

"Down the road a little way." Benj gestured vaguely in the direction away from the village. "You know where that little run comes out onto the road?"

He nodded. Just about a mile from town, then. The run overflowed the road a couple of times a year when the water was high, and the county made vague promises about dealing with it. There was a natural path up into the woods through the shallow depression carved by the stream.

"They were there, anyway. They had flashlights and gas cans." Benj's voice quivered, and Colin heard Rachel take in a sharp breath. "Will told me to carry the gas cans. He led the way up the hill through the woods. There's an old barn up there on top of the hill." He glanced toward Colin. "You know it?"

"No." He was trying to follow them in his mind's eye, trying to figure out exactly where they'd been.

"It's been abandoned a long time, I guess. Will said we were going to set it on fire." He bit his lip. "I didn't know that was what they were gonna do. Honest."

"That's so dangerous." Rachel couldn't seem to keep silent. "You boys could have been trapped, the fire could have spread…what were you thinking? You know how serious a fire could be."

"*Ja*, I know. I didn't want to, but I was there, and I figured I had to go through with it. Will kept saying how everyone in Deer Run would see the fire, it being right up on the hill above town." He rubbed his hands together nervously.

"And what if..." Rachel began, and Colin silenced her with a hand on her wrist. He knew what she was thinking. What if the fire had spread toward the village? Not likely it would have gotten out of control, as wet as the spring had been, but it was still a lot more serious than splashing some paint around.

"Will told us to wait while he went to check it out. So we hunkered down." Benj shivered, as if he were out in the cold night again. "Then we heard an engine—somebody was driving up to the barn. And a man yelled. I was so scared...." Maybe remembering how frightened he'd been made it hard to go on.

"We heard someone running, and then a shotgun blast. And Will yelled to us to run, and we all three ran. The man shot again, but he didn't hit us. We never stopped running until we got clear down to the road." He jerked his head. "Almost across from Rachel's place. I wanted to come, to tell Rachel or Daad or somebody. Will was mad because I left the gas cans, but he said the man couldn't know who we were, and all we had to do was keep quiet. He made us promise." Benj buried his face in his hands. "I'm sorry." His voice was muffled. "I shouldn't have done it."

"No, you shouldn't have." Colin was uncompromising. "I can see why you were scared. But since then—"

Benj dropped his hands to look at them and wiped away a tear. "I kept thinking about the man with the gun. And then Will was gone. Maybe he left me and Joseph to take the blame if somebody found out. Or maybe the man with the gun got him. And when somebody was following me, I didn't know what to do."

Rachel clasped his hands in hers, holding them tightly, as if she could keep him from harm. "Is there anything else that happened? Anything else that's bothering you?"

"Only Daad." Benj sniffled. "You're not going to tell him, are you?"

Colin exchanged a look with Rachel. The boy shouldn't keep this a secret from his father, but on the other hand, Colin wasn't sure what Levi Weaver would be able to do about the bigger issues. The Amish didn't rely on the police to solve their problems.

"We aren't going to tell him," he said finally. "But you had better do it yourself. Just think how much worse it would be if he hears about it from someone else."

"Besides, Will's parents should know that his running away might be more serious than they think." Rachel's face was tight with worry.

"I…I don't know…." Benj looked from Colin to his sister, as if hoping for a miracle to erase what he had done.

"Sleep on it," she said, and Colin could tell that

she was making an effort to smile. "You've done the right thing, telling us. Things will look better in the morning, I promise."

Benj got up and then stood at the table for a moment, hands gripping its edge. *"Ja,"* he said finally. *"Denke."* His eyes were suddenly bright with tears, and he turned and stumbled from the room, rushing up the stairs probably in an effort to shut the door before he started to cry.

"Poor Benj." Rachel wiped away a tear of her own. "I don't know what to think. He didn't really commit a crime, did he?"

Colin shrugged. "Trespassing, at least. They intended to vandalize, even if they didn't succeed."

"I suppose you're right." Rachel rubbed her temples, as if trying to smooth away the stress. "If we go to the police with this story, what will happen?"

"If Benj told Burkhalter the story he just told us, I'm afraid Burkhalter wouldn't look any further than that. The boys would be in trouble, but that doesn't answer the question of why somebody was firing off a shotgun at a bunch of kids in the woods. Even if he just intended to scare them off, it's a dangerous thing to do."

"Do you know who owns that land and the barn Benj was talking about?" Rachel's forehead furrowed. "I can picture where it must be, but I don't think I ever went to the top of that ridge."

"Same here. You'd think, with all the roaming in the woods I did as a kid, I'd know every inch of the area. I've got a vague notion of an abandoned farm up on the ridge, but that's about all. At least that's something I can find out. I look up property in the county records office more often than I'd like."

Rachel managed a smile. "You're a man of many talents, it seems."

"That's right, and don't you forget it." He was relieved by the smile, pitiful as it was. Rachel had enough on her plate without all this worry over Benjamin. "The trouble is that still doesn't tell us who was out in the shed tonight."

"It might not have anything to do with Benj," she protested half-heartedly. "Just someone looking for something to take, or a homeless person wanting a place to sleep."

"Or both of the above," he said. "But I'm finding it hard to believe that the long arm of coincidence stretches that far."

Her expression admitted the truth of that statement. "Whoever he was, I don't think he wanted to hurt me. He was just trying to get away."

"Maybe not." But that didn't seem to alter the concern he felt for her. "But whether he intended it or not, you could have been hurt." He frowned, wondering how much credence to give to Benj's idea that the man with the shotgun was after him. "I suppose it might have been Will or Joseph."

"Will or Joseph? But why would they—you mean they might have been trying to get Benj alone? But Will is gone, isn't he?"

"He's not at home. That doesn't mean he's left the area. You know how kids that age are. He might be hanging out, sleeping in someone's barn or bunking with an English friend."

"I suppose so." She sounded doubtful. "But if either he or Joseph wanted to see Benj, they wouldn't have to go about it in such a roundabout way."

"They might be trying to scare him into keeping quiet. In fact, the more I hear about Will, the more likely it seems for him to do just that. He's the oldest, and it sounds as if he's not exactly new to causing trouble. He's the one who'd bear most of the blame if it came out."

"If that was what they intended, they certainly succeeded in scaring me." Rachel rubbed her arms with her hands. "I could try to talk to Joseph...." She hesitated.

"Better not," he said quickly. "Then he'd know that Benj broke his promise." More seriously, if Rachel were going to be accepted here, she couldn't afford to make waves in the Amish community.

"That's true. I'm afraid I'm not thinking clearly."

"You're tired." He stood, afraid that if he hung around feeling sympathetic he'd wind up doing something he'd regret. "I'll get out of here. Try not to worry. Tomorrow I'll find out who owns that property. Maybe that will tell us who the man with the shotgun was, at least."

Rachel stood and walked with him to the back door. She opened it. He started to leave and then made the mistake of looking at her. Her face was tilted up to his, her expression soft and vulnerable.

"Colin…" She touched his sleeve, seeming to search for words. "Thank you. You're a…a good friend."

His hand closed over hers, pressing it against his arm as longing welled up in him. It was dangerous, being alone with Rachel in the quiet kitchen, the darkness outside isolating them.

"No problem." He tried to say the words lightly and knew he hadn't succeeded. Her face was very close—her gaze wide, her eyes darkening, her mouth soft.

With a sigh, he drew her against him, his lips closing over hers. The kiss was meant to be light, gentle, reassuring, but something far stronger compelled him, giving the kiss an urgency he never intended.

Rachel broke away with an abrupt step back, pushing him out the door. "We can't."

"Rachel, don't—"

"Don't what?" Her cheeks flamed. "Be a prude? Maybe it doesn't matter to you what people say, but I can't afford to have people talking about me."

"I didn't mean to upset you." But he was talking to the door, because she'd slammed it in his face.

Maybe he deserved that. He'd kissed Rachel before, and she hadn't forgotten, any more than he had.

His intentions had been good then, too. He'd been trying to break up her and Ronnie before they did something drastic. He'd only succeeded in making them more determined.

It wouldn't help to start banging his head against the door. He'd better go home before he made any more blunders with Rachel.

ONCE COLIN WAS gone, Rachel's brief spurt of anger burned out, leaving her exhausted. She locked the house and went upstairs with the puppy, hanging on to the railing as if she were an old woman.

Why did Colin have to complicate matters by kissing her? She'd just begun to think of him as a trusted friend, and now he'd ruined it.

The voice of her conscience interrupted what had begun as a promising pity party. She could hardly blame Colin for what had happened. She'd been just as involved as he had.

The upstairs hall was quiet, with the night-light burning where she'd plugged it in next to the bathroom door. Rachel put the pup into the kennel in her room and then went to ease open the door to the room where Benjamin was sleeping.

He lay on his side facing the window, and his deep, even breathing told her he was asleep. She sent a glance toward the window with its easily removable screen, but there was no handy roof for Benj to clamber out on. And as scared as he was, he wasn't likely to wander out into the night.

She moved on to her daughter's room. No need

to be especially careful here, as Mandy had always been a sound sleeper.

Mandy was curled up in the old-fashioned sleigh bed, one arm around the faded stuffed dog that had been her nighttime protector since she was a toddler. As long as Ruffie was awake, Mandy could sleep well.

Rachel smiled, smoothing the quilt over her daughter's small form, feeling the familiar surge of protective maternal love. Mandy's security was what mattered most now. Nothing, including that foolish attraction she felt for Colin, could be allowed to derail her attention from her child. Rachel bent to drop a light kiss on Mandy's hair and went softly out of the room.

Unfortunately, once she gained the sanctuary of her bedroom, she realized that despite how tired she was, she was also too keyed up to go to sleep. She moved around the room, straightening the stack of books she hadn't had time to read, folding back the double-wedding-ring quilt on the four-poster bed.

She'd culled the furniture for her own bedroom from various places in the house. The four-poster would have been perfect for one of the guest rooms had it not been for the broken spool decoration on one of the posts. But if she couldn't use it for guests, at least she could enjoy it herself.

Princess watched her, whining softly. Eventually, apparently deciding Rachel wasn't going to let her out, she curled up in a ball and went to sleep.

Rachel ought to do the same, but before she crawled into bed, she wanted to be sure no one was outside. The bedroom windows looked out to the back, giving her a good vantage point. She switched the light off and then edged the curtain aside and let her eyes adjust to the darkness.

The moon had come out from behind the clouds, and by its light she could see that the shed door hung drunkenly just as they'd left it. Shadows lay deep around the outbuildings, but she couldn't sense anything foreign hidden in them.

Beyond the buildings, the stream caught and reflected the moon's light. Tracing its progress with her eyes, she realized that from this height, she could see the dam and the wide pool below it, gleaming like an oval mirror.

A chill snaked its way down her spine. She and Ronnie had met in various places in their efforts to keep their relationship a secret—her parents' barn, the covered bridge, a nearby clearing in the woods. But never at the dam, until that one time.

Her gaze was fixed on the faint shimmer that was the pool, but her inner eye saw something entirely different. Herself, young and foolish and in love, finding the note Ronnie had left for her behind a loose board in the covered bridge, telling her to meet him that afternoon at the dam.

She'd gone, of course, even though it was risky to meet during the daylight hours, walking down her side of the creek to a shallow spot where some convenient large rocks made it possible to cross without getting her feet wet.

She'd hurried through the woods to the dam, sure Ronnie would be there first, and arrived breathless and eager. But it hadn't been Ronnie sitting on the fallen log who turned to greet her—it had been Colin.

"Hi, Rachel. Surprise." He gave her the smile that had beguiled half the girls in the valley at one time or another.

She eyed him, not sure what to make of his presence. "Colin? Where is Ronnie?" There was no point in trying to hide their relationship from Colin. Ronnie told him everything, she felt sure.

"He'll be here. He sent me to say he'd be late." He held out his hand, indicating a space next to him on the log. "Take a seat. Might as well be comfortable."

If she didn't, he'd think she was afraid of him, and she didn't want that. She wasn't afraid of him, just leery. Colin always gave her the feeling that he was laughing at her. She sat, smoothing her skirt down over her knees.

Like most of the Englisch boys, Colin wore faded jeans that hugged his body and a T-shirt that was equally faded. A shaft of sunlight through the trees touched his tousled dark hair, and his lips quirked in that familiar mocking expression. She looked away quickly, focusing on the water rushing over the dam, but that wasn't much better. A chill slid down her neck.

"What's wrong?" Colin was quick as a cat pouncing on a mouse.

"Nothing." She couldn't help a shiver. "I just don't like it here, that's all."

He lifted an eyebrow. "Thinking Aaron Mast's ghost walks here? He might."

"Don't." The word came out with force, and she clutched her hands together. "Aaron's dying isn't something to joke about."

"Hey, I'm sorry. I wasn't thinking." His voice warmed with sympathy, and he put his hand over her clasped ones. "Did you know him well?"

She nodded, not sure whether that was quite true. She'd always felt she knew him, but maybe that had been just a little girl's fantasy.

"Don't be sad," Colin coaxed. "Ronnie wouldn't have picked this place if he'd known it would upset you."

She wasn't sure that was true, either. Still, it was nice of Colin to say it.

She turned to him, seeing his gaze warm when it rested on her face, wanting to tell him she appreciated his kindness. But the words got all tangled up in the way he was looking at her, and the next thing she knew, his arms were around her and he was kissing her.

A branch cracked, the sharp sound sending her yanking away from Colin, and suddenly Ronnie was standing there, looking at them. She took a step toward him. Where were the words she needed to take that terrible expression from his face?

"Sorry, Ronnie." Colin got in first. "But I guess you know now what Rachel is really like."

She gasped, taking the words like a blow to the stomach. Then she turned and ran blindly into the woods.

Rachel pressed her hand to her midsection, turning away from the window. Ten years ago, and it felt as if it happened yesterday.

Colin had no doubt expected his mean trick to break up Ronnie's relationship with her, but he'd been wrong. In fact, it had probably made Ronnie even more determined to marry her. There had always been a rivalry between those two, despite their friendship. Ronnie had been hotly furious at Colin's action, and it had only increased the sense that it was Ronnie and Rachel against the world.

She wasn't a teenager any longer, and neither was Colin. And Ronnie was dead, smashing his car into a bridge abutment while driving drunk. It was past time to forget. But she still had trouble reconciling the heartless boy Colin had been with the man who seemed to have sacrificed his career to care for his father. And the man who wanted to protect her and Mandy from harm.

She reached out to straighten the curtain and her eye was caught by a movement. She froze, watching. A figure stepped out of the black mouth of the covered bridge, shadow emerging from shadow. It stood for a moment, and she imagined it watching the house. Then it moved, passing quickly along the lane and out of sight into the shadow of the trees.

She took a breath and let it out slowly. The same person, or someone different? If he'd run toward the woods, he might just now be headed back toward the road, thinking it safe because the house was dark.

Well, everything was locked, and Rachel didn't doubt that Princess would raise a fuss, even in her crate, if someone tried to get in. She reached out to pull down the shade when a flicker of light from the other direction caught her attention. Her heart jerked.

That wasn't moonlight reflecting from the pool below the dam. A light flickered and was gone. In that brief moment she'd glimpsed a dark shape, outlined against the water.

Rachel yanked the shade down, moved quickly to the bedside table, and switched on the light. That was enough horrors for one night. Whoever or whatever was out there by the dam where Aaron died, it certainly wasn't Aaron's ghost.

CHAPTER TEN

RACHEL STIRRED SUGAR into a tall glass of iced tea at Millers' market, glad just to be sitting down after a strenuous day of painting and papering with Benj's help. Meredith's call, suggesting they meet, had been a welcome break.

Maybe she could talk to Meredith about whoever or whatever it was she'd seen at the dam last night. She'd be glad to hear someone assuring her that what she'd seen was perfectly normal, and her foolish reaction to Colin made it difficult to turn to him. The flickering light had turned up in her dreams, bringing her wide awake with her heart pounding sometime in the night.

"It's coming along," she said in answer to Meredith's question about her progress on the house. "Benjamin and I started work first thing this morning, and I was surprised at all we accomplished. At this rate, the house might actually be ready by the end of the month."

"That's great." Meredith stirred her tea. "And speaking of the bed-and-breakfast, I thought maybe you could use a little help with the business side of things. If you want to put up a website, or if you need guidance in setting up your tax records, I'd love to do that for you."

The magnitude of the offer took Rachel's breath away for a moment. Then reality set in. That was part of Meredith's business, not a gift.

"I appreciate it." She tried to find the right words to say she couldn't afford it. "I'd love to be able to hire you to do that, but I—"

"Hire?" Meredith's eyebrows shot up. "Who's talking about hiring? I'm a friend. I'm not very good at painting and papering, but this is something can do, and I'd love to." She grinned, her eyes lighting up. "Seems to me we made a vow once to fight each other's battles, didn't we?"

Rachel's throat was so tight she wasn't sure she could speak lightly, but she had to try. "I think that referred to fighting dragons."

"Believe me, the mysteries of the tax code are as fierce as any fire-breathing dragon we ever imagined. Well, how about it? Will you let me in?"

"Of course I will." The thought of having someone else take over that aspect of the business start-up made her giddy. "But I don't want to take time away from your own work."

"No problem. I'm always happy for something that gets me out of the office." Meredith's face tensed a little at the words, and then the expression was gone, as quickly as it had come. "Let me do a little research on how best to set up your records, and then we'll get together."

"Meredith, I...I can't tell you how much this means to me." She no longer felt alone in her plans, and it was surprising how much that mattered.

"It's a pleasure." Meredith, probably trying to change the subject, glanced across the store. "Isn't Mandy with you this afternoon?"

"Benj wanted to take her over to the farm to see the baby goats after we knocked off work. I persuaded them not to take the puppy along. I'm afraid Princess might take it into her head to chase the cows." Her thoughts flickered to the puppy taking off after the previous night's intruder. "She is protective—I'll say that for her."

Meredith chuckled. "You can't fool me. You've fallen in love with that dog already. Getting her was a kind thought of Colin's."

Rachel wasn't so sure she wanted to discuss Colin, not after that kiss. She might give too much away to Meredith's sharp eyes.

"Mandy loves her enough for any puppy, although she's also intrigued by my father's Nubian goats. Once she's seen the kids, she'll probably start trying to convince me that we need one in our backyard."

"It sounds as if your relationship with your parents is improving," Meredith said, an inquiring tilt to her eyebrows.

Rachel shrugged. "Daad is warming up to

Mandy, at least. I'm thankful for that." If she didn't expect too much for herself, she wouldn't be disappointed.

"Your brother just has the two boys, doesn't he? I'm sure the only granddaughter will work her way into your dad's heart quickly. Then it's just a matter of time until things are back to normal between you."

She'd like to agree with Meredith's optimism, but she couldn't. "I'm resigned to the situation for me. As long as they accept Mandy, that's enough. After all, I knew what the cost would be when I ran away with Ronnie."

"No eighteen-year-old really understands the cost of the decisions she makes." Meredith's response was weighted with so much feeling that Rachel stared at her in surprise. Meredith, catching the look, shrugged. "That's my opinion, for what it's worth."

Rachel suspected it was personal experience, rather than opinion, but if Meredith wasn't ready to talk about it, she wouldn't press.

"I looked through the scrapbook last night," she said instead. *And I thought I saw someone down at the dam.* Well, maybe those two comments didn't belong together. "I'd forgotten how detailed those stories of ours were. And the drawings—they were amazing."

"Lainey's work," Meredith said. "I wonder if she

ever did anything with her artistic talent. She certainly had a gift."

Fishing in her bag, Rachel pulled out the sketch she'd brought with her. "Do you remember this one? At first glance I didn't get it, and then I saw what she'd done." She spread the paper out between them, smoothing the brittle edges.

Meredith bent over it, studying the drawing. Lainey had created a scene with Laura as the princess. Her admirers were clustered around her, but the princess only had eyes for the handsome knight, easily recognizable as Aaron.

"Look at the other figures in the picture," Rachel prompted. She put her finger on the plump jester, who was dropping one of the balls he was juggling. "Isn't that Victor Hammond, Laura's husband?"

"Good grief, it is." Meredith started to giggle, putting her hand over her mouth in an attempt to stifle it. "I think he'd better never see this. He's so self-important these days he'd probably sue." She studied the drawing again, still chuckling under her breath. "And this one." She put her finger on a large figure, resplendent in a black-and-gold helmet over a faintly stupid-looking face. "That's Moose Edwards to the life. Did you know him? A tackle on the football team with the intellect of his nickname."

Rachel shook her head. "I don't remember him, but I do know the boys clustered around Laura like bees to honey. But who is this one?" She pointed to a figure standing in shadow, his black robe and pointed hat identifying him as a wizard.

Meredith tilted the paper to the light. "Of course. It's Dennis Sitler. Remember? He was Laura's favorite, I always thought, next to Aaron."

"I'd nearly forgotten he was part of the scene that summer. It's funny that unless you'd mentioned it I wouldn't have thought of it when I saw him the other day."

"Well, he's all grown up now, like the rest of them." Meredith hesitated. "It's sad," she said slowly. "I mean, knowing what Laura is like now. And knowing what happened to Aaron. Life changed for everyone, I guess."

"It has a way of doing that." If she was going to say anything about what she'd seen, now was the time. "I discovered last night that I can see the dam and the pool from my bedroom window."

Meredith gave her a questioning look. "Does that bother you?"

"No, it's not that." She frowned, trying to tread carefully. She didn't want Meredith to think she was imagining things. "I just mention it because I happened to look out last night before I went to bed, and I saw a light down there. It worried me a little. I hope it wasn't kids fooling around. I wouldn't want anyone else to come to grief there."

"I'm not sure there's anything you could do about it," Meredith said, always practical. "The main path to the dam is at the back of our yard, but there are plenty of other ways someone could get there. At a guess, it was local teenagers looking for a quiet make-out spot. Or beer-drinking spot, as the case might be. I didn't hear anything last night."

"You're probably right, but I can't say that makes me feel any better. Now I'm thinking of some kid having too much to drink and deciding he can walk across the top of the dam."

"Teenagers do dumber things than that when they've been drinking." Meredith frowned. "I wouldn't think that was what happened to Aaron, though. As much as we watched him, I don't remember that we ever saw him drinking. He was probably more responsible than most."

Meredith had made the connection to Aaron, just as she had when she'd seen the figure. That place would always be a reminder of Aaron's death in a lot of people's minds.

"Maybe he was showing off," she ventured.

"To whom?" Meredith's brows lifted. "You know, that's really odd now that you mention it. As far as I know, no one ever came forward and said they were with him that night. He was found by an early-morning fisherman, but nobody ever said why Aaron was there."

"To meet Laura?" Rachel voiced the thought that had to be in both their minds.

Meredith's face seemed to grow still, except for the question in her dark eyes. "If so, if Laura was there when he had his accident and she didn't tell anyone—that might explain why she is…well, the way she is."

Rachel could only nod, her heart filled with pity at the thought. Now that Meredith had put the thought into words, she realized that it had been in the back of her mind the whole time. If Aaron's accident had happened that way, it seemed to have destroyed Laura's life just as it had his.

Meredith glanced at her watch with a sudden exclamation. "I didn't realize how late it was getting. I have a client phoning me in a few minutes." She stood, face lighting in a smile. "This was nice. I'll come by soon to talk about the business, okay?"

"Very okay." Rachel put the drawing back in her bag as she stood. "I'll walk with you."

When they reached the door, Rachel started through first, only to be sent stumbling back as someone brushed by her to barge inside. She looked after him, waiting on the walk for Meredith to join her.

"Who was that?" With his low-slung jeans and motorcycle boots, the customer didn't look like the typical small-town boy. Well, not boy. He must be in his mid-twenties, but something about the pouty set to his lips made him look younger.

Meredith sent a glare in his direction. "Believe it or not, that's Franklin Sitler's grandson, Gene. Can you imagine him settling down to life in Deer Run?"

"Not easily, no." They started down the street. "He's surely not living with Mr. Sitler, is he?"

"He is. No one can understand it." Meredith's lips twitched. "Dennis least of all, I hear. He's probably afraid that Gene will edge him out of the old man's will. Honestly, though, I doubt he'll stay around that long. There can't be much for him to do here."

"He looks as if he'd be more at home almost anywhere else. I'd think, given Sitler's insistence on preserving the standards of the past, he wouldn't tolerate a grandson who looked like that."

But maybe that was her own prejudice speaking. Just because Sitler didn't want a bed-and-breakfast across the road from his house, that didn't make him narrow-minded.

"Franklin is getting on in years, and I've heard rumors that his health isn't good. Maybe he feels the need to have someone around to rely on." Meredith turned in at her gate. "I'll see you soon."

Rachel walked on, glancing toward the Sitler place across the street. Meredith was probably right about the elder Sitler needing someone, and that reminded her of Colin's father.

There had apparently been a bit of a hassle yesterday, according to Benj, who'd had it from Lovina. Colin's father had forgotten Lovina was coming and demanded to know what she was doing there. Lovina had handled the situation, soothing him down and reminding him gently. Lovina had a solid bank of good sense beneath her sometimes-pert manner.

Colin had fretted about it when Lovina told him, she'd said. That was natural. Rachel frowned, pushing her gate open. And there she was, thinking about Colin again. No matter what she did, her thoughts kept revolving back to him, it seemed.

COLIN PULLED UP at the side of Mason House in the pickup he'd borrowed from Jake. His sedan, suitable for taking clients to view houses, wasn't right for what he planned at the moment.

He slid out and headed for the back door. Rachel might very well slam it in his face the way she had the previous night. Well, he'd just have to speak quickly and hope he could talk his way in. He didn't want Rachel shutting him out when she was in trouble.

But when she came to the door in answer to his knock, Rachel looked wary, not hostile. "Colin." She held the door, keeping him on the porch. "What brings you here?"

Maybe better to ignore the subject of what had happened between them. "I made a trip to the county records office this morning. It took some digging to identify the right parcel, but I found out who owns that barn."

As he'd hoped, that encouraged her to open the door the rest of the way and gesture him in. She was a little more dressed up than he'd seen her lately, wearing khakis and a soft, long-sleeved shirt that was the same shade of blue as her eyes. It was probably not easy for a woman raised Amish to adapt to modern clothing, and Rachel's clothing tended to be what an earlier generation would call modest.

"Have you been out?" he asked, sitting down at the kitchen table without waiting for an invitation that might not come.

Rachel sat, somewhat reluctantly, across from him. "I met Meredith down at Millers' for a few minutes. Why?"

He shrugged. "No reason. I just noticed you weren't in working clothes. Is Benj here?" He didn't want to have this conversation where the kid would hear.

"He and Mandy are over at the farm." She glanced at the clock. "I don't expect them back before suppertime. What did you find out?"

"The property on the ridge was originally the Mueller homestead. House, barn, outbuildings and about a hundred acres. When the Mueller family died out, it was left to a cousin, who pretty much let the buildings fall to pieces. The property came up for a tax sale about five years ago, and the buyer was Franklin Sitler."

Rachel winced, her lips tightening and her blue eyes downcast as if she studied her clenched hands. Then she met his gaze. "Well, that's that. From everything you've said, it sounds as if Franklin wouldn't hesitate to fire off a gun if he caught kids trespassing on his property. But at least he must not know Benj was involved, or he'd surely have mentioned it when he was chastising me for opening a bed-and-breakfast across the road from his house."

"That's a safe bet. But I'm not so sure Franklin had anything to do with it."

"Why not? You've said it's his property, so who else would be up there at night?"

"That's just the point. Can you seriously imagine an eighty-year-old in poor health tramping around the woods in the dark? I can't."

Her smooth forehead wrinkled, fine lines forming at the corners of her eyes. "Then who would it be? I suppose one of his grandsons could have been checking on the property."

"Again, why then? In the normal course of things, you don't go driving up that rutted logging road in the dark unless you have a darned good reason." He shook his head, dissatisfied. "Look, it just doesn't make sense. From what I've been able to find out, Franklin has been buying up land at tax sales for years. He probably owns half the township by now. But he hasn't done anything with any of it. Just pays the taxes and hangs on to it. Maybe he's waiting for a boom in land prices. Maybe he feels that land is the only real security. Who knows? I'm just thinking that whatever was going on at that barn that night, it might not have anything to do with Sitler or his family." He paused. "That's why I'm headed up there to have a look around."

"I'm going with you," Rachel said instantly.

He should have been able to predict that response.

"I don't think that's a good idea. There's no need for you to tramp around in the woods. I can check—"

She stood, the movement cutting him off. "This is my brother. My business. I'm going." She took a step away from the table, pausing to scribble a note on the pad that lay next to the phone.

Benj, Be back soon. Please stay with Mandy until then.

She looked at him, seeming impatient. "Are you ready?"

He'd anticipated that Mandy would be here and sure she wouldn't either leave the child or take her along. But what harm could come to her in broad daylight with him along?

"All right. Let's go." He followed her outside. "I borrowed Jake's truck, since it has four-wheel drive. The nearest road that goes up there is little more than a log drag."

Rachel nodded, climbing into the passenger seat before he could offer to get the door. Shrugging, he got behind the wheel and started the truck, not without a few grumbles from the engine.

Rachel sent him a questioning look. "Are you sure this thing will get us there?"

He grinned. "Jake always claims the old girl hasn't left him stranded yet. Let's hope this isn't the first time." He pulled out of the driveway and turned away from Deer Run on the narrow two-lane blacktop.

"I'd think a lawyer like Jake would drive something a bit sleeker than this," she said.

"He does. Believe me, his father wouldn't let him call on clients in this thing. But he holds on to it—a relic of his past and a reminder he's a country boy at heart."

"Hunting and fishing and all that?" she said, smiling. "I'll take your word for it. How do we get up to the barn, even with the four-wheel drive?"

"I have a detailed topographic map of the area in the office," he said over the rattle of the truck. "It shows a lane running up to what used to be the farm just off Carter Road. There's actually a better road, but you have to go clear around to the other side of the ridge to access it."

But the lane, when they reached it, was more than the log drag he'd anticipated. A dirt road wound up through the woods toward the ridge. He turned onto it, the truck bouncing mercilessly. Whatever shocks the vehicle had once had must have been shot.

"I thought you said there wasn't a road." Rachel clutched the arm rest, probably trying to keep her teeth from rattling.

"It looks as if someone's been bringing equipment up through here." Frowning, he leaned forward. "I've heard there's some logging going on in Scotch Valley. This can't be an access for the logging trucks, though. They must come up from the other side of the ridge."

"Maybe it was someone connected with the logging who scared the boys." She seemed to be talking through clenched teeth.

He grinned. "Not easy going, is it? But the turnoff to the barn is just ahead. I suppose it could have been something to do with that operation, but nobody logs in the dark."

He turned onto the lane toward the barn, the surface leveling out. In a moment they were through the fringe of woods and into what had once been cleared pasture land.

But not for a long time. The raspberry brambles and sumacs had taken over the pastures first, most likely, followed by a scattering of white pines.

The barn reared upward, its roof nearly gone, timbers jutting jaggedly toward the sky. "It looks as if a good storm would take it down," he said. "Depressing, to see a good German barn deteriorate that way. They were built to last."

He stopped a few yards from the slope of earth that led up to the gaping barn door. There had been a lower level where machinery was kept once, most likely, but that was filled in with fallen timbers.

Rachel leaned forward, staring at the barn, and he suspected she was seeing it the way the boys would have in the dark, looking like a monster set to devour them. She opened the door and slid out without speaking.

He followed suit. "Careful. You don't know what's hidden in the grass, and you don't have boots on." He'd taken the precaution of wearing hiking boots with his jeans.

Rachel didn't show any sign of heeding him. "The boys wouldn't have come up the way we did, would they?"

"Not from what Benj told us. I think they must have followed the creek bed up through the woods in a more direct route." He glanced around. "It sounds as if he and Joseph were hiding somewhere in the woods while Will reconnoitered."

Rachel nodded. "And the headlights they saw came up this way."

"It's the most direct route anybody could drive up here. I'm not sure where the other road comes out—maybe farther up the ridge. I'm going to check out the barn."

She came with him, of course. She hadn't taken more than a few steps before she stumbled, catching the toe of her sneaker on a two-by-four hidden by the long grass.

"Watch it." He grabbed her arm to steady her, and warmth flooded through him at the touch.

Did she feel the same? Maybe, because her blue eyes darkened when she looked up, getting her balance. She pulled her arm away from him.

"I guess the farmhouse and other outbuildings are gone," she said.

She was speaking at random, he suspected, to avoid whatever she felt at his touch.

"The barn's all that's left. That's probably the foundation of the farmhouse over there." He nodded toward the remains of a stone wall. "I wouldn't go exploring. Looks like a perfect spot for snakes and poison ivy."

Rachel shivered, rubbing her arms. "Let's have a look in the barn."

"Right you are." He led the way, careful not to touch her again, but still feeling the warmth. "If anyone is monkeying around up here, the barn seems like the logical place to find something."

"Like what? What are you thinking?" She was so close she bumped into him when he stopped, and then she backed up a hurried step.

"To be honest, I suspected drugs of some sort. Maybe somebody has been planting marijuana in the old cornfields. They supposedly found a patch of it being tilled in the state game lands last year. Or a meth lab, but in that case the door to the barn wouldn't be hanging open."

Rachel stared across what had once been cleared fields or pasture, and he did the same. Not that he was sure he'd know a marijuana plant if he saw one, but there was no sign of any cultivation. The forest was slowly, inexorably, taking over what might once have been a thriving farm.

He stopped in the barn doorway, raising the flashlight he'd brought along for the purpose, and sent its strong beam piercing the dimness inside. It lit up the still-solid timbers of the barn floor and the remnants of stalls on either side. The hay loft above their heads had all but disappeared, its wood rotted away. At the disturbance, a pair of barn swallows fled with their distinctive swooping aerial pattern.

"Nothing here," he said, irrationally disappointed. He'd hoped for a quick and simple explanation, but it looked as if he wasn't going to get one.

"No one's used this place in a long time." Rachel took a step closer to him as the flashlight beam picked out the thick cluster of cobwebs that hung like lace between two decrepit stalls that might once have sheltered work horses.

He nodded. She was right, and yet…what was there about this place that someone would risk shooting a kid for? He walked on through the barn, between the rows of stalls or what was left of them. He sent the flashlight beam upward toward the loft, but it disappeared, caught up in the gaping holes in the roof.

"It's sad," Rachel said suddenly. "This must have been a good farm once."

She was thoroughly Amish still in her attitude toward farms. To them, farming was the closest occupation to God.

"I guess so." He found an access door at the back, lifted the latch and shoved. It shrieked open, and yet another barn swallow took flight above their heads.

He stood still for a moment, frowning a little

in the bright sunlight, and it was only when Rachel pushed him that he realized he was blocking the door.

"Sorry," he said absently. "But look at this. Somebody has been up here in a truck besides us. I didn't notice the tracks on the other side because it was in shadow."

Rachel stared at the marks. "Well, we knew someone came up in a vehicle. Benj said they saw the lights."

"Yeah, but this wasn't your average pickup truck." He squatted, measuring the distance between the marks with his gaze. "This was made by something bigger."

"One of the logging trucks?" Rachel suggested.

"Could be, but what would bring them in here? Unless they were using this as a sort of staging area to keep the trucks. In which case they should have gotten Franklin's permission." He glanced up at her. "He'd probably charge them rent."

"So they might have been parking here without asking." She rubbed her arms again. "That doesn't seem like a big enough deal to warrant firing a gun at anyone."

"No. It doesn't." Colin's thoughts twisted and turned, trying to come up with a logical explanation. He couldn't, and he didn't like that fact.

He rose. Rachel was still rubbing her arms, eyeing the barn as if it might sway toward them, pushed by a sudden breeze.

"It's okay. We'll figure it out." He clasped her arm, intending only to comfort her.

Rachel jerked back as if he'd hit her, and then the color came up in her cheeks. "Sorry," she muttered. "I just—I don't like this place."

He studied her face, not sure what secrets hid behind those deep blue eyes and that vulnerable mouth. "Maybe it's me you don't like."

"Don't be silly." Irritation edged her voice. "You're as bad as…" She stopped, letting the sentence trail off.

"Who?" Anger took him by surprise. "Ronnie? Don't compare me with him."

She sucked in a startled breath, her eyes widening. "I won't. I don't. You…you're not the person I always thought you were, Colin. I know that now. But I still can't get…well, involved with anyone."

He raised his eyebrows, reverting to the sarcasm that was always his defense when someone got too close. "It was one kiss, Rachel. Not a proposal of marriage."

Her color deepened. "I know that. I'm just saying—" She turned away, rubbing her arms again as if for comfort. "I've let down everyone in my life. I can't let down Mandy. She has to be my only concern."

"You let down?" His temper spiked. "It seems to me Ronnie did the letting down, Rachel. And your parents did their share, too. There's no point in beating yourself up over that. Unless, of course, you like being a martyr."

She wheeled on him, eyes blazing. Well, that was better than her looking as if life had flattened her. "You have a poisonous tongue, Colin McDonald, do you know that? Maybe you're more like Ronnie than you want to believe." She marched toward the truck, shoulders stiff.

He stood still, fighting with himself, before following her. He hadn't wanted that or deliberately provoked it. At least, he didn't think so. But maybe it was for the best.

Rachel wouldn't embark on a casual affair because she had to take care of her daughter. And he couldn't get involved in anything serious because he had to take care of his father. So it was best not to start anything at all.

CHAPTER ELEVEN

THE PICKUP TRUCK bounced its way back down the hill, and despite the warmth of the day, Rachel felt a definite chill in the cab of the truck. Her throat was so tight that she probably couldn't carry on a normal conversation, not that Colin was likely to expect that at the moment.

What on earth had happened to cause that stupid flare-up between them? It seemed they couldn't be within touching distance of each other without striking sparks.

She stared through the windshield as they reached the macadam and turned toward Deer Run. This excursion hadn't netted much in the way of helpful information, and it had increased the tension between her and Colin. She should have stayed home and waited for Benj and Mandy to get back.

Would Benj have spoken to Daadi by now? And if he had, how would Daad have reacted? It was possible that he'd feel she had been interfering with family matters. If so, their relationship would head back down in a hurry.

Colin turned into the driveway and parked the

truck. Rachel grabbed for the door handle, but before she could turn it, he'd reached across to stop her with a touch that seemed to shimmer along her skin.

He drew his hand away quickly. "Look, before you go…"

He hesitated, and she thought he searched for words. Unusual for Colin, who always had something to say, it seemed.

"That's a bad habit of mine," he said. "Using sarcasm to put some distance between me and something I don't want to think about. I shouldn't turn it on you."

"You have a right to your opinion, Colin." It took an effort to keep her voice even.

"Even when you think I'm dead wrong?" His lips creased in a slight smile. "Maybe I am. I just don't like to hear you taking all the blame on yourself. That's all."

It wasn't all, but she had no desire to go further toward the truth. If Colin knew the circumstances of Ronnie's accident, he might be eager to put the blame on her.

She stared down at her fingers, twining together in her lap. "Maybe we have too much history between us to be comfortable with each other. About what happened when we were teenagers—I know you were only trying to keep Ronnie from making a mistake. He was your friend, and you wanted to protect him." Rachel pushed the door handle and slid out before he could say anything else. "Thanks for trying to help, Colin. I appreciate it."

She headed for the back door, but she hadn't gone more than a few steps when she realized he was behind her.

"There's no reason for you to come in." She glanced at him. If that sounded inhospitable, she couldn't help it. "Mandy should be home by now, and I have to start supper."

He raised his hands in a gesture of surrender. "I won't get in the way, I promise. But I'm assuming Benjamin is here with her, and I'd like to ask him a couple of questions now that I've had a look around up there."

That sounded reasonable, and she had no excuse for turning him away. She nodded, starting up the steps.

"Just one other thing." His voice seemed strained. "It's true I didn't want to see Ronnie do something rash that could affect the rest of his life. But you have it wrong. It wasn't Ronnie I was trying to protect. It was you."

Shock froze her to the spot. Colin opened the door and stepped inside.

Trying to ignore the feeling that her history had just been turned on its head, Rachel followed him into the kitchen.

Princess, tail wagging, scurried happily toward her, feet slipping on the linoleum floor. But Princess was the only happy being in the kitchen. Benjamin sat slumped at the kitchen table, and the stains of tears were plain on his face. Mandy hovered over him, patting his back the way Rachel would comfort her.

Rachel's heart sank. "Benj, *was ist letz?* Was Daadi angry with you?"

Benj shook his head, wiping his face with his hand. "No. It's not that. I didn't tell him. I couldn't. It's Joseph. He's gone."

She seemed to be stuck in place, her mind refusing to process Benj's words. Colin took a quick step forward, gripping her brother's shoulder.

"What do you mean, gone?" He shook the boy lightly. "Snap out of it, Benj. You have to tell us what happened if we're going to help."

"It's okay." Mandy patted him again, her small voice soothing. "You can tell."

Her daughter was doing a better job than she was. Rachel moved to the table and sat down, pulling her chair close to Benjamin. It was intimidating enough to have Colin looming over him. She had to offer a little warmth.

"Come, Benj. We care about you. You know that. We just want to help."

He nodded, gulping. "I know. I *chust*..." He stopped, his English deserting him for a moment. He took a deep breath. "I heard it from one of the guys. When Joseph's mamm went to call him this morning, he wasn't there."

"Did he say anything to anyone about leaving?"

Colin's thoughts seemed to be racing so fast that they were almost written on his face. "Or leave a note?"

"Not a note, no. But some of his clothes were gone. He…the guy I talked to…he said that Joseph said something to him a couple of days ago about going away for a while."

"Where would he go?" Rachel reached out to clasp Benj's hands in hers.

He shrugged. "Maybe he went to join Will. Maybe he really is down at the shore with his cousin."

She exchanged looks with Colin. She hadn't told Benj what Lovina said about the cousin. Maybe she should have as soon as she heard. She certainly had to do it now.

"Lovina says one of the older boys called the cousin to see if Will got there. According to him, the cousin hasn't heard a thing from Will."

The whites of Benj's eyes showed. "But…if he's not there, where is he?"

"Could he be hiding out around here?" Colin leaned forward, and Benj stared at him. "Think, Benj. Is there anybody who would give him a place to stay, no questions asked?"

Benj shook his head. "I don't know. I don't think so. Why would he stay here? I thought he left because he was afraid."

Afraid of getting into trouble with the police or

afraid of the man with the shotgun who'd seemed to take possession of Benj's imagination? She wasn't sure.

"He could be hiding out someplace," Colin suggested. "Just until he's sure nobody is going to report him to the police. He could have been the person in Rachel's shed the other night."

Benj started to shake his head. Then he hesitated. "Do you really think that was him?" He sounded more relieved than anything else. Obviously he'd rather believe it had been Will than the bogeyman that had been haunting his dreams.

"I don't know," Colin said. "But I know we can't just ignore the fact that another boy has apparently run away." He transferred his gaze to Rachel, his gray stare intense. "You understand, don't you?"

She nodded. Little though she wanted to make this situation public, they couldn't take chances where someone else's child was concerned.

"You think we should go to the police, then?" She made it a question, finding herself cringing at the thought of trying to explain the situation to the police chief.

"Maybe not the police, but Benj has to tell your father." His fingers tightened on Benj's shoulder. "You know that, don't you?"

"Ja." Benj swallowed hard. "I know."

"And then Will's and Joseph's parents must be told what we know." Colin paused. "Maybe that will come best from your dad. They won't want an Englischer coming to them with this story."

"What about the police?" she repeated.

Colin let go of Benj, taking a step back, his face a study in conflicting emotions. "That's my first instinct. It always has been. But I'm not sure either you or I have the right to do that. We really only know what Benj has told us, and in the eyes of the law, he's a minor. I think that decision has to be up to the parents."

Rachel met his gaze. "Amish don't get involved with the police."

"I know." He sighed, rubbing the nape of his neck. "It would be comforting to think we can drop the issue in someone else's hands and walk away, but we can't. So we're stuck, aren't we?"

Colin was including himself, just as he had from the beginning. Judging by her experience with Ronnie, Rachel had thought most men would run the other way when trouble came. Apparently she'd been wrong.

THE DISHES CLINKED as Rachel put a plate into the dish drainer, the sound a reminder of so many hours spent standing next to her mother or one of her sisters, sharing thoughts and secrets as they washed the dishes. Now she was doing the same with her daughter.

Mandy wiped a plate, holding one edge against her chest. The method did seem to keep the plate from slipping, but Mandy sometimes ended up wetter than the dishes.

"Maybe Benj talked to Grossdaadi by now," she said, polishing with strenuous circles. "Maybe everything is all right."

"Maybe," Rachel said. How likely was it that everything was all right? Probably not very. She glanced at her daughter's small face. "Did you understand what Benj was talking about this afternoon?"

Mandy nodded. "About when he and the other boys were chased in the woods by the man with the gun."

So much for thinking she could protect Mandy from the difficult truth. "How did you know about it?"

"Benj told me. He was scared, and he wanted to talk to somebody."

Rachel would rather he'd picked anyone else to confide in, but it was too late now. "You know that's very unusual, don't you? I walked in the woods all the time when I was little, and such a thing never happened to me."

"The boys were going to do something bad, and they got caught." Mandy sounded very matter-of-fact. "Benj knows he shouldn't have done it. I told him it was stupid."

"Good." She touched her daughter's hair lightly. "I mean, I don't want you telling people that they're stupid, but what they were trying to do was both stupid and wrong."

"I know, Mommy. Don't worry." Mandy sounded

as if she'd like to pat her mother on the head. Just who was the mother here, and who was the daughter?

"I'll try not to worry," she said. "But I can't promise. That's what mothers do."

Mandy set the last of the dishes on the countertop. "Can I take Princess out in the backyard?"

Rachel glanced outside, reminding herself that it would be light for a couple of hours yet. "Okay, but keep her on the leash. We don't want her chasing off after a squirrel."

Or an intruder. But Princess had been smart enough to come home again, carrying that scrap of denim in her teeth.

Denim. She and Colin hadn't talked about that, but didn't that indicate the intruder had been Englisch? Still, many Amish boys exchanged their black broadfall trousers for jeans during their *rumspringas*. Will, for instance. Benj had mentioned once that Will liked to dress Englisch.

Mandy, chattering to Princess, who seemed to listen to every word, went out the back door with the puppy. The kitchen fell silent in her wake. It almost felt as if Rachel's mind had been hiding thoughts of Colin, waiting until she was alone to spring them on her.

What had he meant, saying that he'd been trying to protect her by breaking up her relationship with Ronnie? Surely it was Ronnie, his friend, about whom he'd been concerned. Her thoughts spun, trying to find a way to fit this new fact in with her memory of how things had gone. She set the last dish in the cupboard, frowning, and stretched, trying to force herself to concentrate on the movement of her muscles, trying to block out the image of Colin's face.

It wasn't working. She'd almost rather they'd stayed angry with each other. That might be easier to deal with.

The doorbell rang, cutting through the knot in her mind. She went quickly through to the hall and headed for the front door. Meredith had said she'd come over after supper to make a start on the records for the business. She was a little earlier than Rachel had expected.

But when Rachel swung the door open, Dennis Sitler stood there, finger poised over the bell to ring again. She felt heat rush to her cheeks. If he knew where she'd been that afternoon…

No, that was ridiculous.

"Dennis. I wasn't expecting you. Please, come in." She held the door open, trying to sound hospitable. What if he was delivering a message from his grandfather? What if they'd found out about Benjamin?

"Thanks." He stepped inside, his thin face creasing in an apologetic smile. "I hope I'm not interrupting your supper."

"Not at all. We've finished. What can I do for you?"

"Actually, I was hoping I might do something for

you." Dennis moved casually to the table that would be her registration desk, glancing around with open curiosity. "I couldn't get it out of my mind that my grandfather had upset you the other day."

"It's all right." So much else had happened to worry her that she'd had little time to spare for that particular memory.

"You're nice to take it that way. There's no point in telling him he can't go around talking to people like that. Believe me, I've tried." He shrugged, his smile turning rueful, making him suddenly more likeable for the show of vulnerability.

"I appreciate your trying. And really, it's not your fault. We can't change other people." She certainly hadn't succeeded in changing Ronnie, and her efforts had probably made things worse.

"Maybe not, but it still embarrasses the heck out of me when Grandfather gets on that high horse of his, acting as if he's king of the valley."

She smiled, touched by his embarrassment. "I'm sure people still respect his opinion," she said, trying to be tactful.

"Most of them probably don't have any idea who he is." Dennis's tone was blunt. "He and Amanda Mason were two of a kind, I'm afraid, both of them thinking they were the unquestioned moral and social leaders of the community. I hope it doesn't offend you, my speaking of your mother-in-law that way."

Rachel thought of that portrait of Amanda, her

nose tipped just a bit higher than most people's. "I
suspect you're right. But it's a harmless illusion."

"I'm relieved that you see it that way." Dennis did
look genuinely relieved. He must have a tender conscience, to be so concerned about his grandfather's
effect on her. "At any rate, I thought perhaps I'd stop
by and have a look at your progress. Then maybe I
can catch my grandfather in a softened mood and
say something about what a great job you're doing
in restoring the old place."

Rachel was touched. "That's thoughtful of you."

"And maybe a little sneaky." He grinned, and she
was reminded of the teenager who'd hung around
Laura, love-struck like the rest of them.

"I'd certainly rather be on good terms with my
neighbors." She gestured to their surroundings.
"You can see what we've been doing downstairs.
I'm not attempting to change the style of the house,
just freshen things up so that the place will be appealing to people."

"That's the right idea, I'm sure." Dennis walked
into the front parlor, and she followed. "The place
is a perfect example of the best of Victorian archi-
tecture in Pennsylvania, and with any luck you'll
get guests who appreciate that fact. My grandfather
ought to be equally appreciative. He was always
complaining about how Amanda let the place go
in her later years. Not that he's doing much better."

True enough. The Sitler place could use a fresh

coat of paint and some serious trimming of the over-grown foliage around the house.

"I suppose it might seem overwhelming to someone his age to try and keep up the house and grounds," she said tactfully.

"That's what my cousin, Gene, is supposed to be doing." Dennis said the name as if it left a bad taste in his mouth. "As far as I can see, he's made precious little progress in that area."

"I'd heard that Mr. Sitler had a grandson living with him." Maybe it was best not to mention her one encounter with Gene. "I didn't think you had a brother."

"Heaven forbid." Dennis gave her a look of mock horror. "Our fathers were brothers. Grandfather quarreled with Gene's father, the way he quarreled with everyone, and cut him off completely. I'd practically forgotten that branch of the family even existed until Gene turned up here and the old man took him in. Gene doesn't do a bit of work, and he seems to enjoy riling the old man up about his neighbors."

For an instant Rachel thought of mentioning the trucks that had apparently been trespassing on Sitler property. Maybe that would distract Franklin Sitler from thinking of her.

But she just as quickly thought the better of it. Mentioning it would simply lead to questions about why she'd been there in the first place.

"I shouldn't burden you with my family troubles," Dennis said. "I'm sure you have enough of

your own." He paused, almost as if he expected her
to confide in him, his gaze interested enough to
make her uncomfortable. He couldn't know about
Benj, could he?

"My only troubles involve outdated plumbing and
peeling paint," she said lightly. "I do appreciate anything you can do with your grandfather."

"Rachel…" He took a step toward her, his expression suddenly serious, but the front door opened before he could finish.

"Hi, Rachel. Dennis." Meredith looked from one
to the other of them, her gaze questioning. "Sorry,
I didn't realize you had company."

"I was on my way out," Dennis said. "Just stopped
by to admire the progress Rachel is making. How
are you, Meredith? Enjoying having your old friend
back in town, I'm sure." Dennis headed for the door
as he spoke.

"Yes, we've been reminiscing about the old days."
Meredith moved, holding the door open for him. "Of
course some of them are sad memories. Like Aaron
Mast's drowning."

Dennis seemed to freeze for an instant, his hand
on the door frame. When he turned toward them,
his face was wiped clean of expression.

"Aaron Mast." He repeated the name, then shook
his head slightly. "A sad story. I find it's not healthy
to spend too much time thinking about old grief."
Before either of them could respond he went out,

so quickly it seemed he was eager to leave them behind.

Rachel stared after him for a moment and then turned the look on Meredith. "Why on earth did you bring up Aaron's death in front of Dennis?"

Meredith shrugged, letting the oversize bag she carried slip from her shoulder. "I haven't been able to stop thinking about our conversation. If our speculation was right, and Aaron's accident was the result of showing off for Laura, then—"

"Let's go back to the family room." Rachel interrupted her, glancing toward the door. "I don't want anyone walking in on this conversation."

Leading the way, she took Meredith through the hallway to the room at the back of the house that had probably once been a maid's room. She'd decided early on that the parlor and dining room were far too formal for comfortable use.

The small, square room was furnished with comfortable castoffs from the rest of the house, ruffled Cape Cod curtains and a small television. Two windows looked out on the backyard, where she could see Mandy and Princess playing. Mandy hadn't let Princess off the leash, true, but she wasn't holding it, either. She ran in circles, the puppy prancing after her, leash dragging.

Meredith dropped into one corner of the chintz sofa, setting her bag on the coffee table. Rachel took the rocking chair opposite her.

"Now, talk," she said. "What was the point of mentioning Aaron's death to Dennis?"

"I wanted to see his reaction. And he did react, didn't he?" Meredith's dark eyes sparkled with interest. "His face turned into a blank screen."

"True, but I'm not sure it means anything." Rachel visualized the frozen expression on Dennis's narrow face. "Maybe you just caught him by surprise."

"Maybe." Meredith's skeptical tone said she didn't believe it. "But think about that summer. Dennis was always around, always in the background. Lainey caught it perfectly in that picture she drew."

"He had a crush on Laura. All the boys did." Odd, wasn't it, that Laura had picked Aaron? Maybe he had represented the lure of the unknown. Or the ultimate challenge.

"Dennis must have known that Laura and Aaron met by the dam," Meredith said. "He was around all the time. When word came out about Aaron's death, he had to wonder."

"I guess so. Maybe Aaron's death was one of those things that all the kids knew something about and yet never mentioned. Teenagers can be secretive creatures." Nobody knew that better than she did.

Meredith leaned back, crossing one leg over the other. "You look worried. Mandy's surely not keeping secrets from you already, is she?"

"No, thank goodness." Although Mandy had known about Benj's misadventures and never men-

tioned it. Maybe she didn't know her daughter as
well as she thought.

"Is it your brother, then?"

Shock took Rachel's breath away for a moment.
She'd been so sure no one else knew.

"What…what do you know about Benj?"

Meredith brushed a strand of hair back behind
her ear, the simple gold hoops she wore swaying.
"I haven't been prying, honestly. But I hear things.
You can't help but hear things when you work with
clients in Deer Run. Two Amish teenagers have run
away within a week of each other, and Benj is going
around looking scared out of his wits." She leaned
forward to put her hand on Rachel's arm. "Don't
tell me anything you don't want to. But if you need
a listening ear, I'm safe."

"I know you are." Rachel had come home to find
support in unexpected places. "I haven't said anything because Benj confided in me, and that put
me in an awkward position with my parents. He
was involved with the other boys in trespassing, and
they were seen by someone who scared them." She
skimmed over the details. "He's supposed to be telling Daad the truth about it, and that's a big relief."

"I'm sure it is. Maybe if Laura and Aaron had
confided in some sensible adult instead of the other
kids, things might have turned out better for them."

Meredith, seeming to dismiss the topic from her
mind, pulled a laptop and several files from the bag

on the coffee table. Rachel found she couldn't seem to turn her thoughts away so easily.

A twenty-year-old tragedy. A frightening encounter only weeks ago. They were unrelated, surely. But the same people kept coming up in connection with each of them.

Maybe that was the price of living in a small town. Sooner or later, everyone and everything connected in one way or another.

CHAPTER TWELVE

COLIN DROVE TOWARD the basket, evading Jake's attempted block, and sank the shot. Jake jogged toward him, panting.

"Man, you're playing like you're back in high school again. What's got into you?" Jake bent, hands on his knees.

"Just getting some much-needed exercise." Colin dribbled the ball slowly, his muscles protesting. "You getting old, Evans?"

"No older than you," Jake retorted. "You act like a man trying to keep himself busy so he won't think too much."

"Psychoanalyzing, now, are you? They teach you that in law school?" He was jeering, but Jake had actually hit too close to the truth. Pushing himself physically was the only thing that kept him from thinking too much of Rachel. And of the situation with Dad.

The trouble was that he couldn't manage to keep going long enough to wipe his problems out of his mind.

"A lawyer has to understand his clients." Jake

adopted a pedantic tone, meant to mimic one of his law-school profs, Colin assumed. "I've known you all your life. You're an open book to me, McDonald."

He certainly hoped not.

"Save it for someone you can impress," Colin retorted. He walked toward the bench at the edge of the court where they'd left their towels.

Not that it was actually a court, exactly. The town fathers figured it was foolish to waste the parking lot at the township building just on cars, so they'd erected tennis nets and lined out a court on the macadam, along with a painted square for four-square and a hopscotch pattern.

The place was popular with kids earlier in the day, but most of them had been called home by now. Dusk was drawing in, and when Colin tilted his head back, he could see a few stars.

Benjamin was supposed to have talked to his father by now, and he couldn't help but dwell on how it might have turned out. Would it make matters worse between Rachel and her dad? That was what he feared.

"Do you know anything about that timbering that's going on up on the ridge above town?" he asked abruptly.

Jake was pulling a sweatshirt over his head. He emerged, his eyes bright with curiosity. "Now why, I wonder, would you be interested in that?"

"Never mind why. Do you?"

"Funny thing about that timbering." Jake sat on

the bench to pull on a pair of sweatpants over his shorts. "Franklin Sitler asked us to look into the pros and cons of donating that piece of property to the state game lands. He told us he wanted to be sure the woods above the town were always protected." Jake grimaced. "I figured it was more likely he was looking for a tax advantage. But anyway, next thing I knew, a firm was taking timber off that patch."

"So maybe he wasn't pleased with the answers you gave him. If he saw a better chance of making money off the land…"

Jake was shaking his head. "We hadn't even given him our opinion yet. But Sitler may be trying to have it both ways. It looks like the timbering operation is primarily on the other side of the ridge."

"True." It was odd, even so.

"Like I said, the timbering can't be spotted from town, which makes me wonder how you come to know about it." He raised his eyebrows. "Does this have anything to do with you borrowing my four-wheel drive and bringing it back muddy?"

Custom demanded he come back with a snappy retort, even though his heart wasn't in it. "Listen, that vehicle of yours was so filthy a little more mud wouldn't hurt it."

Jake just looked at him, waiting.

"Okay, okay, I admit it. I was curious. I went up there and had a look around." He wasn't about to say anything about Rachel's presence on that little jaunt.

"You were curious," Jake repeated. "Why? And

don't bother telling me to mind my own business, because you know I won't."

He couldn't tell Jake the whole thing. But he'd love to get Jake's take on the situation.

"Suppose, just hypothetically, that you found out someone had been shooting at trespassers up in that area. What would you think?"

"I'd think that particular someone was breaking the law," Jake said promptly. "Despite what a lot of the old-timers believe, even out here in the country you can't take potshots at someone because they're on your land. There has to be an actual threat of harm before potential deadly force is justified. And even then, if you can get away, you should."

"True. But like you say, a lot of folks around here wouldn't agree. Or would say they were just trying to scare the trespassers off."

Jake shrugged. "I'm telling you what the law says, not what a possible jury might say if such a case ever came to trial. If I knew about this hypothetical situation of yours, I'd urge the party shot at to report it to the police. The chief might not be entirely sympathetic, but I'd think he'd at least try to put the fear of the law into the shooter."

Easier said than done. "Suppose the trespasser declined to go to the law?"

Jake put his foot on the bench to stretch his hamstrings. "By that I deduce that the party in question was Amish. Rachel's kid brother, was it?"

He'd given too much away, but the secrecy was

starting to wear on him. "What makes you think that?"

"People talk. You know what it's like around here. Everybody gossips, not necessarily maliciously. They notice things—things like the fact that two Amish teenagers have run off, and that young Benjamin is acting like he has something to hide."

"Benjamin's a good kid."

"I'm not saying he isn't." Jake stretched the other leg. "But he's looking bugged about something, and you're asking questions about Franklin Sitler's land and somebody shooting, and you've got that look you get when you're thinking of Rachel."

It was like being hit in the stomach by the basketball. For a second Colin couldn't catch his breath. "You don't know what you're talking about."

"Maybe not." Jake bent to touch his toes, his voice muffled. "But I'd say you've got feelings for Rachel. And what's wrong with that? It's about time you dropped that detached-onlooker routine and fell hard for someone."

"Not Rachel." He had a feeling he didn't sound definite enough. "She has a daughter to consider."

"So? The little girl's a nice kid, from what I hear. And you were just reminding me that you were once her daddy's best friend. What's wrong with being a stepfather?"

Seemed to him that Jake was hearing entirely too much. "You gossip like an old woman. I'm not cut out to be a stepfather. And even if I were, there's my dad to consider. I couldn't ask a woman to take on that responsibility."

Jake stopped stretching and looked at him, eyes serious. "Know what? If it was the right woman, you wouldn't have to ask."

For once, a snappy comeback escaped him, because Jake just might be right.

MIDMORNING, and Rachel still hadn't heard anything from Benjamin or any other member of their family. Surely Benj would have told Daad by now.

Why wasn't Daad reacting, one way or another? If he thought she had been at fault in keeping Benj's secret, she might have destroyed whatever small progress she'd made in healing the breach with her family.

She crossed to the kitchen window and glanced out. Mandy and Princess were in the backyard, as they should be, but they were not alone. Another girl, probably about Mandy's age, was kneeling to pet Princess.

Curious, Rachel went out to the porch. Both girls looked up at the sound of the door.

"Hey, Mommy, guess what? This is Emily, and she lives just down the street, and she'll be in my grade when school starts." The information came out in an enthusiastic gush of words.

Rachel smiled at the child. "It's nice to meet you, Emily. I'm so glad Mandy met somebody her age." And that was something she should have seen to before now. Obviously Mandy needed more company than adults could supply.

"Emily Forrest." The child supplied her last name with a twirl of her curly dark ponytail. "My daddy says he remembers you from when you were Amish."

The innocent words set up a pang in her heart. But that was true, wasn't it? Anyone she'd known here in Deer Run would identify her that way.

"Would your father be Mickey Forrest?" Mickey had been one of Ronnie's friends.

Emily nodded, ponytail bobbing. "That's him." She looked down at Princess, seeming to lose interest in her father, and patted her denim shorts. Princess pranced to her. "Mandy's so lucky to have a puppy. I can't have anything but stupid old goldfish because my stupid brother is allergic."

"That's too bad." And obviously not the brother's fault, but Rachel didn't bother pointing that out. "Princess likes you."

Emily's pixie face lit in a smile. "She does, doesn't she?"

"It's okay if Emily stays to play, isn't it, Mommy?" Mandy beamed possessively at both dog and friend.

"It's fine, as long as her parents know where she—" Rachel stopped, catching movement out of the corner of her eye.

Emily's father, coming to look for her? No, this man was obviously older than Mickey Forrest would be. Middle-aged, probably, wearing khakis and a plaid sport shirt, he carried a clipboard and looked around, frowning when his gaze lit on her.

"Mrs. Mason?"

"Yes, I'm Mrs. Mason." She moved to meet him, realizing that she was stiffening automatically, as if any stranger had to be carrying bad news. "How can I help you?"

"Matthew Carter." He flashed an identification card, so quickly it barely registered. "You applied for a permit to run a bed-and-breakfast on these premises. I'm here for your safety inspection."

She hadn't thought she'd be caught off guard again. First the tourist bureau rep arrived unexpectedly and now this man. "I was told that I would receive two weeks' notice of the safety inspection."

Carter removed his dark glasses, maybe the better to frown at her. "I don't know anything about that. I just come out when the office tells me to, and you're up today. Shall we get on with it?" He turned toward the house.

Her mind raced. "This must be some mistake. I have a few more repairs to make before I'll be ready for an inspection."

"Makes no difference to me." He sighed, rather elaborately. "But if you don't have a preliminary inspection today, I don't know when I'll be able to get you on the schedule again. I always have to figure on a follow-up visit to be sure everything's been taken care of. We don't start today, it might be Labor Day before we're done with the process."

She couldn't afford to wait that long to open. Her bank balance was running precariously low as it was. She didn't have a choice.

"Fine. Come this way, please."

A half hour later she was standing in the same spot while Carter ambled to his car. She stared, appalled, at the list he'd insisted she initial before he gave her a copy. Things she had to do before she could open—way too many things.

"Was ist letz?" Her father's voice sounded so close that she jumped. "Who was that man, and why did he make you look so upset?"

Rachel made an effort to swallow the lump in her throat as she turned to her father. "He's a safety inspector from the state. He gave me a list of all the things I have to fix before I can open the house to guests."

She gestured with the list. Daad, seeming to take that for an invitation, took it from her hand. He bent his head, studying the paper in that deliberate way he had, as if he had to absorb every word before he could understand what he'd read.

Finally he put his finger on the list. "Most of these things Mose and I can do for you. Except the electric, *ja?* And for that, you must call Davey King. He is honest, and he will do *gut* work for you, that's certain sure. *Chust* remind him that you are my daughter."

She could only stare at her father. Here was the sort of response she might have expected if she'd never gone away.

"*Denke*, Daadi." She found her voice. "That would be *sehr* kind of you. But you and Mose have your own work to do. I can't ask—"

"Don't talk foolish." His voice was gruff, and he didn't look at her. "We will do this first. It makes no matter."

"*Denke*," she said again, her voice clogged with tears she didn't want to shed. Daadi would be embarrassed if she started to cry. He'd never known how to cope with women's tears.

He cleared his throat. "About Benjamin—you saw that something was wrong with the boy. I should have been the one to see that, for sure. You're a *gut* big sister to him, Rachel."

"I love him," she said. It was all she could manage.

"*Ja. Gut.*" Daadi fell silent, still not meeting her gaze.

A spark of hope fluttered. Daad wouldn't say he had been wrong to oppose her marriage. That wouldn't be true. But maybe, if he was willing, they could go on from here.

Her father cleared his throat. "I will talk to the parents of the other boys. It is right that they should be told. Benj says that Colin McDonald said so." He gave her a look that contained a question.

"Colin…" How to explain Colin's presence in

this whole thing? "Colin was worried about Benj. He helped me to get Benj to tell us the whole story."

"*Ja?* Well, he has taken an interest in Benj, since the boy works for him."

She nodded, relieved that she wasn't called on to explain her relationship with Colin any further. "Do you think…" She hesitated, but if she didn't ask, who would? "Will you go to the police about the man shooting at the boys?"

The lines in Daad's face seemed to engrave themselves more deeply. "We do not go to the law to settle our problems. I will see to Benj's punishment myself."

She'd known that would be his answer, but she had to try and get him to see the other side of the issue. "The man, no matter who he was, should not have shot at the boys."

"We will not go to the law." That was clearly his final answer.

"Mommy, Grossdaadi!" Mandy came running toward them, Princess bouncing at her heels. "Did you know there's going to be a festival? Emily told me. Can we go, Mommy? Please?"

"The volunteer fire company festival," Daadi said in explanation. "It will be open evenings all week, and then all day on Saturday." He smiled at Mandy, resting his work-roughened hand lightly on her hair. "You will like that, *ja?*"

The gesture seemed to squeeze Rachel's heart. Once Daadi had looked at her that way.

There was no point in yearning for something that wouldn't come again. She and Daadi had traveled miles today. She was content with that.

"Yes, I guess we'll have to take in the fair tonight," she said, smiling at her daughter. "You can tell Emily you'll see her there."

"Wow, that's terrific." She whirled and darted across the lawn, light as a firefly.

Benj had told Daad the whole story, and she was no longer burdened with the secret. Maybe just the fact that it was known would free her from the oppressive sense that something threatened.

Maybe.

THE PARKING LOT and grassy area around the cinder-block fire hall sported three rows of booths, a couple of trailers and a small merry-go-round, along with a flatbed truck set up as an improvised stage. Somehow Rachel wasn't even surprised when the first person they met was Colin. Maybe she'd become used to the fact that he kept showing up. If so, she'd better get unused to it.

"Colin." She nodded. His father was with him, requiring an extra measure of warmth on her part. "Mr. McDonald, it's nice to see you."

"Good to see you, as well, Rachel." He remembered her name without effort this time, which must mean that he was having a good day.

"Hi, Mr. McDonald." Mandy grasped his hand in

her excitement. "Isn't this a neat festival? I've never been to something like this before."

"It is neat," he agreed solemnly, his eyes twinkling. "It seems to me if this is your first time, you ought to see if you can win a few prizes. What say we try the ball toss?"

"Wow, that would be great. Could I really win something?"

His smile widened. "I can practically guarantee it." He glanced at Rachel. "Is it all right if I take this young lady off your hands for a bit?"

Rachel hesitated for a second, but the fire company grounds were so small Mandy would find it hard to get out of her sight. And when she was Mandy's age, she'd been free to wander around the festival with her friends, even without an adult in attendance.

She nodded. "That's kind of you."

"The pleasure is all mine." He was at his most courtly, a tantalizing flash of the man he used to be. He and Mandy headed for the ball-toss game.

Rachel glanced at Colin, catching an expression of longing and sorrow on his face. Her heart clenched.

"He's having a good day," she said softly.

"Yes. Thanks for letting Mandy go with him. His doctors say that the more normal his activities, the better. I'm not supposed to hover over him or try to take away his independence. But it's a tough balancing act sometimes." Colin seemed to make an effort to pull his thoughts away. "He's given me a chance to ask you. Did Benj tell your father?"

"Yes, thank goodness. Daad came over today to let me know Benj had told him. He…he was grateful to me for seeing something was wrong with Benj. And to you, too, in fact. Of course, he's blaming himself for not seeing it first."

Colin lifted an eyebrow. "I see you come by your talent for blaming yourself honestly."

She stiffened. "Naturally a parent feels responsible for a child." She didn't bother adding the corollary. And a child for a parent. That was obviously what drove Colin.

Colin didn't pursue the subject. Maybe he remembered that their last conversation about self-blame had ended badly. "Is your father going to talk to the police?"

"No. He'll talk to the other parents, but that's all."

"Well, it's what we expected, I guess." But he sounded exasperated. "Is he going to be here tonight? Maybe I can talk to him."

"I don't think so." She was just as glad. A confrontation between Colin and her father wasn't on her wish list. "The family usually just comes the last day."

"A compromise?" His voice was faintly mocking.

She shrugged. "Amish don't go to carnivals. But since this is called a festival, and since all the proceeds go to the fire company, which the Amish support…"

She let the statement die out. Really, she didn't
have to explain this to Colin. Amish life was one
long series of compromises, she sometimes thought,
a trick of adopting the new only after careful consideration of its effect on the family and the church.

A familiar squeal had her turning to see Mandy
clapping her hands.

"It looks as if Mandy won something. I didn't
think she was good enough tossing a ball," she said.

"That's the Boosters' Club stand," Colin said.
"They never let a kid go away empty-handed. And
one of Dad's cronies is running it, so I suspect she
got a bit of extra help."

Of course. She'd forgotten that such things in
Deer Run typically ran on volunteers and kindness.
Mandy was jumping up and down as the volunteer
put a stuffed panda in her arms and Mr. McDonald
looked on, beaming.

Rachel's throat tightened. This was the life she
wanted for Mandy. No matter what obstacles were
in her path, she had to make this work.

"You're not going to get all weepy about a stuffed
bear, are you?" Colin's hand closed on her arm, and
she felt its warmth travel straight to her heart.

She looked up at him, eyes wide, and saw his
darken in response. The noise and movement around
them began to fade, until she saw nothing but his
face, heard nothing but the quick catch of her breath.

"Hi, Rachel, I hoped you'd be here." Meredith's
voice shook her out of her momentary paralysis.

Rachel turned to her friend with relief, catching a similar relief on Colin's face. Then he was murmuring an excuse and strolling off.

"Did I scare him away?" Meredith asked.

"N-no." Rachel sucked in a breath. *Get control of yourself,* she ordered. "I think he might have seen someone he wanted to talk to."

"Hmmm." Meredith invested the syllable with a wealth of meaning. "Well, to business. I've done some work on a webpage for you, keeping it fairly simple to begin with. We can add more bells and whistles later if needed. I should take some digital photos as soon as possible if you hope to start taking guests by the end of the month."

The reminder brought her back to earth. "That may not be possible. I had an unexpected visit today from a state safety inspector."

"Unexpected?" Meredith's eyebrows lifted.

Rachel shrugged. She wasn't going to start imagining a conspiracy to chase her away.

"I thought I was supposed to get two weeks' notice, but apparently not. Luckily a lot of the work is stuff that my father and brother are going to do. But some of it is electrical, so I have to hire someone." She should have called the person Daad mentioned. She'd have to do that first thing tomorrow.

"Your dad and brother?" There was a question in Meredith's voice.

She nodded. "Daad offered." She didn't need to

explain anything more to Meredith, who would understand.

"I'm glad," Meredith said softly.

"Look at the two of you together. It's just like old times, isn't it?" Jeannette Walker's voice seemed to contain an edge. She had stopped a few feet from them, wearing a smile that didn't seem to reach her eyes.

"Rachel and I have always been friends," Meredith said. She smiled. "I'm glad you remember that."

"It's nice you can be reunited. So few friendships seem to last anymore. Not like my day, when people didn't run off so readily." She patted her tight curls and turned her gaze on Rachel. "I noticed you had a visit from the state safety inspector today. I do hope he's not going to prevent you from opening on schedule."

She noticed? How would Jeannette have noticed that, when the man had come and gone from the back door?

"It won't be a problem at all." Meredith jumped in before Rachel could respond to that frontal attack. "We already have the necessary repairs scheduled."

"We?" Jeannette's carefully plucked eyebrows lifted.

"Didn't you know?" Meredith's tone was all innocence. "I'm helping Rachel with the bed-and-breakfast."

Jeannette's lips tightened briefly. "Really? I'm surprised your little home business and taking care of your mother gives you enough spare time to take on something else."

With that shot, Jeannette strolled off, her outsized handbag swinging from her arm.

"Poisonous woman," Meredith said, not troubling to lower her voice.

"Be careful," Rachel murmured, mindful of people passing. "Someone will hear you."

"Maybe that would be a good thing." Meredith shook her head so fiercely that her silver earrings jangled. "Sometimes I'd just like to stir things up so much they'd never be the same again."

"You don't mean that." Rachel couldn't prevent a sense of shock. Meredith was always so cool and controlled. Who would guess that such rebellion lurked underneath that serene exterior?

"Maybe not." Meredith seemed to take a calming breath. "I shouldn't say things like that. I wouldn't, to anyone but you." Her gaze suddenly seemed to sharpen. "That's an interesting picture, isn't it?"

Rachel followed the direction of her gaze, side-stepping to avoid a small crowd of children running toward the merry-go-round. A few yards away there was a space of calm in the eddying crowd.

Laura Hammond stood there, wearing a filmy dress that looked more appropriate for a four-star restaurant than the fire hall parking lot. Her husband, Victor, hovered at her elbow, seeming to urge her to do something. Beyond them, Dennis stood, face impassive, watching.

Rachel let out a slow breath. "Except for Moose, it's like the drawing."

"Without Aaron," Meredith said softly. "And with the addition of Jeannette."

She was right. Jeannette approached and took Laura's arm as if to steer her away, but Laura shook her off.

"I'd forgotten," Rachel said, trying not to stare. "Jeannette was always Laura's best female friend. I wonder why? They seem such an unlikely pair."

Meredith shrugged. "Some pretty girls like to have plain friends, I guess."

"More likely they knew each other from the time they were toddlers," she said, hating to think Laura might have been that calculating. "Would you like to take a walk around? I have to collect Mandy from the ball toss."

Meredith nodded, but before they could move, a commotion broke out in the small cluster around Laura.

"No!" Laura's voice was high enough to draw stares, but then eyes were quickly averted. "I don't want to go home. Stop pawing me."

Victor, pudgier than ever, took a step back, his round face flushed. "Laura, you don't feel well—"

But his comment was addressed to empty space. Laura spun away from her husband and headed straight for Rachel and Meredith.

Straight wasn't exactly the right word, Rachel realized, her heart filling with pity. Laura wove her way toward them, as if the ground were spinning under her like the carousel.

Laura reached them, grasping Rachel's arm, staring into her face with pupils that were contracted to tiny pinpoints. "You remember, don't you? You remember." She wavered, nearly losing her balance.

Rachel caught her by one arm, while Meredith grasped the other.

"It's all right," Meredith soothed.

"You remember," Laura repeated. "You two." She frowned, shaking her head. "No. Three. There were three of you. You remember."

"We remember," Rachel said quickly. She'd say anything to comfort her, to take away the terrible, stricken look from Laura's face. "It's all right now, Laura."

Victor reached them, puffing a little. "My wife isn't well," he said, avoiding their eyes. "She doesn't know what she's saying. I must take her home."

"No. Have to talk to them. They remember." Laura repeated the words, but with less assurance. She wavered, as if about to slip out of focus.

"It's all right," Rachel repeated. "We remember." It seemed the least she could do for the tormented woman.

"Come on, now, Laura." Jeannette took her arm in a firm grasp. "Time to go home. You'll feel better tomorrow."

Between them, they steered her off toward the

parking lot. Dennis stood where they'd left him, watching them go, his face expressionless.

Rachel realized she was shaking. She wrapped her arms around herself. "That poor woman."

"She's using again." Meredith sounded just as shaken but not surprised.

"Using again?" She wasn't sure which word startled her more.

Meredith nodded. "It happens. Every once in a while Laura goes off on what's billed as a 'spa vacation.' Everyone knows she's actually going into rehab, but we all pretend to believe it."

"That is so incredibly sad." She'd once thought that Laura, the beautiful golden girl, had everything. "How long has this been going on?"

"Years, but worse lately." Meredith shook her head. "What do you suppose she thought we remembered?"

"Not what," Rachel said, sure she understood. "Who. She meant that we remember Aaron."

Before Meredith could respond, Dennis approached them. Rachel managed a smile.

"Evening, Rachel, Meredith. Enjoying the festival?" Dennis seemed determined to ignore what had just happened, though he could hardly be unaware of it. Just like the drawing, he'd stayed in the shadows, watching.

"I'm sure the fire company will do well this year," Meredith said, seeming to regain her sense of tact.

"I hope so," Dennis said. "That tanker truck will have to be replaced before long, and I doubt we can hope for much help from the state, given the current economy."

"Are you a volunteer firefighter?" Rachel asked, curious. It somehow didn't seem a likely fit with him.

"I can't be, unfortunately. Since I work and live in Williamsport, I'm too far away. But all of us can and should support them financially."

"Making a speech, cousin?" Gene Sitler emerged from a passing group and elbowed Dennis, who looked less than pleased at the interruption. Rachel wasn't surprised, given Dennis's outspoken comments about his cousin. "Introduce me to the pretty ladies."

Dennis stiffened, his narrow face a mask of disapproval. Still, he could hardly refuse, no matter how much he might want to. "Meredith King, Rachel Mason, this is my cousin, Gene Sitler. He's staying with my grandfather right now."

Gene ignored him, his dark eyes zeroing in on Rachel's face. "Sure, I've seen Rachel around. She's the one with the little girl. Cute kid." He glanced around. "Where is she, anyway?"

Something in his tone had Rachel spinning to scan the crowd. Colin's father still stood at the ball toss, leaning on the counter. But Mandy—Mandy wasn't there.

CHAPTER THIRTEEN

PANIC SEIZED RACHEL by the throat, cutting off her breath. She bolted toward the ball toss, battling her way through a flock of teenagers who seemed oblivious to the presence of anyone else. Mandy…she should never have let Mandy go off with Colin's father, Mandy didn't have anyone but her, she had to keep Mandy safe….

Rachel forced her way through the last few people between her and her destination, heedless of startled, annoyed looks. Colin emerged from the crowd in the opposite direction, his expression making it clear he knew something was wrong. He caught her arm before she reached his father.

"What is it? What's wrong?"

"Mandy." She yanked herself free. "She was with your dad. Where is she?"

Colin's expression seemed to freeze. He clasped his father's shoulder. "Dad, where is Mandy?"

His father turned toward them, a puzzled frown creasing his forehead. "Mandy?" He glanced around, confusion clouding his eyes. "Was she with me?"

The man behind the counter, his face vaguely

familiar, seemed to catch on. "The little girl who was with your father? She went over that way." He gestured toward his right. "I figured she was going back to her mother. I'm sorry, I didn't realize…"

His words trailed off as he looked from the confusion on James McDonald's face to the terror that must surely be plain on hers. "Listen, I'll close the stand and help you look for her. She can't have gone far."

"No need." Colin clasped her arm, his grip firm. "Just keep Dad with you, okay? Rachel and I will find her."

She would have darted through the crowd, panic driving her, but Colin tightened his grasp. "Don't run off half-cocked. Think first."

Rachel had an atavistic urge to strike at him. "She's gone. I shouldn't have let her out of my sight. I shouldn't have trusted—"

She stopped, but Colin clearly knew where that sentence was going. His jaw turned to granite.

"Is there anything she wanted to do? Anyone she expected to see here?"

His questions seemed to penetrate the fog of fear.

"Emily Forrest. Her new friend. But she wouldn't just go off—" There was no sense to the words, since Mandy had clearly done just that.

"You go to the right, I'll start around to the left. If you see anyone you know, get them looking, too." Some emotion broke through the frost in his face. "We'll find her. This is Deer Run, not a city street."

Nodding, she pulled free and headed to the right. Colin meant well, but she knew better. Bad things could happen anywhere. She had plenty of evidence of that, didn't she?

It took control to keep from running mindlessly, but she had that now, maybe thanks to Colin's rational approach. Resentment flickered through her. Colin didn't understand. He didn't know what it was like to be solely responsible for your child.

She peered between stands and scanned the crowd without success. Panic rose again. This wasn't doing any good, she had to—

Music interrupted her. The carousel had started, its faintly tinny music drifting across the fire-hall grounds. Mandy would have been drawn to that, and even as Rachel's gaze searched the crowd around the carousel, she spotted Mickey Forrest, Emily's father, half a head taller than most people around him. Relief flooded through her. The combination of her new friend and the carousel might have been too much for even so obedient a child as Mandy.

Rachel hurried toward the carousel, dodging the stream of people moving the other way. There was Mickey, holding a cone of cotton candy with a resigned expression on his face while his wife wiped off Emily's hands. But Mandy wasn't with them.

"Emily?" The little girl turned at the sound of her voice. "Have you seen Mandy?"

She shook her head, sending Rachel's heart plummeting.

"You're Rachel Mason, right?" Mickey said. He seemed to catch on quickly. "It's easy enough to get separated. We'll help—"

Before he could finish, the music cut off and a voice boomed over the loudspeaker.

"Mandy Mason. Come to the carousel right now. Your mother is waiting for you."

Rachel spun, eyes searching the carousel until she spotted Colin, microphone in hand, repeating his announcement. Hope leaped in her heart. Surely Mandy would hear—the speaker carried even over the chatter of the crowd.

Please, please…an almost wordless prayer rising in her mind. *Please.*

Her eyes caught a flicker of movement by the nearest food stand, and then Mandy was running toward her.

In a few steps Rachel had her arms around her daughter, hugging her so tightly that Mandy protested.

"Mommy, you're squeezing me."

"I should do more than squeeze you." She stooped, bringing her face to Mandy's level. "What do you mean by running off like that? You were supposed to stay with Mr. McDonald. It was very naughty to go off."

The carousel began playing again, and Colin stepped lightly from the moving platform. He moved to stand between them and any curious glances. "Did somebody call you away, Mandy?"

Mandy shook her head, mouth set in a mutinous pout. "I wouldn't have gone, but it was Princess, I know it was."

Rachel found herself exchanging glances with Colin. "What do you mean? Princess is at home in her crate."

Mandy shook her head, and with a pang Rachel realized there were tears in her eyes. "I heard her. I know Princess's bark. She was back behind the stands, but when I went back there, I couldn't find her, so I had to look."

A chill finger seemed to touch the back of Rachel's neck. "Princess couldn't have gotten out of her crate and out of the house, sweetheart. It had to be some other dog you heard."

"It was Princess." Mandy was stubbornly determined. She clasped Rachel's hand and tugged. "Come on, Mommy. We have to find her."

"Tell you what," Colin said. "Let's walk over to the house and see if she's there first. I'll bet you'll find her safe and sound. Okay?"

Mandy wavered for a moment, but then she nodded, obviously willing to give up any pleasures for her pet. "Okay."

"You don't need to come—" Rachel began, but Colin was already shaking his head. "Just let me tell Ralph we found her and ask him to take Dad home. I'll catch up with you." He was off before Rachel could protest.

Clasping her daughter's hand, she headed for the

street. The aftermath of the fear she'd felt seemed to drain all her energy, and she longed to call it a day, no matter how early it was. She had to make Mandy understand the seriousness of her actions, preferably without scaring her.

"Even if it had been Princess, which I'm sure it wasn't, you were wrong to run off from Mr. Mc-Donald that way."

"Mommy, I tried to tell him it was Princess, but he didn't understand. And she's my pet, and you told me I had to be responsible."

Why did children always choose to remember what you didn't want them to? "I meant you should be responsible about feeding her and walking her. And if Mr. McDonald didn't understand why you were worried about her, you should have come back and told me."

"But Mommy—"

"No more 'but Mommys', please," she said, her tone sharpening. "You know you should have come to me, don't you?"

Mandy paused for a long moment—long enough for Rachel to hear the quick footsteps behind her and know they were Colin's. For an instant Mandy's expression reminded her of Ronnie's when she'd insisted on the truth from him.

"Yes, Mommy," Mandy said finally. She stopped, then turned and threw her arms around Rachel's waist. "I love you, Mommy." Her words were muffled against Rachel's shirt.

Heart squeezing, Rachel wrapped her arms around Mandy. "I love you, too." Over her daughter's head Colin's gaze, serious and almost somber, met hers.

"Well, let's have a look and see what Princess is up to," Rachel said, trying for a lightness she didn't feel.

"I hope she's in her crate." Mandy skipped a few steps. "Can I have the key, please, Mommy? I want to run fast and check on her."

Rachel fished the keys from her bag and handed them over. "I'll be right behind you, but you can open the door."

Mandy hurried on ahead, and Colin fell into step with Rachel. Rachel's tongue seemed stuck. She should apologize for snapping at him. She'd implied that his father was to blame, even if she hadn't come right out and said it, and that wasn't fair.

"I had a quick look behind the stand where Mandy said she heard Princess," Colin said, his voice pitched low enough not to reach Mandy, who was hurrying on ahead of them to the gate.

Rachel raised a no-doubt startled gaze to his face. "Why? Princess wasn't back there. She couldn't have been."

"No. There was no sign of any dog back there, and I couldn't hear anything."

"Then why—"

They started up the walk, but her eyes were on

Mandy, flitting up the steps and putting the key in the door with an air of importance.

"Mandy could have heard some other dog, I suppose," he said slowly. "She must have. But she seemed so convinced she recognized Princess's bark."

The foreboding was gripping her again, seeming darker each time she felt it. "What are you thinking, Colin? Just say it."

He met her gaze. "I'm thinking how easy it would be to tape the dog barking sometime when she was out in the yard with Mandy. And how easy it would be to play it and lure Mandy away."

A cold hand seemed to squeeze her heart. "But why? Why would anyone want to do that? Anyway, nobody was there. No one tried to harm her."

"No. But it scared you plenty, didn't it? Maybe that was what he or she wanted."

"Why?" she said again, wanting desperately to push the entire subject away.

"Why any of it? Why did someone shoot at the boys? Why did someone hide in your shed? Why did Will and Joseph run away? Why?"

"I don't know, but no one would deliberately try to lure Mandy away—"

The idea was too monstrous. Halfway up the steps she swung around to tell him so, grasping the railing for balance.

The railing gave under her hand, shrieking in

protest. Off balance, she swung with it, losing her grip, falling—

Hands grasped her, arms closed around her, and Colin drew her roughly against him, his heart thundering in her ear as she pressed her head against his chest. His grip tightened, and he held her as if he'd never let her go.

And she didn't want him to. She wanted to stay safe inside his embrace, feeling his arms holding her close—

"Mommy! Are you okay?" Mandy ran across the porch.

Colin released her, his hand steadying her until he was sure she had her balance.

"I'm fine. Don't come on the steps until we see what's wrong," she added.

"That's right." Hand on Rachel's elbow, Colin guided her carefully up the steps, across the porch and into the front hall.

Over their heads, Princess burst into a volley of barking, obviously hearing them.

"Princess!" Mandy exclaimed, and darted toward the stairs.

"Go with her," Colin urged. "I'm going to have a look at that railing."

Now it was her turn to clasp his hand. "I don't understand. That railing was shaky, but I fixed it. It should have been fine."

"I know." Colin's face was grim. He gave her a little push. "Go on. See to Mandy."

A FEW MINUTES later Colin squatted next to the porch steps, having detoured through the kitchen to pick up the flashlight he'd seen Rachel kept there. He'd noticed the shaky railing the first time he'd come to the house.

But Rachel said she'd fixed it, and on recent visits he hadn't noticed anything wrong.

Frowning, he shone the light on the upright that had given way. He could see the brightness of the nails Rachel had used to reinforce the two-by-two. He grasped the skirting board, half-expecting to find it rotted through, but it was solid under his hand.

He didn't like this, not one bit. There was no reason he could see for the railing to have failed like that. He sat back on his heels, frowning, muted carousel music an incongruous accompaniment to his thoughts.

Using the tips of his fingers, Colin explored the place where the new nails had pulled free of the board beneath. Did he, or didn't he, feel the slight gouge that a pry bar might have made? He couldn't be positive, and the flashlight beam wasn't strong enough to be sure, but he'd be coming back in daylight to see what that board might tell him.

Moving the broken railing to one side, he mounted the steps, testing each one with his weight, and then checked the railing on the other side. It looked solid, but he wasn't going to risk any more accidents.

Once he'd satisfied himself that it hadn't been

tampered with, Colin went into the house. Rachel hadn't exactly invited him to hang around, but he had to be sure she was taking this evening's events seriously.

He ran a hand through his hair and rubbed the back of his neck. What on earth had Benj and those boys stumbled onto to make someone so nervous? Or wasn't this string of actions against Rachel related to that at all? Maybe someone else wanted Rachel Mason out of Deer Run. Or wanted to put an end to a new bed-and-breakfast in town.

Rachel came down the steps just then and he looked up, studying the evidence of strain in her face. "You and Meredith," he said abruptly. "What were you doing to attract Laura Hammond's hysteria tonight?"

Her blue eyes expressed nothing more than confusion as she came the rest of the way down the stairs, her hand resting lightly on the railing as if she feared it, too, might give way.

"Nothing," she said. "Well, nothing that could have anything to do with what happened."

Colin let out a frustrated breath. "That's just the trouble. Nothing that's been happening seems to tie together, but one thing is clear—whether it's related to Benj or not, someone isn't happy that you've come back to Deer Run. And that unhappiness is strong enough to make him or her take action."

Her gaze flew to the door, as if she could see through it to the porch railing. "The railing—you mean that was deliberate." She didn't even sound very surprised.

"I can't be positive, but it looks that way to me. I'll have another go at it in daylight. But I think that while you were out, someone slid a pry bar behind the upright you fixed and pulled it free enough that as soon as someone put their weight on the railing, it would give way."

Rachel shook her head in quick denial. "Surely not. They'd have risked being seen."

"Not much of a risk. The bushes hide that area, and it wouldn't take more than a few seconds to do it."

Now it was Rachel's turn to rub the nape of her neck, as if tension had settled there. His fingers tingled with the image of doing it for her, of running his hand along the long, sweet curve of her nape, of drawing her toward him, of Rachel tilting her face up, unresisting, for his kiss…

Whoa. Back up. Hadn't he just seen tonight how impossible a relationship with her was? Dad had been with Mandy for no more than a few minutes, and he'd managed to put her at risk.

"Look, are you going to tell me about Laura Hammond? Maybe it has nothing to do with anything, but I'd like to know what reasons anybody might have for wanting to see the last of you."

A chill slid along his skin even as he said the words. That sounded a lot more final than he'd meant it.

But Rachel didn't seem to take it that way. She sighed, then flipped the lock on the front door and headed toward the kitchen, motioning for him to follow her.

"Let's go in the kitchen. I told Mandy I'd make some hot chocolate. We're giving up on the festival for tonight. We'll try again tomorrow."

He followed, taking a seat and watching as Rachel poured milk into a saucepan and set it on the stove. Once she'd put out a mug she sat down across from him.

"All right," she said. "I'll tell you, but you'll see it's nothing." She clasped her hands together and looked down at them, as if marshaling her thoughts. "It was twenty years ago, the summer I was ten. I spent a lot of time with Meredith and another girl who was staying here for the summer—Lainey Colton. That didn't usually happen, but Mammi was busy with a sick relative, and nobody was paying much attention to any of the three of us."

He nodded, understanding. It wasn't that Amish and Englisch didn't become friends, but there were boundaries—boundaries that had apparently been stretched that one summer.

He listened, his gaze on her face, as she told him of their fanciful adventures of that summer, of the way they'd watched the romance between Laura and Aaron, investing them and those around them with mythic properties.

"We didn't realize we were spying on them, you

understand," she said at one point, fixing him with that serious blue gaze. "We were just playing."

"I understand." He'd been totally preoccupied with baseball that summer, as he recalled, and had been just as obsessive about it as the girls had apparently been about their fantasy.

"Anyway, when I came back, it seemed so many things were reminders of how Aaron died." She spread her hands wide. "Meredith and I started talking about it, remembering more together than we ever would have separately. When I saw what had become of Laura, I wondered…we wondered…if Aaron's death had anything to do with it. Usually we knew if they were meeting down at the dam, but if it was late in the evening, I'd have been home already, and Meredith had gone someplace with her parents that day."

It took him a moment to realize where she was going with that. "You think that Laura and Aaron were together when he died."

Rachel's face tightened defensively. "It would make more sense than Aaron being there by himself and somehow falling in. But if they were both there, and he was showing off for her, the way kids do, he might have fallen in and gotten caught in the current."

"She never spoke of it, if that's the case."

"No. She wouldn't have wanted to cause trouble, maybe. And she'd have felt guilty for not saving him." Rachel's voice quivered on the last sentence, and the hands that had been loosely clasped on the table were suddenly clenching together so fiercely that the knuckles were white.

"It could have happened that way," he said carefully, not sure what was going on. "But Laura wasn't to blame for what happened to Aaron."

"She'd have felt responsible. It might have made her turn to...to anything...that would make her feel less guilty." The hands strained against each other.

He couldn't stand it. He clasped her hands in both of his, holding them warmly. "What is it, Rachel? What do you feel guilty about?"

"Nothing." She shook her head, but her eyes were already brimming with tears. "I can't." She tried to turn away. "The milk. I'll burn it."

He got up, moved the pan off the burner and sat back down, pulling his chair close to hers. "You might as well tell me," he said. "You know I'll keep on guessing until I know. You feel guilty about Ronnie, the way you're convinced Laura feels guilty about Aaron. Why?"

She held out against him for another second, and then the tears spilled over. She wiped them away with her fingers, like a child, and his heart twisted.

"I sent him away," she whispered. "I loved him, and we were so happy together at first. But after Mandy was born, and there wasn't enough money, things just turned sour. I finally told him we couldn't live together any longer. He was gambling, drinking...Mandy was getting old enough to notice, to understand, and I couldn't let her down. I'm all she has."

She didn't need to fill in all the blanks. He could imagine the rest of it. Rachel hadn't mentioned women, but he didn't doubt that there had been other women, where Ronnie was concerned. Ronnie had been a charmer—fun to be with and generous, but careless with money, careless with his property, careless with his family, and ultimately careless with his life.

"That was the right thing to do. Your first responsibility was to your child." He said the words firmly, even knowing it was that responsibility that would keep her from any involvement with him. "Ronnie was a grown man. If he wanted to throw away everything that should have been important to him, you couldn't stop him."

"I should have." Her fingers clenched again. "If I hadn't kicked him out, if Mandy and I had been with him—"

"You and Mandy would be dead, too." Harsh words, but the truth was often harsh. "Wake up, Rachel. You weren't responsible for Ronnie's bad choices. If you think you could have prevented them, that's like thinking you're God. Nobody could stop Ronnie when he wanted something."

Anger flared in her eyes at that, but before she could say what she undoubtedly thought of him, a little voice called down the stairs.

"Mommy? Is the hot chocolate ready yet?"

"Almost," she called, pushing her chair back with an abrupt movement. She seemed to take a steadying breath before she looked at him.

"Forget about what happened between me and Ronnie. That's not your concern. And you may as well forget about Laura and Aaron, too. Even if Laura knew we'd guessed, what could she do? It's crazy to think of her out front prying at the stairs."

"Maybe." He rose. "I'm inclined to think you're right. She'd have trouble keeping two thoughts in her head long enough to accomplish that, but anyone could do it. It doesn't take much strength or skill."

"I don't believe it," she said.

He wondered if she still saw Laura as the enchanted princess from that long-ago summer. Actually, he hadn't been thinking of Laura. He'd been thinking of Jeannette, who might not be above pulling a trick or two to discourage her competition if she was sure she wouldn't be caught.

"Somebody did," he said soberly. "So lock the doors, please. I'll be back to look at the steps in the morning."

"You don't need to." She busied herself with the hot milk, as if to give herself an excuse not to look at him. "Daad is coming over, and he'll fix it."

"I'm coming," he repeated. She ought to know she wasn't getting rid of him that easily. "Has anything else happened that I should know about? No anonymous phone calls or nasty notes?"

"No, but—" She stopped, as if something struck her.

"But what?" Was he going to have to drag everything out of her? She was as bad as Benj.

"That grandson of Franklin Sitler's. Not Dennis, the other one. Gene."

"The one that looks like a hood? What about him?"

"He was at the fire-hall grounds. They all were." The words came slowly, as if she were visualizing what had happened. "I was distracted by Laura, and then they started talking to me. Dennis introduced me to Gene. And Gene said something about knowing who I was, and knowing I had a little girl. And then he said where was she, and something about the way he asked frightened me. That's when I looked around and saw that Mandy was gone." She shook her head. "But that's ridiculous. Why would he go to all that trouble? What could he have against me?"

Colin managed a smile, but it was a tight one. "The trouble with you, Rachel, is that you think the best of everyone. Now me, I tend to think the worst. And I have a feeling Gene Sitler wouldn't disappoint me."

Rachel straightened. "I don't want to think about people that way."

"Then it's a good thing you have me around to do it for you," he said. Quickly, before he could talk himself out of it, he seized her shoulders, pulled

her toward him and gave her a quick, hard kiss on
the lips.

Rachel looked a little dazed when he let her go,
but not more dazed than he felt. He shouldn't have
done that, but he couldn't seem to stop himself.
Quickly, before he could let himself kiss her again,
he went to the back door.

"Lock this behind me," he ordered, and walked
away.

CHAPTER FOURTEEN

THE NEXT MORNING, the sound of hammering was punctuated by the occasional murmur of Amish voices as Daad and Mose turned up bright and early to start on the repair work. Rachel reminded herself that she should be delighted by the noise, even if it sometimes seemed they were hammering in time with the pounding in her head.

Too little sleep and disturbing dreams hadn't helped matters, but for the most part she'd been reliving those moments in the kitchen with Colin the previous night. She'd revealed her deepest pain to him, and he'd responded with harsh, almost angry words.

She could give in to being angry in return if it weren't for the fact that a small voice in the back of her mind kept asserting that Colin just might be right.

If you'd been with him, then you and Mandy would be dead, too.

Much as she tried to dismiss everything Colin had said, the words lingered, haunting her.

The screen door rattled, and her brother Mose

walked in. He was a full head taller than she was now, but she could remember when he'd been furious that she'd actually been an inch taller for one whole school year. With only eleven months between them, they'd been more like twins than just brother and sister.

But her "twin" was a grown man now, his short chestnut beard attesting to the fact that he was a married man. He looked at her stiffly, as if he didn't quite know what to make of her, either.

"Daad says do you have a Phillips screwdriver," he said in Pennsylvania Dutch, as usual slipping the Englisch name into the flow effortlessly. Most Amish did that—incorporating Englisch words into the language for anything that had come along since the eighteenth century.

"I think so." She led the way to the trunk filled with tools that took up so much space in the back hallway. "It looks as if all the tools are in here." She lifted the heavy lid.

"*Ach*, what a collection." Mose's frostiness turned into awe. He picked up an old-fashioned square-cut nail. "The old lady must never have thrown anything away."

"I guess not. You should see the attic. More crowded than even Great-aunt Mattie's used to be."

Mose smiled in response, maybe remembering, as she did, hours spent playing in the clutter when they were supposed to be cleaning it up for Mamm's elderly aunt.

The smile touched her heart, but before she could speak the smile had been replaced by a chilly, guarded expression. Mose might as well come out and say that even if Daad had softened toward her, he wasn't convinced.

Mose pulled a screwdriver from the strap that held it to the lid of the box. "This is what I need." His mouth clamped shut, and he turned away.

Rachel lowered the heavy lid carefully. She'd seen a glimpse of her brother, and it had just made her more aware of the fact that he was lost to her.

The bell on the front door jangled, yanking her into the here and now. She went quickly to answer it, planting a determined smile on her face. If it was Colin...

But Dennis Sitler stood on her front porch, peering through the rim of frosted glass that surrounded the stained-glass medallion in the door. She pulled it open, trying not to let herself feel foreboding at the sight of any member of the Sitler family.

"Good morning, Rachel. I hope you don't mind my stopping by." He stepped inside as he spoke, leaving her no choice but to close the door behind him.

"Of course not." *And why are you here?* She left the question unspoken, but maybe he read it in her face.

"I just wanted to be sure your little girl is all right after getting lost at the fire hall last night."

He didn't leave her in doubt as to his reason for

coming, but she couldn't help wondering if that was his only motive in stopping by. She was getting as bad as Colin, suspecting everyone of hiding secrets.

"Mandy is fine, thanks. It's good of you to be concerned."

"I'm sure it was scary for the child, realizing she was lost in a crowd."

Dennis's expression was filled with sympathy. So why did she keep picturing him as the shadowy wizard Lainey had drawn all those years ago?

"Honestly, I'm not even sure she realized she was lost. She thought she heard her puppy barking, and she chased after the sound."

"That's good." He hesitated, and she sensed there actually was something else on his mind. Maybe Colin had a point about questioning people's motives.

"Is something else worrying you?" She'd rather ask him outright and hear the truth.

He blinked. "Well, to be honest, I did wonder if my cousin was bothering you in some way."

Now it was her turn to be surprised. "What makes you say that?"

"I guess I'm not very good at sounding out people," he admitted with an expression of candor that disarmed her. "I don't know why I even try. The truth is, I thought it was rather odd that Gene said something about your little girl last night just when you realized she was missing. Almost as if he knew something about it and was taunting you."

That took her breath away. She studied his face, reading nothing but concern there.

"It was odd," she admitted carefully. "But why would he be taunting me, as you put it?"

Dennis shrugged. "I'm not sure why Gene does anything. I knew almost nothing about him before he turned up here and moved in with my grandfather."

"Yes, you had mentioned that. But surely your grandfather can handle him." Franklin Sitler certainly intimidated her, but possibly Gene was made of tougher stuff.

"I'd say that about most situations." His forehead furrowed. "Frankly, I've been looking into Gene's past, and what I've found hasn't been very reassuring. He's been involved with the police several times, mostly on drug-related offenses." His frown deepened still more. "I don't like saying anything negative about a relative, but Gene seems malicious enough to enjoy scaring you. I wouldn't want that to happen."

"It won't," she said with more assurance than she felt, given the bombshell he'd just dropped about his cousin. "But thank you. I appreciate the fact that you are concerned."

His worried expression cleared a little. "Well, that's all right, then. Maybe I'm worrying needlessly, but I led a pretty placid life before my cousin arrived."

Had he? For the first time she found herself wondering about Dennis. He had that habit of effacing himself that Lainey had captured so well. Since he didn't live here in Deer Run under his grandfather's eyes, he could do as he pleased. She glanced at his hand, resting on the registration table, noting that he didn't wear a ring.

"It can't be easy, feeling responsible for your grandfather," she ventured. "Is there anyone to help you?"

"Afraid not. No wife, no kids, no siblings. Just Grandfather. And now Gene." His mouth twisted a little on his cousin's name. "Still, I'm better off than a lot of the old gang. You got a good look at Laura and Victor's problems last night, and as for Jeannette—well, I think she's married to her precious business."

She hadn't expected him to bring up Laura, but since he had, should she ask him anything? Meredith would undoubtedly say she should take advantage of the situation, but she wasn't Meredith.

"I was so sorry," she said after an uncomfortable pause. "For Laura, I mean. Seeing her like that…"

Dennis shook his head sadly. "You know, many people have troubled teen years, but they manage to grow out of their problems. Poor Laura seems stuck in hers."

That was more candor than she'd expected from him—practically an admission that Laura's current issues stemmed from Aaron's death. Or was she reading more into it than he intended?

"It was tragic, having the boy she loved die in such a senseless way," she said. "I wonder if she felt somehow responsible." She certainly knew all about that kind of responsibility.

Dennis seemed to consider her words. "That's possible, I guess. Survivors often do, I've heard. I suppose we'll never really know the whole story."

"I guess not." All their suppositions were just that. "It's too bad. It might bring some closure to Aaron's family to understand how it happened."

"Maybe. But sometimes not knowing is for the best." Dennis turned, heading for the front door. "Goodbye, Rachel."

Rachel stood staring after him, wondering. Had those last few words been meant as an observation? Or a warning?

"Why are you standing there as frozen as Lot's wife?" Colin's voice came from the door behind her.

She turned, trying to regain her balance. She should have been expecting him. He'd said he'd be here this morning.

"Lot's wife wasn't frozen. She was turned into a pillar of salt," she informed him. "I was just thinking…" She let that trail off.

She'd like to discuss Dennis's words with someone, but she didn't think Colin was necessarily the right choice. "Why did you come in the back way, if you want to look at the front steps?"

"I saw Mose and your father out back and stopped

to talk to them. Mose is going to have a look at that stair railing with me."

"*Ja.*" Mose, wearing a tool belt, emerged from the kitchen behind Colin. "Let us see what made it break." He spoke naturally to Colin. Just not to her.

There wasn't much to choose from in deciding which one bothered her most—Mose, with his reminder of the mistakes she'd already made, or Colin, tempting her to make yet another one with his compelling presence.

"I'd better check on Mandy," she said, and fled up the stairs.

"TAKE A look at that." Squatting next to the porch steps, Colin pointed to the scrape marks, visible now in the daylight. "If those weren't made by somebody prying that railing post loose, I'll eat it."

"*Ja.*" Mose ran work-roughened fingers over the faint indentations, seeming to read them with his hand. "A crowbar would do it, or a tire iron. Or even a claw hammer, but that would be harder, ain't so?"

With his attention caught by the evidence, the coldness had disappeared from Mose's face. Colin hadn't missed the way he'd looked when he'd spoken to Rachel. Or the hurt in Rachel's eyes as a result.

His jaw clenched. Not his business, as Rachel would be quick to tell him. But he couldn't help but remember how close Mose and Rachel had been as kids. Too bad that when she could really use her brother, he persisted in cutting her off.

"Maybe we should show this to the police," he suggested, knowing already what Mose's response would be.

"Amish don't go to the police to solve their problems," he said, predictably. Then he seemed to have another thought. "Not that Rachel is Amish anymore."

"She's still your sister." That was getting dangerously close to interfering in a way no one would thank him for.

"Ja." Mose said the word heavily. "I am thinking that if Rachel brings in police about this, it will make it harder for her to be accepted."

A few harsh words about Mose's own lack of acceptance hovered on his tongue, but he bit them back. That would probably make things worse, not better.

"And maybe it was some teenagers, monkeying around," Mose said, obviously following his own train of thought. "Making a fuss might upset the Englisch, as well."

"If it was, teenagers arc getting up to worse than we did," Colin said. He nudged Mose. "I seem to remember one beer bash in particular, down by the dam."

Mose reddened under his tan. *"Ach,* don't remind me. I pray my boys will never hear of it. If you hadn't let me stay in your garage until I sobered up, Daadi would have given me such a licking."

"You and me both. Although I never did feel like I fooled my dad."

Mose looked at him, curious. "Did he find out about you hiding me that time?"

"If so, he never said. But I think he knew a lot I didn't give him credit for." That was an unhappy reminder of Dad as he was now, and he pushed the thought away. He was trying to mend things for Mose and Rachel. Better stick to that.

"Teenagers are always trying to hide things from adults," he said, not looking at Mose. "Like Ronnie and Rachel. All the kids knew about them, but nobody told, even though we probably all knew that would just lead to unhappiness for them."

"Ja." Mose busied himself getting out a hammer and nails.

"I tried to break them up," Colin said, keeping his voice casual as he held the upright. "It didn't work, of course."

Mose's hand seemed to freeze on the nails he held. "I did not know you tried to help."

"Well, I didn't want people to know. Stupid, but that's how kids are. I always felt guilty, though. I could have saved Rachel a lot of grief if I'd done something more."

Mose darted him a quick look. "Their marriage—it was not happy?"

"No." He could be blunt about that. "It started all right, I guess, but it sure didn't end up that way. So if I can do anything to help Rachel now, maybe it'll make up for failing her then." He shrugged. "You must feel the same, I guess—guilty that you couldn't protect your little sister."

Mose studied the hammer as intently as if he'd never seen one before. *"Ja,"* he said, his voice gruff.

It wasn't much, but it was enough. Maybe he'd done something about Mose's feelings. He certainly didn't seem able to do anything about his own.

They worked side by side for several moments without talking. Mose was a more skillful carpenter than he was, so Colin contented himself with holding the uprights and the railing while Mose worked.

They'd nearly finished before Mose spoke again. "My sister Lovina really likes working at your place. She's getting *sehr* fond of your daad. Says he's a *gut* man."

Apparently satisfied that he'd said what he wanted to, Mose turned back to the railing. *He's a good man.* Colin repeated the words in his mind. That was true, and it was one thing the illness hadn't robbed him of. He was a good man. Maybe that was the best anyone could hope to have said of him.

RACHEL KEPT BUSY upstairs until she no longer heard pounding from the area of the front stairs. Good. With any luck, Colin would have gone back to his business and Mose would be occupied with Daad. By the sound of it, they were working on something in one of the guest bedrooms.

She'd like to go over the fledging website Meredith had set up for her, but somehow she didn't feel quite comfortable working on the computer when Daad might walk in on her. That was just another example of fuzzy thinking where her status was concerned, but she couldn't seem to help it. She decided instead to make a coffee cake. Mandy would be delighted to help bake, and surely the least she could do for the free help was to provide coffee and cake.

Mandy was sprinkling streusel over the top of the batter with abandon when Mose came into the kitchen.

"*Ach*, looks like you have a *gut* helper in the kitchen, Rachel." He came to look over Mandy's head at the cake pans. "Streusel cakes, yum."

"They're for you and Grossdaadi to have with your coffee, Onkel Mose." Mandy tried to look very grown-up in the apron that enveloped her. "They're almost ready to go in the oven."

"We will look forward to that for sure," he said, resting his hand lightly on Mandy's shoulder, but he looked at Rachel. "I was… Anna and I were thinking maybe you two could come for supper tomorrow night. Give the little ones a chance to get to know each other, *ja?*"

"*Ja.*" Rachel had to blink back a tear at this sudden change of attitude. "We would like to come over, wouldn't we, Mandy?"

"*Denke*, Onkel Mose." Mandy was showing off

her limited knowledge of Pennsylvania Dutch. "I'd like to meet my cousins."

"They're not so big as you," he said. "A couple of little schnickelfritzes. Do you know what that is?"

Mandy shook her head.

"Ask your mammi," Mose said, grinning as he headed out the back.

"You mean you got *kinder* just like you," Rachel called after him. She turned to Mandy. "A schnickelfritz is a mischievous child. Let's get these pans in the oven now, and then you can take Princess out in the yard. Okay?"

"Okay." Mandy began to unwrap herself from the apron. "When will the streusel cakes be ready?"

"About half an hour. I'll call you," she promised, knowing Mandy wanted to see the cakes come out of the oven.

Mandy darted for Princess's leash, and the puppy scrambled after her, feet slipping on the floor in her hurry. The screen door slammed behind them.

Rachel had barely slid the pans into the oven before the kitchen door swung again and Colin came in.

Ignoring the thump her heart gave at the sight of him, she shook her head. "This place is as busy as the farmers' market on a summer Saturday," she said. "I thought you and Mose had finished the railing."

"In other words, why am I still here?" He raised an eyebrow in that infuriating way he had as he crossed the kitchen to her. "Just wanted to report what we found. As I suspected, the railing had been tampered with."

"I see." She took off the apron she'd tied over her jeans, not looking at him. She didn't need to look, did she? Every line of his face was engraved on her mind.

"Mose doesn't want to tell the police, of course." Colin leaned back against the counter next to her. "I have to say I agree with him. The police couldn't do anything except stir up some unpleasant publicity, which you don't need."

She darted a quick look at him. "What did you say to Mose?"

"What do you mean?" He did a good impression of not understanding, but she wasn't fooled.

"You said something to him about me. I know you did. He was entirely different toward me after you talked to him."

Colin shrugged, as if disavowing responsibility. "We were reminiscing about our teen years. I pointed out that I felt guilty for not doing more to protect you from Ronnie. Maybe that reminded Mose that he felt the same."

There were a lot of things she could say to that, including that it wasn't his responsibility to protect her, then or now. But if he had seen what was really causing Mose's issue with her, how could she blame him for that?

"Thank you," she said, her voice husky.

"Anytime." The words themselves were light, but the tone in which Colin spoke them wasn't.

If Colin could be trusted with her family situation, surely he could be trusted with what she'd learned from Dennis.

"Dennis Sitler stopped by earlier," she said abruptly.

"You have had a busy day." Colin accepted the change of subject without argument. "What did Dennis want?"

"He said he came to see if Mandy was all right after getting lost last night."

"But…?" His eyebrow quirked.

"I'm not sure," she said slowly, "but I think he really wanted to tell me…warn me, maybe…about Gene. He said that Gene has been arrested several times for drug involvement."

"Interesting. Did he say why he was investigating his cousin?"

That wasn't the response she'd expected. "He implied that he was concerned for his grandfather. And he thought what Gene said to me about Mandy was odd. So I wasn't the only one to think so."

"Relax, Rachel. I agree that Gene is an unsavory character. I'm just trying to figure out why he would have something against you."

"Don't you see?" She turned to him, frustrated that he didn't see what jumped so readily to the eye. "If Gene was doing something involving drugs up at that old barn, that would give him a reason to chase the boys away with a gun and to ensure they stayed quiet. He's right across the street—he could easily be aware of how much time Benj spends with me. He might think a threat to me would frighten Benj out of speaking."

A little shiver went down her spine at the thought. She'd thought she'd left the threat of drugs behind when she came back to Deer Run.

"Kind of convoluted reasoning on his part, but what would Gene have been doing?" Colin's voice was annoyingly calm. "We were in the barn. There was no sign of anything. If he'd had a meth lab up there, believe me, there'd have been some sign."

"I…I don't know." Her excitement at having found an answer began to evaporate. "We only looked right around the barn. We didn't go any farther. There could have been marijuana growing someplace farther away."

"I don't know a lot about growing marijuana, but it seems to me the plants wouldn't do well under that dense growth of trees."

She had an urge to shake him. "You're just ignoring the idea because you didn't think of it."

"I'm not ignoring it. I'm trying to think of the best way to deal with the possibility. I know a guy whose brother is with the state police narcotics division. Maybe I can drop a hint without involving Benj. You don't want the state police coming to call at the farm, do you?"

"No, of course not. I just feel as if I have to do

something. I can't just keep waiting for another bad thing to happen."

To Benj. To Mandy. Her heart shuddered at the thought.

"Okay, I get it. Just don't rush off and make things worse. I'll try to get in touch with my friend's brother."

"Thank you," she said, her voice chilled. That wasn't the first time Colin had used that expression toward her. She didn't like it any better now.

CHAPTER FIFTEEN

BENJ TURNED UP at the house a short time after Colin left, determined to help, and the old house fairly buzzed with activity. Rachel discovered Mandy in the dining room, holding the leg of a chair Mose was mending.

"Like this, Onkel Mose?" She steadied it with both hands.

"*Ja*, just right." With a few gentle taps of the hammer, Mose reinforced the crosspiece. "*Gut* job." He placed the chair down and held it by the back. "See? No more wiggling."

"*Gut* job," Mandy echoed with a look of satisfaction.

Rachel had to swallow a lump in her throat. That was how an Amish child learned what would be expected of him or her in life—by working alongside a patient adult.

"That is good work," Rachel said. "Benj is out back working. I'll bet he could use some cold lemonade."

"I'll take it," Mandy said, and whirled out of the room.

Rachel's gaze met her brother's. *"Denke,"* she said softly. "For taking time with her."

"She is a sweet child." He grinned, eyes crinkling so that she saw again her companion in so much childhood mischief. "And as stubborn as her mammi, I think."

"Probably," Rachel admitted. "Sometimes when she and Benj are talking, it sounds as if she's his big sister."

He chuckled, nodding. "I see Benj is trying to help without catching Daad's attention. Just like we used to when we had done something we shouldn't."

She'd noticed the same thing. "Daad has already forgiven him. Benj just hasn't noticed that yet." She hesitated. "Those other two boys, Will and Joseph. What do you know about them?"

Mose grunted. "Enough to know Will Esch is mighty close to jumping the fence. And Joseph is foolish enough to try and do whatever Will says."

"You think they really have run off to try living Englisch?" She'd actually find it comforting to know they were safely working at some hamburger stand.

"Wouldn't be surprised." Mose checked the next of the set of ten dining-room chairs.

"Their parents must be worried." She'd be frantic, not knowing where her child was.

"*Ja*, well, boys will go off during their *rumspringa* years. They soon find the outside world isn't where they want to be."

True enough. That was what parents counted

on, even as they worried and prayed their children through adolescence. "I guess you're right."

"I think those two are the sort who'd be quick to run away to avoid trouble," he added. "At least Benj has better sense than that."

That was reason enough to be glad. Even if Benj had been tempted to run, he'd known better. That said something good about the kind of man he'd be.

Later, when Daad and Mose headed back to the farm, Mandy went with them, skipping along between them. Rachel watched until they'd disappeared into the covered bridge. Then she went in search of Benj.

She found him putting a coat of wood polish on the front door. "I noticed this needed doing," he said when he realized she was watching him.

"That's great. *Denke*, Benj." She hesitated, wondering if she should bring up the question in her mind. But Mose was right—Benj did have enough sense to deal with it.

"I was talking to Dennis Sitler earlier. Do you know who he is?"

Benj sent her a sidelong glance and nodded. "*Ja*. Mr. Sitler's grandson. The one that works in a bank."

"He told me that Gene Sitler, the one that's staying with old Mr. Sitler, has been in trouble over drugs."

Benj didn't move for a moment, but then he nodded. "*Ja*. I heard some talk about him."

She moved to the side so that she could see his

face. "I wondered if he could have been the man with the gun. If he'd been doing something involving drugs up there, he might have reason to chase you boys away."

Benj's hand slowed and then stopped its polishing. "I did not think about that," he said.

"Could the man you saw have been Gene?" she persisted.

To her relief, Benj didn't get that frightened look. He closed his eyes, as if trying to visualize what he'd seen.

"It could have been," he said finally. "All I could see was a dark shape." He put the cap back on the wood polish. "There's been some talk about people growing marijuana up in the woods. Even on the state game lands."

Colin had said something about that incident, but she hadn't expected to hear it from Benj. Amish fourteen-year-olds must be more sophisticated than they'd been when she was fourteen. She doubted she'd even heard of marijuana then.

"How do you know about it?"

He shrugged. "Kids talk. Maybe just bragging that they've seen it, though."

Rachel's thoughts raced. Was this logical? If Gene had thought his summer spent in Deer Run was a good opportunity to grow a crop of marijuana somewhere near the old barn, he'd be eager to keep people away. She felt reasonably sure that Franklin Sitler would have no tolerance for such activity.

Of course, Colin had discounted it because they hadn't seen any in the overgrown field around the barn. But had they searched enough?

"Would you know what marijuana looks like when it's growing?" she asked.

Benj shook his head. "What are you going to do?" His eyes widened with apprehension.

"I'm not going to just do nothing and wait for something bad to happen."

She'd said more or less the same thing to Colin, and he'd told her to wait. Not go rushing off. But this had been in the back of her mind since Mandy had gone missing the night before. She couldn't just wait, letting things happen. She had to act.

"First I'm going to find a picture of a marijuana plant on the computer, so I'll know what I'm looking for. Then I'm going to the barn to see what's worth making someone take such desperate action."

"No." Benj paled. He grasped her hand. "You can't. What if he's up there?"

"I'll be careful. I don't think he's going to shoot at me in broad daylight."

Benj just stared at her for a moment. "You can't go by yourself." He seemed to grow taller in front of her. "If you are going, then I am going, too."

Rachel squeezed his hand. "You don't need to do that, Benj. I know it scares you."

"I won't let you go alone." His face was pale, but the set of his jaw was determined. "We will both go."

Benj led the way, walking down the road away from the village for about thirty yards before cutting up into the woods. Rachel followed, already questioning whether she should have attempted to drive the car up the logging road the way Colin had taken her.

But Benj seemed doubtful her car would make it, and remembering the bone-shuddering jolts even in the four-wheel-drive vehicle, she had to agree. Glancing to the right, she could just make out the Sitler house through the trees, its windows like so many eyes staring at them.

"This is a shortcut," Benj said, brushing past a growth of blackberry brambles. "It's the way we came when…that night."

When the man shot at you. She finished the thought. Maybe she should have insisted Benj stay behind, but she doubted that he would have. He seemed determined to make up for the fear that had been terrorizing him. Well, if he could put that nightmare to rest, so much the better.

The brambles caught at her clothes, and she was glad she'd changed to jeans, a long-sleeved shirt and old sneakers for this trek. Benj, of course, already wore the black broadfall trousers, long-sleeved shirt and sturdy work shoes that he wore every day.

When Colin found out about this expedition, as he undoubtedly would, he'd be furious. She couldn't help that. He didn't seem to understand her need to act. He'd rather do what he always did—attempt to protect her. Just when she thought their relationship was moving forward, he'd default back to the same attitude that had made them enemies at eighteen. She was responsible, not Colin, and she couldn't let herself depend on him or anyone else.

Not that she wanted a relationship with him. And even if she did, it was impossible. He might not have said the words, but his attitude said that Colin couldn't take on more than his father. Certainly not a widow with a child who had to be the center of her concern.

A dogwood branch caught at her hair, and she stopped long enough to untangle it. That served her right for letting herself think about Colin. She should know better.

Benj extended a hand to pull her up a steep bank. "Easier walking ahead, where the pines are thicker." He spoke softly, as if afraid someone might be there to overhear.

She found herself on alert, listening for the slightest sound that was out of place, but heard nothing other than birdsong and the whisper of the breeze in the trees.

They moved out of the thick growth of brambles and bushes and under the shelter of the trees, where the air was instantly cooler. A dense mat of pine needles underfoot made walking easier, even though they were still moving steadily uphill. The needles deadened the sound of their footsteps, as well, and the woods seemed more silent here, more ominous where the sunlight didn't penetrate.

"Is this the way you came when you ran away?" She deliberately spoke in a normal voice, hoping to dispel the apprehension that was settling on both of them, she suspected.

Benj gave a nervous jerk at the sound of her voice and then nodded. "*Ja*, I think so. We were running, and it was dark."

Dark. Yes, indeed, she didn't like to think about how dark it would be under these trees at night.

"Look!" Benj seemed to come alive, and his pace quickened. "See, here is where we hid, behind this log."

She caught up with him. "Are you sure? I thought you said you left the gas cans here." There was no sign of any cans now, and the thick carpet of leaves and pine needles seemed undisturbed.

"I'm sure. You can see the barn from here." He pointed, and she saw the old barn, seeming to collapse in on itself, jagged timbers pointing upward in places where the roof was sagging.

"But the gas cans…"

"The man must have taken them." Benj's voice dropped again, and the haunted look returned to his eyes.

She couldn't blame him. She was visualizing the scene only too clearly in her own mind, seeing the boys crouching behind the log, cold, excited, scared, straining their eyes to make out what was happening to Will. And then the gunfire, shattering the night into a thousand echoes.

"You can stay here while I look around," she said abruptly. "It's okay."

"No." His reply was quick, and he clasped her hand. "We are together, *ja?*"

Heartened, she smiled and squeezed his fingers. "*Ja*. Let's go."

They walked toward the barn. Rachel could feel the tension tightening her shoulders, her neck, even her scalp, but she kept going. They couldn't end this problem by running.

As they neared the barn a woodpecker swooped past them in a flash of black and red. Settling on the barn, he began tapping, the rat-a-tat echoing cheerfully through the woods. That was oddly reassuring. Rachel marched up to the barn door and yanked it open. With a reproachful look, the woodpecker flew away.

Benj approached more hesitantly, but there was nothing to see.

"It looks just the same as it did when Colin and I were up here," she said. "Whatever someone is doing, they're not actually using the barn."

"I guess not." Benj glanced up at the holes in the roof. "But the car or truck did pull up beside the barn. We saw the headlights."

"Which side? Show me."

Benj led her straight to the side where she and Colin had seen the truck tracks. It didn't look as if any new marks had been made since they'd been here, but it was hard to tell. One tire track looked much like another to her.

"Colin thought the logging trucks might have been pulling in here," she said.

Benj looked doubtful. "Maybe. But this is where we saw the lights."

That didn't seem to get them any farther. Rachel reminded herself she'd come up here to look for signs of marijuana cultivation. "Where could someone plant something up here that it would get enough light to grow?"

Benj gazed around, as if looking for inspiration. "The farmhouse was over there before they tore it down." He pointed to the foundation stones she'd seen on her earlier trip. "Seems to me I heard there was a hay field on the far side of those trees."

The trees he indicated were a narrow band of hemlocks. Planted as a windbreak, maybe? This hilltop didn't really seem a very welcoming place to farm. Maybe that was why no one had taken the farm over after the family died off.

"Let's have a look." She led the way toward the trees, sensing Benj's reluctance as he followed. Her own enthusiasm evaporated as they moved farther away from the route home.

But she'd come up here on a wave of determination to do something, anything, that would resolve the situation. She couldn't give up so easily. If Gene Sitler were involved in something centered on the deserted barn, surely they could spot some evidence of that fact. Only then would Benj be safe.

And Mandy. Colin's suggestion of someone taping Princess's barking and using that to lure Mandy away had seemed the stuff of fantasy at first, but the more Mandy insisted she'd heard Princess, the more likely it became in Rachel's thoughts. Whether Colin's guess was right or not, she couldn't let Mandy be put in danger.

As they neared the band of trees, Benj brushed past her, his gaze fixed on something. "There is a path," he said. "Look, someone has been through here."

Her stomach clenched. Benj was right. The grass was flattened, the earth disturbed in a line that led from the area where the tire tracks were into the trees.

She'd come up here to find something. Now that she had, she wasn't sure what to do with it. Go back and tell—who? Colin? The police? Who would take it seriously?

"We'd better have a look and see where it leads." She was a little surprised to hear the words coming out of her mouth, but they'd come this far. They shouldn't turn back now.

Benj nodded, his face tense but not, thank goodness, wearing that terrified expression. Rachel led the way, moving cautiously. Somehow the hemlocks held a silence even more ominous than any they'd experienced yet. Not even a bird disturbed the stillness.

The trees thinned, and sunlight streamed ahead of them. Alert for any sound, Rachel moved forward. The field was there, just as Benj had said. But it seemed to grow nothing any more dangerous than grass. Lush, green, but nothing like the illustrations of the marijuana plants she'd looked at.

"Nothing." Benj stood beside her. He shook his head. "I don't get it. Why would someone come up here? It's just grass, ain't so?"

"I guess so." Rachel took another step and stopped when her sneaker sank nearly to its top. "Watch out. It's boggy here." She pulled her foot back, releasing an odor that assaulted her nostrils. "Ugh. What is that?"

Benj sniffed. "Maybe the old septic tank from the house was here. Or they might have had a buried oil tank."

Rachel wasn't sure which she'd dislike most on her shoes. She stepped back onto the solid ground of the path. "Well, it looks as if we've come up with nothing."

"I think—"

A gun shattered the silence, swallowing the rest of Benj's words. Birds lifted in a raucous cloud from the trees.

For a second she was frozen. Then she gave Benj a shove back into the relative shelter of the trees. "Run!"

They pelted back along the path, Rachel's mind racing faster than her feet. Maybe it had been someone target shooting, not knowing they were there. But another shot exploded, and a branch snapped off the tree some ten feet over their heads.

Her heart jolted. Not an accident, then. Someone shooting at them. She had her evidence that something was going on up here, if only she could survive long enough to tell someone.

They reached the edge of the band of trees and stopped. Rachel pressed a hand against her chest, trying to catch her breath.

Benj grabbed her hand. "He's behind us," he whispered urgently. "We can't stop."

Her little brother was wiser than she was. They didn't dare stop, not if the man was following them. He'd been somewhere across the field, so it would take him time to reach this spot. They had to cover the exposed ground around the barn before he was in position to have a clear shot at them.

"We've got to get the barn between us and him," she said, voice urgent. "Then head down through the way we came. You know it better than I do—I'll follow you." She stopped any argument with a push.

Benj took off and she followed, trying to stay between him and the person with the gun. Benj was only fourteen—she was responsible for him. She had to keep him safe. If something happened to him, she could never forgive herself.

And if something happened to her, then she had let Mandy down in the most final way possible.

Best not to think. Just mutter silent prayers and run as fast as she could.

They reached the far side of the barn without any more shots being fired and stopped for breath. She bent over, winded, but Benj seemed all right. He pointed silently toward the woods. That must be the way they'd come up.

Ready? He mouthed the word, her little brother growing into a man before her eyes.

She nodded, and they took off again. Any hope she might have cherished that the shooter had given up was destroyed when the gun cracked again, a bullet thudding into a tree trunk above their heads.

Was that deliberate? Was he just trying to scare them? She wasn't foolish enough to try and find out.

They ripped through the thicket they'd bypassed coming up, the brambles tearing at their clothes. Something stung Rachel's cheek, and she realized one of the brambles had opened a scratch there, but it was the least of her worries as another shot sounded, so close its echoes seemed to surround them. They weren't going to make it, he could pick them off no matter how bad a shot he was—

Then someone was shouting, an angry male voice sending its own echoes through the woods. Grabbing Benj's arm, she veered in the direction of the voice. Someone was there, someone shouting at the shooter, a witness, a savior—

They slid down an embankment, stumbling and falling, and she saw who it was—Franklin Sitler, his shock of white hair seeming to stand straight up, shaking his cane toward the woods.

"Stop that shooting, I say! You're on private land, I'll have the law on you! Stop it!"

Silence. Whoever the shooter was, he apparently didn't want to tangle with Sitler.

Gene? She allowed herself to try putting a name to the man. Maybe. But she'd never had so much as a glimpse of him, and there had been no evidence of anything drug-related anywhere near the barn. She could hardly accuse him without evidence.

Sitler came hurrying toward them, leaning heavily on his cane. "You all right? Here, boy, help your sister up. She's hurt."

"I'm all right," Rachel said quickly, wiping the blood from her cheek. "He didn't hit us."

"Ignorant trespassers," he muttered, and Rachel saw to her relief that he wasn't talking about her and Benj. "Think they can go target-shooting in anyone's woods. Think they're big deals because they have a gun when they don't know the first thing about shooting. You sure you're all right?"

Rachel nodded. "We're fine. Just a bit shaken."

"Well, I should think you would be after a scare like that." He gave her a surprisingly gentle look. "You go on home and take care of those scratches. Don't you worry. I'll report those idiots to the police. You just tend to yourself." He patted her shoulder somewhat awkwardly. "Sorry this happened. I'm just glad your little girl wasn't with you. Wouldn't want her thinking this isn't a safe place."

She nodded. Sitler was feeling responsible, apparently because the person shooting was on his land.

How would he feel if it turned out to be his grandson? She couldn't possibly say anything about that to him. Not even to the police without evidence, but surely even the township police knew something of Gene's background. If not...

Reaction was setting in. She realized she was shaking, and both Benj and Sitler were looking at her with some concern. "I'll be fine," she said, answering their expressions. "I guess I had better go home."

Home. At this moment, she was relieved to know that Mandy was safely at the farm.

CHAPTER SIXTEEN

BENJ TOOK RACHEL'S arm as they went into the house, supporting her as carefully as if she were a very old woman. Now that she thought of it, that was how she felt.

Even if the gunman had only intended to frighten them, a ricocheting bullet could go anywhere. She knew that well enough from the lectures Daad had given them every year when deer-hunting season started. A hunter himself, he didn't think too highly of the outsiders who flooded the county on Thanksgiving weekend, some of them so eager to bag their first buck that they forgot the simplest safeguards.

She straightened, finding the energy to smile at her brother as they reached the kitchen. "You should go on home now, Benj. I'll just sit here and have a cup of tea before I have to talk to Chief Burkhalter."

Worry didn't set easily on his young face. "I should maybe stay with you, *ja?*"

She set the kettle on the stove, using the excuse to turn away from his concerned gaze. "If you're here, you'd have to talk to the chief as well, and Daad wouldn't like that. Best to let me deal with it."

She turned back to him, seeing that her words had hit home. But then he shook his head.

"I should stay. I should take care of you."

Touched, she put her palm on his cheek, cradling it for a moment. "You've already done that, Benj. I'll never forget how strong and brave you were when we were in danger. But you'd better let me handle the police. We don't want to worry Daad and Mamm more than necessary, right?"

He nodded, looking as if he were still not completely convinced. "I'll go. But if you need me, I will *komm*."

"I know. Go now, *schnell*." Rachel gave him a quick kiss on the cheek. "Everything will be all right."

Once Benj had left, she thought how foolish those words sounded. How could she possibly guarantee that anything would be all right? Her mind skipped from her father, who would surely be upset that she'd led Benj into danger, to Colin, who'd be equally upset that she'd taken action without him.

The kettle whistled, and she lifted it off the burner and poured the steaming water into the mug, the familiar action seeming to steady her.

Maybe she'd best clean herself up first. She didn't have any doubt that Chief Burkhalter would be showing up at her door. He wouldn't ignore a summons from Franklin Sitler, that was certain.

She'd barely had time to wash the blood and dirt from her face and hands before she heard heavy footsteps followed by a knock on the door. The chief had come even more quickly than she'd imagined.

She swung the door open.

"Rachel." Chief Burkhalter nodded, looking faintly harassed and redder than usual in the face. "Franklin Sitler tells me you've had some trouble with trespassers up in his woods. You okay?"

She gestured for him to come in and led the way to the front parlor. "I'm fine." Her hand went to her cheek automatically. "Just some scrapes and bruises from coming down the hill too fast."

"Well, it's probably a good thing you did." Burkhalter sat on the tapestry-covered love seat, removing his uniform cap and balancing it on his lap. "Franklin was all for charging up into the woods and chasing those fools off himself, but I got him calmed down."

She collapsed into the corner of the sofa. "I'm glad he listened to you. He certainly shouldn't be wandering up into the woods today." Or any other day, but she wouldn't want the job of telling him what he could and couldn't do.

"Right. Folks that would go target shooting on someone else's property most likely don't have sense enough to know how far a bullet can carry. Like I always told my boys, you don't go shooting a gun until you know exactly what you're going to hit."

So Chief Burkhalter had already opted for the easiest explanation. She couldn't say she was surprised.

"Yes, that's what my daad always told us kids when he took us hunting."

"Your father's a sensible man. Not one to let his kids go off into the woods alone with a gun." He shook his head, his color fading to its usual ruddy hue. "I told Sitler I'd investigate, and naturally that's what I'll do. But it's mighty hard even to tell where someone was shooting, the way the sound echoes in these hills."

In other words, he wouldn't do more than take a cursory look around. "It seemed to me—" she began, but stopped when the front door flew open. Colin charged inside, not bothering to knock.

"Colin." Chief Burkhalter almost sounded as if he'd been expecting him. "You can come in and sit down, but don't go upsetting Rachel. She's had enough for one day, I expect."

Colin ignored him, striding into the room, his eyes never leaving Rachel's face. Whatever he saw there must have satisfied him, because he sat down next to her on the sofa, leaving a cautious couple of inches between them.

"Now, then, Rachel, you were saying it seemed to you…" Burkhalter paused, inviting her to finish her statement.

"I thought that the person with the gun was above us on the hill." She chose her words carefully. "As if he wanted to chase us away."

Burkhalter frowned. "Sitler said one of your brothers was with you. What did he make of it?"

"Benjamin, the youngest. He thought the same as I did. We ran down toward the road as quickly as we could, afraid we'd be hit."

"Benjamin's about fourteen, right?"

She nodded.

"Well, I'm sure the two of you felt as if the shooter was after you, but most likely he didn't know you were there at all." He smiled indulgently. "What were you doing up there, anyway? Looking to pick berries, were you?"

For an instant she was tempted to say that was just what they were doing, if only to get out of this increasingly awkward conversation.

"Not exactly," she said, trying to find the words that would be true without causing trouble for her family, who certainly wouldn't welcome a visit from the police. "Benj had been frightened by someone chasing him near the old barn one evening a week or so ago," she said carefully. "I thought if we went up in daylight and had a look around, we might see some reason for it."

Burkhalter raised his eyebrows. "Seems like a funny thing to do. Did you find anything?"

She could sense a sharpening of Colin's already intense focus. "No. Nothing."

"Well, then…" Burkhalter planted his hands on his knees and got to his feet. "I'll go up and have a look around myself. If I find anything that leads me to the person who was shooting up there, you can trust me to put the fear of God into them. I don't see that there's much else I can do."

"What about the two Amish boys who have gone missing?" Colin's voice rasped with impatience. "Can you do anything about them?"

Burkhalter looked blank for a moment. "You mean Will Esch and that buddy of his? I heard they'd run off, but their folks haven't asked me to do anything about it. Shoot, if I started an investigation every time a teenager decided to have some fun, I wouldn't get anything else done. What do they have to do with somebody target shooting up in Sitler's woods?"

"They were with Benj when someone chased them away from that barn."

Colin was saying more than she would have— more than either her parents or the parents of the other boys would want. But there was nothing she could do to stop him.

Burkhalter's face reddened. "If and when I get a complaint from one of those boys or their parents, I'll look into it. In the meantime, just you do your job and let me do mine."

Rachel could almost see the tart response that sprang to Colin's lips, and she rose hurriedly to cut him off. "Thank you for your concern, Chief Burkhalter. I appreciate it, and I'm sure Mr. Sitler does, as well." It certainly couldn't do any harm to invoke Franklin Sitler's name again.

Burkhalter grunted something that might have been an acknowledgement. With another glare for Colin, he stalked out.

BURKHALTER'S REACTION HAD been just about what Colin expected, but he'd had to give it a try. He'd been heading back to the office when he'd seen the police car in front of Rachel's place, and his reaction didn't bear thinking about.

Colin managed to contain himself until he heard the police car pull away. Then he shot off the sofa, propelled by a mix of anxiety, anger and protectiveness that he didn't care to look at too closely.

"What were you thinking?" It took an effort to keep from shouting. "Why would you go up there? Didn't I tell you I'd deal with it?" He tried to grasp her wrists but she eluded him, her face just as furious as his probably was.

"I had to answer Chief Burkhalter's questions, but I don't have to answer yours. If you've come here to bully me, you can just go away again."

The words were said defiantly, but he heard the faint tremor in Rachel's voice, and the deep scratch on her cheek seemed to slice at his heart.

Rachel was teetering on the edge of her control, and he couldn't let himself push her over. He took a deep breath, reaching for control.

"Sorry." His throat nearly closed on the word, and he reached out to touch her cheek gently. To his surprise, she didn't pull away. "That looks nasty. Maybe you should have it checked."

Her lips trembled for an instant, as if the gentleness of his response had gotten under her guard. "It's nothing. Just a scratch. I think we must have blundered into every blackberry bramble on the side of the hill trying to get away."

He kneeled down in order to take her hands in both of his, and again she didn't try to evade him. "Are you hurt anywhere else?"

"Just a few bruises." She tried to smile. "You should see the other guy. Isn't that what the saying is? Only we never did see him. Again."

He led her to the sofa, pushing her down gently. There were more questions he had to ask, but Rachel needed a little comforting first.

"I'll get some ice to put on that cheek. Maybe it will help keep it from bruising." He strode toward the kitchen before she could argue.

By the time he returned with the ice pack he'd found in the freezer and wrapped in a dish towel, she was leaning back, eyes closed, her face drained. He sat down next to her and pressed the ice pack lightly against her cheek.

"How's that?"

"Good." She opened her eyes, surveying him with what seemed like caution. "Before you say it, I will. I should never have taken Benj up there."

"Actually, I was thinking you shouldn't have taken yourself." He kept his tone mild. "Do you feel like telling me about it? The real thing, not the expurgated version you told Burkhalter."

She was silent for a moment, as if gathering her thoughts. Or her strength.

"The more I thought about the possibility that Gene was involved with drugs, the more convinced I became that something had to be going on up there," she said, her voice drained, the words coming out with an effort. "I know we didn't see any signs when we were there, but I wanted to look again."

She seemed to be waiting for a sharp response to that, but he was determined not to give her an excuse to shut him out.

"How did Benj get into this expedition?"

Rachel repositioned the ice pack a little more firmly against her cheek. "I asked him if he'd heard any rumors about Gene and drugs. Sometimes teenagers know more about things like that than anyone, don't they?"

He nodded. "What did he say?"

"Just that he'd heard rumors. And that there was some talk of people growing marijuana out in the woods, like that patch you said they found on the state game lands last month."

"So Benj figured out what you had planned and insisted on going with you?" He didn't doubt that Rachel would have left her little brother out of it if she could.

She nodded and then winced at the movement,

making him wince, as well. "He was determined. Maybe trying to prove something to himself."

"I'm not surprised." Benj was struggling into manhood, it seemed.

"Anyway, we walked up. Nothing had changed since you and I were there, but we found a path leading into that strip of woods near where the farmhouse used to be. It's not really dense woods, more of a windbreak. There's a field on the other side, but nothing seemed to be growing there but grass. That's when the shooting started."

He couldn't stop himself from taking her free hand in his. "You're sure he was shooting at you?"

"If he was target shooting, we were the targets, believe me. Although…" She hesitated, looking thoughtful. "It almost seemed as if he were deliberately shooting over our heads."

"Chasing you away, like he chased Benj and the other boys. Still, you can't be sure he wasn't trying to hit you." The thought made him cold.

"No, I wasn't about to take that on faith." Her voice was growing stronger. Maybe it was good for her to talk about the experience. "We ran, and when we neared the bottom of the hill, we heard Mr. Sitler. He'd heard the shooting as well, and came a little way up the hill from his yard, yelling at the person. He was furious that someone was shooting on his land. He called the police."

"Who won't do anything." He got to his feet, unable to sit still any longer. "Burkhalter is always going to favor the obvious explanation, and we don't have any proof that it's anything else. If you told the police everything—"

"You did that, and you saw the result." There was something like a snap in her voice. "No Amish parents are going to appreciate having the police show up at their doors. I have to make a living here, remember?"

"*Live* is the operative word." The fear he'd been trying to suppress came surging to the fore. "You could have been killed out there today, don't you realize that?"

"Of course I do." She shot to her feet, as if unwilling to have him looking down at her. "I had to do something. I couldn't just wait for bad things to happen to me and the people I love."

"I told you I'd look into the drug connection, and I did. I talked to my friend's brother, and he wants to meet with me. Couldn't you just—" He stopped, his attention riveted by something he hadn't noticed before.

Rachel wore jeans and sneakers, as she often did when she was working around the property. Those sneakers had started off navy blue. Now they were blotched and speckled with white where the color had been bleached right out of them. There were even some white stains on her jeans, where something must have splashed on them.

"What happened to your shoes?" He shot the question at her.

Rachel looked at him blankly, and then glanced down at her feet. "I…I don't know. They weren't like that before." She reached down, as if to feel them.

He caught her hand. "Don't touch it. You must have stepped in something that bleached the color out of them."

"That field I mentioned—it was boggy. I sank in to the tops of my shoes before I realized it. What is it?"

"Some kind of chemical, at a guess. I don't know much about meth production, but I know it requires chemicals. Better take the shoes off, but try not to touch the bleached spots with your skin. I think my state-police contact might want to see this."

"But you said there was no sign of that, and it would require a building of some sort, wouldn't it?" She toed her shoes off and handed them over carefully.

His mind was racing. "A trailer maybe. The barn wouldn't be suitable." He should have had a more thorough look around when he had the chance. Why hadn't he taken it more seriously?

He took the shoes, holding them by the insides. "I'm going to try and set up a meeting as soon as possible. I'll probably have to go into Williamsport." He was already heading for the door, mind totally preoccupied with the best way to avoid endless bureaucracy and get someone to act. "Stay home, stay out of trouble and keep your doors locked. I'll be in touch as soon as I know anything."

He hesitated, remembering the way he'd kissed her the previous night. Her gaze was cautious, questioning.

He almost reached for her, almost gave in to the longing to feel her lips under his again. The panic he'd felt when he saw the police car in front of her house flooded through him again.

He couldn't do this—couldn't jump into making the commitment that someone like Rachel would expect. His guilt over past failures, his responsibility for his father, most of all his history with Rachel…at that moment they seemed insurmountable barriers.

He stepped away. The best thing he could do for Rachel right now was to resolve this situation so she and her family would be safe.

"Take care," he said again, his voice husky.

He hurried out of the house and jogged toward his car, pulling out his cell phone. Surely this latest incident was enough to get an investigation started. Once that happened, the person or people involved in this would be too busy to bother Rachel again.

STANDING AT THE window and staring after Colin as he drove away was not an option, Rachel decided. Maybe the walk to the farm to pick up Mandy would clear her head.

Heading upstairs, she stripped off the shirt and jeans she'd worn, looking with distaste at the white drops on the bottoms of the pant legs. She lifted the jeans to her nose and sniffed cautiously.

Sure enough, it was that odd smell she'd noticed when they'd moved into the field. She should have repeated Benj's ideas about a ruptured septic or oil tank to Colin, but he'd been so caught up in his own interpretation that she hadn't thought of it.

She changed quickly, trying to keep her mind off Colin, and hurried downstairs and out the back door, reminding herself to lock it. The sun hovered in the western sky, lengthening the shadows of the out-buildings as she scurried past them. She'd have to do a thorough clean-out there, too, but it was far more important to get the house ready for guests first.

Always assuming she had any guests, of course. For each step forward she made, like the help from the family and from Meredith, it seemed there was an equal step backward. If she didn't make some money from the bed-and-breakfast this summer, how would she and Mandy get through next winter?

She could always take Colin's offer and try to sell Mason House, even though everything in her rebelled at the idea. And she wasn't going to think about Colin, remember?

Too late. His face filled her thoughts, and she couldn't seem to deny him entrance, any more than she'd been able to keep him out of her life since she'd returned.

Her steps slowed as she approached the covered bridge. Maybe it was time to face facts. Colin obviously regretted having kissed her—she'd seen that for herself in his reaction. He was drawing a line in their relationship. So far and no farther.

Unfortunately it was only now, facing that fact, that she realized how much she'd grown to care for him in such a short time.

Or maybe not such a short time. She stopped at the bridge entrance, glancing toward the dam. Maybe that was where her feelings had actually started, in the place where Colin had kissed her for the first time.

It hadn't meant anything then, and it didn't mean anything now. She stepped inside the bridge, feeling the chill that seemed to reside there. Her footsteps echoed hollowly.

As a child, she'd taken the bridge for granted. It had been the dividing line between home and the outside world, but there had been nothing frightening about it. Meredith, always so cool and brave, had been the one who'd found it scary. They had been convinced that Aaron and Laura were leaving messages for each other in the covered bridge, just as she and Ronnie did years later, and had set about trying to find the hiding place. That is, she and Lainey had looked. Meredith had hung back in the entrance, urging them to hurry.

They'd never found the hiding place, if there had been one, and that was probably just as well. Laura and Aaron had deserved that much privacy for a relationship that seemed destined to fail, just as hers and Ronnie's had probably been.

Thinking about her failure with Ronnie might be a good antidote for dreaming of something that was obviously not meant to be with Colin. Her focus in life now was Mandy, and that required all she had to give.

She emerged from the bridge to see Mandy and Daad coming toward her, with Mandy juggling a basket as well as Princess's leash. Seeing her, Princess made a determined effort to run and greet her, nearly sending the basket to the ground. Daad rescued it, and Mandy darted to her, the puppy running along with her.

"Mommy, guess what? I helped Grossmammi make apple dumplings, and she gave me some to bring home."

"That's great, Mandy. I love apple dumplings."

Daad handed the basket to her without a word. A glance at his face had Rachel's heart sinking. Clearly he'd heard from Benj about their adventures, and just as clearly he hadn't liked what he'd heard.

"Mandy, why don't you give Princess a run? It looks as if she could stand to burn off some energy. I'll bring the basket."

"Okay." With a quick wave to her grandfather, Mandy let the puppy tug her into a run, and they raced through the bridge.

Rachel met her father's gaze. "I'm sorry about what happened with Benj. I shouldn't have let him go with me into the woods."

Her father looked as if she'd taken the words right

out of his mouth. "No. You should not have done that. I saw the police at your house."

"Franklin Sitler called them." It was just as well to make that clear, but she hoped it didn't sound like an excuse. "I tried to answer all their questions, so I hope the chief won't want to talk to Benj."

"Gut." He said the word with emphasis, the lines of his face tight. "I am thinking it best if Benjamin stays close to home for a bit."

In other words, away from her. She couldn't blame Daad for that. In fact, she agreed with him. Home was the safest place for her little brother right now. But still, it hurt.

"That's probably best," she said. She turned, eager to leave before he saw the pain in her eyes. But there was one more thing she should say.

"When we were in trouble, Benj was very brave. Very responsible. I thought you should know that."

Her father nodded, but his expression didn't change. Why would it? She had single-handedly wrecked the fragile peace that had been growing between her and her family. There was nothing more to say.

CHAPTER SEVENTEEN

"You NEED anything, Dad?" Colin switched on the television and handed the remote to his father, who'd just settled into his favorite chair to watch the evening news.

"I'm fine." The response seemed distracted. Lovina had said he'd been that way all day.

She'd been calm and cheerful about it, and the girl's patience seemed endless, despite her youth. Every issue was met with the same patient reply. *It makes no trouble.* It had been his lucky day when Lovina had come to work for them.

That thought led to Rachel, who was responsible for Lovina's presence in his home, and he really didn't want to think about Rachel right now.

Naturally that conviction brought her image to his thoughts—her lips curving slightly in a smile, her eyes widening when she looked at him.

The doorbell rang, cutting off a futile train of thought.

"That'll be the fellow I'm meeting with," he said, but his father didn't seem to have noticed the doorbell.

Banishing the worry to the back of his mind, he went to the door. Chuck Mowery, his buddy Pete's brother, was right on time.

"Hey, Colin, good to see you again." Chuck was as tall and rangy as he'd been when he'd played forward on the basketball team of their biggest high-school rivals. He still had that innocent, cherubic look that had always led the opposition to underestimate him. Colin couldn't help but wonder if that was an asset or a problem for a cop.

"Thanks for coming here. I appreciate it." He waved Chuck toward the kitchen. Dad didn't look up as they passed the living room archway.

"No trouble at all." Chuck's unexpectedly keen gaze seemed to take in his surroundings in a comprehensive sweep. "Situations like the one you describe are sometimes better discussed informally, so word doesn't get around."

"Coffee?" Colin lifted the carafe as Chuck settled himself at the table.

"Not for me. I'm trying to cut back." He grimaced. "Cops and medical people drink way too much of that stuff."

Colin nodded, sitting down opposite him.

"So." Chuck planted his elbows on the table and leaned forward. "Tell me what makes you think someone's got a drug operation going in Deer Run."

Colin grimaced. "When you put it like that, it sounds impossible."

"Don't you believe it," Chuck said quickly. "You'd

be surprised if you knew the number of raids we've pulled out in the boonies. No place is immune these days." He stopped, obviously waiting for Colin.

He'd given this a lot of thought, and there was nothing for it but to tell Chuck the whole story. Nothing else would convince him that there was something worth investigating.

"It started a couple of weeks ago." It seemed more like a lifetime, but it had been even less time since the day he'd walked into Mason House and seen Rachel again. "Three young Amish teens were up on that hill that overlooks the village." He hesitated, but it was all or nothing now. "It must have been past midnight, and the truth is that the oldest kid was planning some vandalism. He wanted to torch what remains of an abandoned barn."

Chuck grinned. "Don't worry. I don't look into vandalism cases."

"No. Well, they didn't count on running into anyone there. You have to understand, there's nothing else around, and no reason for anyone to be up there at night. But they spotted vehicle lights, and apparently they were seen. Next thing they knew, someone was shooting at them."

"I assume no one was hit, or the local cops would be on it by now."

Colin nodded. "You assume right. They got away, didn't tell their parents because they knew they'd be in big trouble for what they'd planned. Over the next few days, both of the older boys disappeared—it's assumed they ran away for a taste of the Englisch life as part of their *rumspringa*. The youngest kid is only fourteen. He works for me, taking care of the yard." He deleted a reference he'd been about to make to Rachel. That wasn't relevant, was it? "Anyway, I could see he was scared about something, and eventually we got the story out of him."

"We?"

It looked as if Rachel was coming in, whether he wanted to mention her or not. "His older sister. She was married to a friend of mine, and just recently came back to town."

Chuck pulled something from his pocket, unfolding it, and Colin realized it was a topographic map of the area, similar to the one he had consulted. "Can you show me where the incident took place?"

It took a moment to orient the map, but then he found the spot without difficulty. "Right there."

Chuck put a light *x* on the map. "This kid who told you the story—would you say he's pretty reliable?"

"Very. He's Amish, kind of quiet and not even old enough to be involved with the other kids, who are already into their running-around years."

He didn't have to explain further to Chuck. Chuck had lived in the area all his life, so surely he knew about *rumspringa*.

Chuck nodded. "Something more has happened since then?"

"Several minor things." Colin frowned, hoping

Chuck was taking this seriously. "None of it was very threatening, but things that would upset and scare the boy and his sister. I went up to the barn and had a look around myself. Nothing much there, but it looked as if some heavy trucks had been in there."

Chuck looked up at the mention of trucks. "Is there anything to account for that?"

"I figured it had to do with some logging they're doing on the other side of the hill. Until today." He felt his throat tighten at the prospect of talking about the danger Rachel had been in. "The boy and his sister went up to the barn this afternoon. Someone started shooting at them. According to Rachel, they were chased down the hill. Enough shots were fired to rouse the owner of the property, Franklin Sitler, who lives at the base of the hill. He came out shouting, called the local police. Chief Burkhalter attributed it to somebody target shooting."

Chuck's expression suggested he wouldn't say anything negative about another peace officer. "Anything else?"

"This." Colin picked up the bag in which he'd put the sneakers and dumped them onto the table. "Rachel wore these. She obviously stepped into something strong enough to drain the color right out of them."

Chuck's attention seemed to sharpen. "Interesting. I'll see what the lab can make of this, if you don't mind. If it's been done by a chemical used in drug processing, they should be able to identify it."

"That's what I hoped you'd say." He dropped the shoes back into the bag and handed it over.

Chuck rose. "Guess I don't need to tell you to keep this quiet." His lips creased slightly. "Except maybe for the owner of the shoes."

"There is one more thing." He stood as well. "Neither of them can identify the person doing the shooting. But there is recent arrival in Deer Run who apparently has a record of drug involvement. His name is Gene Sitler."

"A relative of the Franklin Sitler you mentioned?" Chuck's eyebrows rose.

"A grandson."

"Interesting." He extended his hand. "Thanks for the information. I think I can promise you that my department will pursue it."

"Good." Maybe then he could stop worrying about Rachel. And Benj, of course.

They headed toward the front door. As he passed the living room, Colin looked in automatically. His heart did a stutter step. Dad stood in front of the television, the remote in his hand, looking at it with a baffled expression.

"Dad? What's wrong?" Colin moved toward his father.

"Why won't this work? Did someone take the right one?" He shook the remote at the television, his mouth trembling.

"It's okay," Colin said, taking it from his hand.

"Maybe it needs a new battery or something. I'll fix it. Do you want your game show on?"

Dad just stared at him for a moment, looking lost. Then he nodded. "That would be nice." He went back to his chair.

"I'll let myself out," Chuck said quietly, and the pity in his eyes was almost more than Colin could stand.

Colin turned to the television, adjusting it to the game show that was his father's favorite. He sat down in the chair opposite his father, the one that had always been Mom's chair. Already Dad's expression had cleared, the momentary confusion passing quickly, as it always seemed to.

For the moment, they could manage. Lovina was now coming in the morning and staying until supper, and she was a wonder. Doris Brubaker, their next-door neighbor, kept an unobtrusive eye on things when Colin went out.

But Dad's condition would get worse, eventually, despite the medication that seemed to have slowed the progress of the disease. Eventually he'd have to have full-time care. It was another reminder, not that he'd needed one, that he couldn't get involved with Rachel.

RACHEL CURLED UP in the corner of the family-room sofa after supper, trying to keep her mind on her list of things that had yet to be finished before the bed-and-breakfast could open. Mandy, already in pajamas, sat cross-legged at the other end, her attention seemingly divided between the half hour of cartoons she was allowed to watch each day and the antics of Princess, who wanted her attention.

An Amish household didn't depend upon electronic entertainment, and Rachel was making a determined effort to keep Mandy's reliance on television at a minimum.

Of course she'd had her brothers and sisters to keep her company as a child, and when they wanted indoor entertainment there had been a stack of board games and plenty of books to keep them busy.

But Mandy wasn't growing up Amish, and somehow Rachel had to strike a healthy balance in raising her. It was a balance that constantly tipped one way and then another, making Rachel sometimes long for the clear boundaries of Amish life.

Setting the laptop on the table, she stretched, wincing as she discovered a few more bruises and aching muscles. The show came to an end. She reached for the remote but Mandy had it before her, clicking the television off with no sign of regret.

"Can I practice fetch with Princess a few more times before bed? Please, Mommy?"

Mandy was attempting to teach the puppy a few tricks, but it seemed to Rachel that it was Mandy who did most of the fetching.

"Just five minutes, all right? Then it will be time for bed."

Mandy nodded, running to grab the soft rubber ball. Rachel welcomed the noise and distraction of child and dog, she realized. It kept the dreary thoughts about Colin and her family at bay.

"Princess, bring me the ball." Mandy's command had no effect.

"She's good at chasing it, but not so great at bringing it back," Rachel said.

The ball rolled through the open doorway to the front hall. Princess scrambled down the hall to the front stairs, ears flopping. Mandy ran after her and Rachel followed, laughing in spite of herself. If any actual training was going to get done, she had a feeling she'd have to take a hand.

"I've got you now." Princess had run behind the coat stand in the corner, and Mandy blocked her way. "Give me the ball, Princess."

The puppy cocked her head, surveying the situation, holding the ball in her mouth. Then she darted right through Mandy's legs and raced toward the kitchen. Giggling, Mandy went after her just as the doorbell rang.

Trying to control her own laughter, Rachel opened the door and instantly sobered, wishing she hadn't. Gene Sitler leaned on the bell.

Before she could shut the door he grabbed it, his sleeveless black T-shirt showing off muscular arms. The shirt was emblazoned with the mildly profane name of a rock band.

"Rachel. You don't mind if I come in, right?" He stepped inside as he spoke, forcing her to retreat.

She took a deep breath, telling herself that the ripple of panic she felt was unwarranted. "As a matter of fact, I do mind. I'm busy with my daughter."

As if on cue, Mandy and the puppy ran back into the hall and then stopped dead, staring at the visitor.

Gene stared back. "So, kid, you gotten lost again lately?"

Mandy shook her head, her gaze wary, as if she didn't know what to think.

Rachel knew all too well what she thought—that she didn't want Gene Sitler anywhere near her child. She stepped between Sitler and Mandy. "Mandy, go on back to the family room, please."

"Looks like she's ready for bed. Cute pajamas." It was the kind of thing any visitor might say, but coming from him it sounded sinister.

"As I said, I'm busy." She stalked to the door and yanked it open.

"That's not exactly neighborly. I thought people in small towns were supposed to be about good neighbors, right?" His smile didn't reach his eyes. "The old man sent me over. Wanted to make sure you're all right after your little adventure in the woods. You want me to tell him you kicked me out?"

Was it likely that Franklin would send Gene on such an errand? He probably didn't sense the menace Rachel did in his grandson.

"Please tell your grandfather that I'm fine and I appreciate his asking. Good night." She held the door firmly.

"He'll be glad to hear that." Gene slouched toward the door. "It can be dangerous, out in those woods. You don't know what you might run into." He stopped, no more than a foot from her. "You wouldn't want to risk leaving your little girl alone. Unprotected." His gaze seemed to narrow on her cheek. "Nasty cut that is. It'd be a shame if it left a scar." He reached out, as if to touch it.

She recoiled, unable to prevent her revulsion from showing. His face darkened, and fear took her in a cold grip.

Princess rushed toward him, barking and snarling, her fury obvious. She nipped at his legs, forcing him to stumble out onto the porch through the open door.

Heart thudding, Rachel grabbed the dog's collar, holding her with one hand while she slammed and locked the door with the other.

"Princess!" Mandy scrambled toward the puppy, dropping to the floor to hug her. "You're a hero."

Still shaking a little over the transformation of the friendly puppy into fierce guard dog, Rachel kept a hand on the collar. But Princess licked Mandy's face in an extravagant gesture of love. Clearly Princess knew who the enemy was.

As did she, Rachel thought. The question was, what could she do about it?

"YOU SHOULD have called the police." Meredith sat across the kitchen table from Rachel the next morning, her dark eyes snapping with indignation. "Honestly, Rachel, the man is a menace."

"Maybe so, but I doubt that Franklin Sitler sees his grandson that way." Rachel took a swallow of coffee, hoping it would counteract the effects of a mostly sleepless night.

"That's all the more reason for someone to let him in on his grandson's behavior," Meredith snapped. She'd arrived to drop off some questions she needed answered for the website and stayed to drink coffee and commiserate. Much as Rachel appreciated her support, Meredith didn't seem to understand how precarious Rachel's situation was.

"Maybe so, but not me. I have a business to get off the ground, remember? I can't afford to alienate someone as important as Franklin Sitler."

Meredith shook her head, the corners of her lips quirking. "I suspect Franklin would only be considered important in a place like Deer Run. Like Jeannette." She paused. "I've been wondering whether I should tell you this or not, but I think you should know."

"Know what?" Her muscles tightened. More bad news?

"I started thinking about that unannounced visit from the safety inspector. I happen to know one of the women who works in that office—she went to college with me. So I sounded her out. It seems someone called to suggest that they might want to hurry up a safety inspection, implying you were going to start having guests without it."

Rachel felt as if she'd stepped in a hole. "Jeannette?"

"The caller didn't give a name, but it turns out their system keeps a record of calls, and my friend was able to access it. The caller was Jeannette, all right. She probably called the tourist bureau as well, but unfortunately I don't have any old friends there." Meredith gave her a cautious smile, as if still wondering whether she should have told her.

"So that's it." She was surprised, and maybe she shouldn't have been. "I wonder if she's the person who wrenched the railing loose, too."

"I wouldn't put it past her as long as she thought she wouldn't get caught," Meredith said. "There's just as much envy and malice in a place like Deer Run as in any upper-crust suburb, I expect. And as many secrets." Her face sobered, and Rachel suspected she was thinking about Aaron and Laura. Then she shook her head, as if shaking off a troubling image. "Well, to business. If you can get the rest of this information to me, I can have the website ready to go live in a few days."

"That soon?" She hadn't expected such speed, and she grappled with the prospect. "But I can't possibly be ready to open that quickly."

"No, I realize that," Meredith said. "But you want to start taking reservations, don't you? We can just set the opening date for July first or whenever you can get that final inspection scheduled. The important thing is to get the information out."

"I...I don't know." Putting up the website made the bed-and-breakfast seem so irrevocable. What if she couldn't be ready? What if the situation with her family continued to worsen? What if she just couldn't do this?

"You're having opening jitters, aren't you?" Meredith patted her hand. "It's written all over your face."

"I guess I am." Rachel managed a shamefaced smile. "After all my fine declarations of how I was going to do this no matter what anyone said, now that it seems a reality, I'm scared. I guess I really am a coward."

"Don't be ridiculous. You're far braver than I am," Meredith said instantly. "You had the courage to follow your heart, no matter where it led." Something that might have been regret flickered across her face. "All you have to do is take it one step at a time. It's not as if you'll be flooded with guests from the first day. You'll have time to get used to the operation gradually. You can do it."

"I hope so." What was she saying? She couldn't just hope. She had to make this happen. She had to provide for Mandy, and she didn't have the skills to do it any other way. "I guess you're right. We may as well—"

A pounding on the back door cut off her words.

With a startled look at Meredith, Rachel got to her feet and headed for the door.

"Look first. If it's Gene Sitler, I'm calling the police," Meredith said.

"It's my sister." Rachel was relieved, but a little surprised, to see Naomi this early. She swung the door open, but before she could say anything, Naomi had grasped her arm.

"Is Benj here? Have you seen him?"

"What? No, he's not here." Rachel drew her inside. "Daad said he was keeping Benj at home for a few days." Naomi's obvious anxiety began to affect her, and her voice sharpened. *"Was ist letz?"*

"Everything." Naomi sent a glance toward Meredith, who had come to join them when she realized something was wrong, but the presence of another person didn't deter her. "Benj is gone." A tear slid down Naomi's cheek. "He's gone."

Rachel tried to process the words. "What do you mean, he's gone? When did he go? Where?"

"We don't know." Naomi let herself be led into the kitchen. She wiped the tear away with the palm of her hand. "I'm sorry. I'm acting all *ferhoodled*, but I'm that worried—"

"It will be all right." Rachel put her arm around her sister's waist, longing to comfort her. "Just tell me what happened."

Naomi gulped. Nodded. "Benj went up to bed early last night. He was upset, I guess because Daad was still not saying much. Lovina peeked in at him

when she went to bed, and she said he was just sitting at the window, looking out."

A chill touched Rachel's heart. Benj had gone
out that window the night all his troubles started.

"Anyway, Daad went to call him this morning to
help with the milking, and he wasn't there. His bed
didn't look as if it had been slept in."

"Did he leave a note?" Meredith asked.

Naomi shook her head. "Nothing. He didn't say
a word to anyone. None of his clothes are gone, except what he had on. He was just gone."

Like Will, Rachel thought. *Like Joseph*.

"What did Daad do?" Surely her father had taken
some action by this time. He would have been up
before dawn to do the milking.

"He had us search all over the farm, thinking
Benj might be in the barn or one of the outbuildings. And then he said maybe Benj had taken a walk
to think things over, and he'd be back by breakfast.
But he didn't come." The tears started again. "Rachel, are you sure he's not here? You wouldn't hide
him…."

"Of course I wouldn't," she snapped, exasperated
that Naomi even asked the question. "He couldn't be
in the house without my knowing." She thought of
Benj hiding in the old stable. "We'll have to check
the outbuildings."

"I'll help," Meredith said instantly. "Surely he
can't have gone far. We'll find him."

But no one had found Will or Joseph, despite

their parents' conviction that they were just having a *rumspringa* lark. And Benj wasn't old enough for that, anyway. If he'd disappeared, it meant something far direr.

"I should go back to Mamm." Naomi whirled toward the door. "She insisted Lovina go to work because Mr. McDonald would be counting on her, but I don't want to leave her alone." She turned back to grab Rachel in a quick hug. "You'll come to the farm once you've looked, *ja?* Either way, Mamm needs you."

Rachel patted her sister's back, longing to comfort her but not knowing how. "We'll find him," she said at last, fearing it wasn't true but needing to say it. "I'm sure we'll find him."

But she wasn't sure at all.

CHAPTER EIGHTEEN

COLIN STEERED HIS car carefully through the covered bridge and accelerated up the narrow lane to the Weaver farmhouse. He'd stopped by the house to check on his father after lunch with a client and heard the news from Lovina.

Benj missing. His jaw clenched. Why hadn't Rachel called him about it? Weren't they in this together anymore?

He stopped the car short of the back porch. By the time he got out, Rachel was hurrying to meet him, and any anger he felt at being left out disappeared when he saw her face. Anguish battled hope when she looked at him.

"Have you seen Benj?" She clasped his arm. "Has he been around your place?"

"No." He covered her hand with his, trying to soften the impact of the word. But he knew better than to offer false hope. "I haven't. You should have called me."

She blinked, looking a little startled. "I thought Lovina would tell you."

"I'd left for a meeting before she arrived. I didn't

find out until just now, when I stopped back at the house. What's been done to find him?" Selfish to be thinking of his own feelings at a time like this, but he was relieved to know she hadn't intentionally left him out.

"We've searched every place we can think of on the farm and at my house, too. There's no sign of him." She choked back a sob. "He's just vanished."

He tightened his grasp on her hand. "Has anyone notified the police?"

"Daad won't hear of it." He saw the same frustration on her face that he felt. "But Mose has gone to get some of the brothers started searching."

That's what the Amish would do, of course. Form search parties of their own before calling in the authorities. "Are they looking up in woods on Sitler's property?" Chuck probably wouldn't like that, but it was the least of his worries at the moment.

She shook her head. "Daad is sure Benj would be too scared to go back up there. They are concentrating on his friends, trying to see if any of them are hiding him." She bit her lip. "What if he's not hiding? What if someone took him?"

"Take it easy. No one could have gotten into the house without setting the dogs barking, could they?" The boy could have been lured out in some way, but he didn't want to put that fear into her mind. "What about his room? Was there any disturbance?"

"No. None of his clothes are missing except what he was wearing. It's as if he just walked out.

But why would he?" Her fear was so intense that it seemed he felt it, too.

"I guess we'll know that when we find him." He tried to sound more confident than he felt. "What about you and Mandy?" He softened his voice. "Are you all right?"

"I'm glad Mandy has the farm animals to distract her." A ghost of a smile slipped across her face and was gone. "I'm just trying to keep Mamm from fretting too much. It seems to comfort her to have me here."

"That's the best thing you can do." He cradled her hand in both of his and then let it go when he saw Rachel's father coming toward them. Levi looked as if he'd aged ten years in a day.

"Colin. It is *gut* of you to come. Have you seen anything of Benjamin?"

"I'm sorry but I haven't, Levi. I was just telling Rachel that I think you should call the police. After all, Benj is only fourteen, and…" He let that thought fade away, because Levi was already shaking his head.

"It was my fault," he said, his voice gruff. "I was too harsh with the boy, and he has run off to hide from me. Bringing in the police will only make him more ashamed to come home."

Colin wanted to argue, but a look at Levi's face dissuaded him. It would do no good. "I'll drive along the roads leading out of town," he said instead. "It's possible he's out there trying to hitchhike."

"That would be *gut* of you." Levi turned away quickly, as if afraid of showing too much of his pain. He hurried toward the house.

"Thank you," Rachel said softly. "Do you think it will do any good?"

"Probably not," he said bluntly. "Look, I've already told the state police investigator everything we knew as of last night. I've got to tell him about Benj's disappearance, and I'll start searching. Do you have your cell phone with you?"

She nodded. "Daad wouldn't like it, but yes, I have it."

"Good. I'll stay in touch." He hesitated, but it was just as foolish to touch her now as it had been yesterday. Maybe more so, because of how vulnerable she was. "Until later," he said, and slid back into the car.

BY SUPPERTIME, Rachel was convinced this was the longest day she'd ever experienced, with the overcast skies contributing to the gloom. Even the shock that Ronnie had died in a car accident had come quickly, out of the blue, with no anxious hours of waiting. Instead the news had come with the knock on the door from the state police officer.

One by one the searchers reported back, disheartened, having found no sign of Benj anywhere. Colin called in once to let her know that he'd searched the road toward Williamsport and was circling around to come back by the route to the north of town. He was waiting for a call back from his state police contact.

Neighbors began showing up as the news spread, the men to take over the farm chores, the women bringing enough food for an army. No one seemed to question her presence there, and for that, Rachel could only be numbly grateful. As she worked around the kitchen, setting food in the refrigerator or the oven, exchanging soft comments in Pennsylvania Dutch with the other women, she felt as if she'd truly come home.

Mamm came back into the kitchen from a quiet talk with Mary Kline, the bishop's wife, bidding her goodbye at the door and then turning to look at the clock.

"It's late," she said, straightening her shoulders as if picking up a burden again. "We must put the food on the table, girls. Folks must eat, to have strength to go on."

Rachel exchanged a glance with Naomi, knowing they were thinking the same thing—that Mamm needed to rest, but she wouldn't. Not until Benj was found, anyway.

"It's all ready, Mamm," Naomi said. "Just call any who are outside while Rachel and I get the hot dishes on."

Her mother nodded, and in a moment the long table in the kitchen was crowded with people, just like long-ago Sunday afternoons when extended family came to supper. Rachel saw Mandy to a seat at the bottom of the table with a few young cousins and then hesitated. Her usual seat was at Mamm's right, but it had been a long time since she sat at this table.

"Komm." Mamm gestured to the place next to her.

Daad halted in the act of pulling out his chair. He looked at her and seemed about to speak. But Mamm tugged at his hand.

"Sit, Levi." Her voice was soft, but every person in the room heard it. "Rachel is not under the *bann*. She can eat with us. Would you deny me the comfort of having my oldest daughter here?"

Daad patted her shoulder in wordless comfort. He nodded to Rachel. "Sit, Rachel."

She sank into her place. Daad bowed his head in the silent prayer which preceded the meal, and Rachel didn't doubt that Benj was the subject of every prayer.

An eternity later the kitchen had been cleaned up and people had scattered, the men to go on searching while the women took children home to bed.

Her mother was sitting in her rocking chair, a bit of mending lying forgotten in her lap. Her face was so drawn that the bones stood out. Heartsick, Rachel went to kneel by the chair.

"I'm sorry, Mamm. If it hadn't been for me, Benj might never have run off." She tried to keep any other possibilities from her mind.

Her mother patted Rachel's cheek, her work-worn

hand as gentle as it had been when Rachel was a small child. "What happens is God's will, not our doing, my Rachel. We must trust and pray."

"I will. I am." She blinked back tears and rose. "I should find Mandy and get her home to bed. Please, send to me if you hear anything."

Mamm nodded. "*Komm* in the morning, *ja?*"

"*Ja*, Mamm. I will."

She hurried her steps, wanting to get out of the house before Mamm could see the fear in her eyes. Would Benj be here in the morning?

Trust and pray, Mamm had said. Rachel felt the drive to do more, but what?

"Mandy!" Calling her daughter, Rachel walked toward the barn. Knowing Mandy, she'd most likely be where the animals were. "Mandy, it's time to go home."

The only answer was a frenzied barking, but it wasn't coming from the direction of the barn. She turned, scanning the field below the house.

The barking broke out again, echoing, and she realized it was coming from the covered bridge. Her heart in her throat, Rachel ran to the bridge. Dusk was settling over the valley, but it was already dark inside the bridge.

Princess was a blur of movement as she jumped, barking until the sound seemed to be inside Rachel's head. "Hush, I'm coming. Are you stuck, foolish puppy?"

She reached the center of the bridge, trying to

keep the dog still while she untangled the leash. "Where is Mandy?"

Her heart twisted on the words. Why would Mandy leave her precious pet in the covered bridge? Her fingers touched the end of the leash—not stuck, but tied to one of the braces. And just above it, stuck into a crevice in the wood, was something white.

Rachel grabbed it, her breath catching painfully. Grasping the leash, she hurried out off the bridge so that she could see what it was.

Mandy's careful cursive sprawled across the page. The message was short. *I think the bad man took Benj. I'm going up to find him. Mandy.* Beneath her signature, she'd printed three more words. *I love you.*

Rachel's heart seemed to stop and then began beating so fast it might jump out of her chest. She wanted to run, scream—

She sucked in a breath, sending up an anguished plea for calm. Think. What to do first?

She glanced toward the farmhouse…no, not Mamm, she couldn't tell her. Where was Daad? The barn? She didn't see him, but one of her cousin's boys, among those who'd arrived to take over the chores, was just coming out of the double doors.

She ran toward him. The boy seemed to catch her anxiety, because he raced to meet her.

"Find my *daad* or my brother," she demanded. "Tell them I think Mandy has gone up the hill to the old barn." She pointed across the valley, making sure he understood. "I'm going now. Tell him to bring some of the searchers and *komm. Ja?*"

"*Ja*, I w-will." The boy almost stammered in his need to help. "Right now." He took off, running, toward the back of the barn.

Satisfied that he'd do what had to be done, Rachel ran the other way, the puppy bounding along at her side as if Princess, too, had picked up on her fear.

What else? Rachel's feet pounded across the bridge. Colin. She snatched her cell phone from her pocket, pressing in his number as she ran.

But the call went straight to voice mail. He must be out of range, easy enough in the succession of ridges and valleys.

"Mandy is gone." She nearly choked on the words. "She thinks she knows where Benj is. I'm sure she's gone up to the barn. I'm headed there. Please come."

The first fat drops of rain were falling as she clicked off. She pounded up the steps to the house, hitting 911 as she plunged in the door, repeating the information to the dispatcher. The woman tried to keep her on the line, but she had no time for more explanations.

Shove the dog into the house, grab a windbreaker and flashlight, and then run.

Crossing the road, Rachel headed straight up the hill, using the direct route she and Benj had taken on their way down the previous day. It was rougher than the other path, but shorter. She scrambled up the bank, relieved that the branches they had already broken would show her the way.

Concentrate on little things, she ordered herself. The falling rain, the muffled padding of her feet through the pine needles, the loud thumping of her heart—anything to keep her from picturing her baby in the hands of whatever was waiting up at the old barn.

She couldn't be wrong about what Mandy had meant, could she? Fresh panic ripped through her. What if she was sending everyone in the wrong direction?

But Mandy had a lot of common sense for a nine-year-old. She'd assumed her mother would know where she'd gone, she'd used the word *up* and the place that had figured in their conversation lately had been the old barn.

Please, God, please, God… The thudding of her heart seemed to beat time with the words. Nothing mattered more than caring for her child. If she failed Mandy, her other failures paled in comparison.

She stumbled, regained her balance, pushed on, legs aching. Darkness grew under the pines, even though they protected her from the worst of the rain. She switched on the flashlight. Probably not wise to use it when she got closer, but surely here it was safe.

With the circle of light moving ahead of her, she made better time, but it still seemed to take agonizing hours until she reached the spot by the fallen log where the boys had hidden.

Noise alerted her. She switched off the flashlight, heart thudding, and dropped to the ground behind the log. Holding her breath, she peered over it.

Two…no, three tanker trucks were pulled up beside the barn where they had seen the tire tracks. She narrowed her eyes, trying to distinguish what she was looking at. Trucks, their headlamps off. Moving figures around the trucks.

Where was Mandy? There was no sign of her small figure. Had the men seen her? She could be in the barn or sheltering in the trees, like Rachel.

She hesitated, biting her lip, not sure what to do next. She didn't want to draw the men's attention to her. Whatever they were doing, they'd taken enough trouble to keep it private.

She edged a little closer, trusting that her dark jacket would let her fade into the darkness under the trees. She stopped, her fingers pressing into the rough bark of the nearest tree.

They'd been wrong in their suppositions, it seemed. This was no drug operation. A long hose-like affair wound from the first truck along the path they'd followed through the stand of trees, and if she hadn't figured it out from that, the acrid aroma would have told her the answer. They were dumping chemical waste in the field beyond where the old farmhouse had been.

No wonder they'd been so eager to go undetected. Something like this would have the whole valley up in arms. The chemicals could leach into the groundwater, turn up in wells, harm goodness knew how many animals and people in the process. Who—

She saw the answer even before the question formed in her mind. Gene Sitler appeared from around the rear of the truck. He gestured to the man who seemed to be in charge of the hose. She couldn't quite make out his words, but his gestures were clear. *Hurry up!*

Obviously Gene would be getting a substantial payoff from someone to allow the dumping on his grandfather's property. Enough, probably, to make him desperate to keep it quiet. The rain streaked down her face like tears. If he'd found Mandy...

She couldn't let herself think that way, or she'd be useless. If she could move a little farther to the right, she'd have a better view—a branch cracked sharply behind her. She whirled, ready to run, ready to scream—

It was Mandy. Joy leaped through her as Mandy rushed into her arms. She cradled her close, hugging her fiercely, and then freed herself enough to yank off the windbreaker and wrap it around Mandy.

"Mommy—"

"Hush, we mustn't let the men hear," she whispered. "We have to get away quietly."

She had to get Mandy down the hill to safety. Once they were out of earshot, she'd call the police.

"We can't," Mandy whispered back, tugging on her hand. "It's Benj. I found him. We have to get him out."

"Where? Where is he?" Rachel's mind moved frantically. *Get Mandy to safety.* But she couldn't desert her little brother.

"Over here." Mandy led her through the trees, moving closer and closer to the remains of the old farmhouse and closer as well to the men handling the hose.

"Stop." Rachel caught her hand. "Just tell me where Benj is, and I'll get him. You have to get away from here."

She'd brought her child home to Deer Run for safety, but safety was in short supply.

"I have to show you." Mandy pulled away. "He's under the ground. I can hear him, but I can't move the door."

Rachel hurried after her, trying to puzzle out what she meant. A cellar of some sort, maybe, under the farmhouse, or even a separate root cellar. Had Benj run there to hide and been trapped, or had Gene imprisoned him there?

Mandy slipped along the low wall that marked the remains of the farmhouse, stepped over it and stopped. "Here," she whispered. "Benj is down there. I heard him."

A heavy wooden trap door was sunk in the crumbling remains of the floor, weighted down with two cement blocks.

Rachel grasped her daughter by the shoulders. "Go and hide behind the wall," she ordered. "I'll get Benj out. Your job is to make sure nobody sees you, okay?"

Mandy's heart-shaped face firmed, and she looked older than her years. "I'll help."

Doubt tore at her. The men could spot them at any moment. If she took Mandy to safety, what might happen to Benj in the meantime?

There was no answer. She grabbed the nearest block and dragged it, praying the sound of the trucks would mask its scraping. Mandy's small hands were suddenly next to hers, and together they pulled it free.

Then the second one, and she fumbled with the broken handle of the door. She'd have expected a lock, but when she raised the door, she saw why Gene hadn't needed one. There was a straight drop to the cellar floor, and any steps that had been there once were long gone.

"Benj," she whispered, and then her eyes adjusted to the darkness enough so that she could make out what was beneath the door.

Benj looked up at her, his face a pale oval in the gloom. But he was not alone. Two more faces tilted toward her—Will and Joseph. They were all there, and they were alive.

But maybe not for long, if she didn't find a way to get them out. Raising the door had released an acrid wave of fumes. One of the boys doubled over, coughing, and she realized Benj held a piece of his shirt over his nose and mouth.

"Rachel." His voice broke on the word.

"Hush," she murmured urgently. "The men aren't far away. We've got to get you out. Is there anything you can stand on?"

"Some broken shelves," he whispered. "We tried climbing up, but they weren't high enough."

"Maybe if you get on them, I can reach your hand." She lay flat, squirming to the edge of the opening. "Try it."

A scraping sound came from below, and a mutter of voices. Then Benj was climbing on top of a pitifully small pile of wood, teetering as he reached toward her groping fingers.

Not enough. She edged farther over the hole, stretching as far as she could, fingers grasping until they met her brother's, met and grabbed and held.

A fresh wave of fumes caught her in the face, and she struggled not to cough. She pulled, frantic in her haste. She had to get him out, get all of them out. The fumes must be seeping into the cellar somehow, if she didn't get them out they could die before help came, but she wasn't strong enough, there was nothing for Benj to push against, she was going to fail.

And then someone was there next to her, reaching down, grabbing Benj's hands and hauling, and she knew without even looking that it was Colin.

CHAPTER NINETEEN

COLIN'S HEART HAD nearly stopped when he'd seen Rachel so close to Gene and his crew. It didn't take much imagination to piece the story together. Just how far would Gene go to keep his secret? Colin didn't want to find out at the cost of someone's life.

No point in telling Rachel to leave. She wouldn't go until Benj was safe. He certainly knew that about her.

"You, Joseph, give Benj a boost." He kept his voice low, praying no one from the dumping crew would look this way.

Joseph nodded, coughing, and managed to shove Benj up from beneath. Colin caught the boy under the arms and with Rachel's help hauled him out.

Benj struggled to his knees and sucked in a breath. "We…we couldn't breathe…Will's ankle… I think it's broken…we have to get them out."

"We will," Colin promised. He looked around. "We need something like a rope to help lift the boys," he muttered, half to himself.

Mandy darted from behind the wall, stripping off

the sopping windbreaker that was wrapped around her. "Can this be a rope?"

"Good girl." He grabbed it. "Get back, now."

Rachel gave her daughter a gentle push. "Hide, quick." She dropped back down on the ground. "You came," she murmured to Colin.

He nodded. He'd come, but not in time to keep her and Mandy out of danger. He wrapped one end of the windbreaker around his hand and dropped the other into the hole. "Can you reach it?"

Even as Joseph reached for the dangling sleeve, Colin heard a shout. Then, shocking in its volume, a gunshot.

He shoved himself to his knees. One of the men was struggling with Gene for the gun, the others scrambling to get the hoses back to their trucks.

Colin grabbed Rachel, hauling her to her feet. "Take Mandy and Benj to the woods. Hide." Surely the rain and dark would keep them safe.

"I can't leave you—"

"Go." He had to stay between Rachel and the gun. "I'll try to make Gene see sense."

"The others—" Benj reached for the hole. "I can't leave them."

"The police are on their way. They'll get the boys out." Colin darted a glance toward the trucks. Gene yanked the weapon away from the man who was trying to stop him and swung toward them. "Go," he ordered again.

Rachel grabbed Mandy and Benj by the hands.

In an instant they were running toward the safety of the woods.

Colin took a step toward Gene, praying he could keep the man's attention on him.

"Stop and think, Sitler," he called. "You don't want to do this. The cops already know. They're on their way."

"You're lying." Gene's face twisted.

"I'm telling you the truth. You other men better think what you're doing. If you let Sitler shoot anyone, you're an accessory. You want to go to prison for him?"

One or two of the men hesitated, and for an instant Colin thought he'd won. Then they scrambled into the trucks, opting to run instead.

Gene lifted the weapon. Colin held out his hand, palm out, as if that would stop a bullet. At least Rachel and the kids would be safe—

"No!" Rachel's voice, and Rachel was running to him. Why hadn't she stayed where it was safe? "Stop it. You can't."

"Rachel, go back—"

"Gene!" Dennis Sitler raced past the trucks, coming from the lane. He must have followed them. His face was distorted with disbelief. "What are you doing? Let those boys go. Put down that gun."

"Stay out of it," Gene snarled. His face dark with fury, he swung the barrel of the weapon at Dennis. In an instant the cousins were struggling, the gun between them.

Colin launched himself forward. *Help Dennis, get the gun away—*

Another shot exploded, obscene as it ripped through the woods. The two figures seemed frozen. Then, almost in slow motion, Gene slid to the ground, red blossoming on his shirt.

Colin caught Rachel, turning her face into his chest, keeping her from looking. The image would be burned into their minds as it was.

An engine roared, and one of the trucks began to back up. It stopped, just as suddenly. A township police car, lights flashing, pulled into the clearing, followed by a state police car. They filled the narrow lane, blocking retreat.

Too late. That was all Colin could think. Too late for Gene. Too late for Dennis, who stood with his head bent, looking down at his cousin's body.

Colin averted his face, not wanting to intrude on the man's grief. He saw movement in the woods, and touched Rachel's shoulder.

"Look." Her father and several other Amish men emerged from the woods. Benj and Mandy raced toward them, to be gathered into Levi's arms.

Rachel took a step and then stopped, as if unsure. Her father looked at her. Held out his arms. And Rachel ran, to be drawn into the embrace as well.

Colin rubbed his face. He was wet, cold, muddy and tired. But there were still two more boys to retrieve from their underground prison, and then, no doubt, hours of questions and explanations.

At least the danger was over. The guilt, he suspected, was still to come.

"LET ME DO THAT." Meredith took the hot chocolate pan from Rachel's hand. "You must be exhausted."

"Actually, it feels better now that we've both had hot baths." Rachel sank down on a chair at the kitchen table, next to Mandy, who looked surprisingly bright-eyed after all she'd been through.

Meredith sent a cautious glance toward Mandy as she poured steaming cocoa into mugs. "It must have been frightening."

"I was scared," Mandy admitted. "Can I have a marshmallow in my chocolate?"

That quick transition surprised Rachel into a smile. "You sure can." Mandy couldn't be too traumatized if her mind was on marshmallows. Still, she ought to talk it over, to be sure there weren't any lingering questions or fears.

Meredith provided the marshmallow and sat down with them. "How did you figure out where Benj was, Mandy? That was pretty smart."

Rachel sent her a thankful look. Meredith seemed to understand what was needed, and she'd asked the question in a more matter-of-fact way than Rachel possibly could.

"I remembered when I walked Princess down by the covered bridge." Princess looked up at the sound of her name from her place on the floor near

Mandy, and her tail thumped. "I thought it was a dream, but I guess it wasn't."

"Thought what was a dream, sweetheart?" Rachel hoped she didn't sound as confused as she felt.

"Looking out my window when it was dark." Mandy took a gulp of cocoa and licked foam from her lips. "There was somebody coming from the farm, and a shadow came out of the bridge and grabbed him."

Rachel and Meredith exchanged glances. Gene. It must have been.

"And then I was riding a pony across the field, and I know that part was a dream." Mandy's logic was impeccable, it seemed. "So I thought the part about the shadow was, too. But when I went to the covered bridge, I remembered, and I knew I'd seen it. The shadow came out our side, and he was carrying something, and when the moon came out, I knew it was the same man Princess chased."

"So you thought he'd taken Benj to the old barn, and you went to see for yourself." Rachel clasped her hand. "Mandy, you know that was wrong, don't you? You should have come to me or to Grossdaadi, not gone on your own."

"But Mommy, I left you a note," Mandy protested. "I thought I should go right away once I remembered, and when I found the note in the bridge, that made me think of writing to you."

"Note in the bridge? What note?" Rachel was starting to feel dizzy.

"I found it when I tried to tie Princess up, and she pulled the board loose. I wrote on the back of it, didn't you see? I had a little pencil in my pocket, but no paper, so I used it."

"A note," Meredith whispered. "Do you think…"

Rachel stood, going to the shelf by the back door where she'd left Mandy's note. She brought it to the table and spread it out, revealing Mandy's writing.

She turned it over to reveal the writing on the other side. The ink had faded, but the words were still readable. She and Meredith bent over the paper, heads together.

Not a love note from Laura to Aaron, as she'd immediately assumed. *Laura doesn't want to be with you anymore*, it read. *She laughs at you behind your back. Leave her alone. From a friend.*

Meredith let out a long breath. "Do you think Aaron saw this?"

"I don't know." Her mind was so full it seemed about to explode. "If he did, or even if he didn't and it was true, we might be completely wrong about what happened."

"What happened to who, Mommy?" Mandy surveyed them, her eyes bright with curiosity.

The last thing she wanted was to get Mandy questioning that old tragedy. "It's just something that happened a long time ago, that's all. Now, listen. I want you to promise me you'll never run off like that again." She held up her hand to cut off debate. "I know you did it to help Benj, but it was still wrong, understand?"

"Yes, Mommy." Mandy was wise enough not to push. "I promise."

"Good."

Meredith's cell phone rang, almost simultaneously with a knock on the back door. Rachel headed for the door, trying not to let herself think that it might be Colin.

It wasn't. She opened the door to her sister Lovina.

"Mamm sent me over." Lovina's pert face was filled with curiosity. "She didn't like you and Mandy being alone."

"Perfect timing," Meredith said, slipping her phone in the pocket of her jacket. "I'll have to leave. My mother—" she glanced at Mandy and seemed to edit what she was about to say "—needs me. I'll stop by first thing in the morning. You take care." She gave Rachel a quick, hard hug and left.

Lovina grinned at Mandy. "Hot chocolate, yum. I'll make some more. We're going to have a pajama party, *ja?*"

"Cool." Mandy's face brightened. "Do you want to play a game?"

"Sure." Lovina sounded almost as excited at the idea as Mandy.

"I'll get some." Mandy slid off her chair and ran for the stairs, Princess galloping along beside her.

"I'm glad you came." Rachel patted her sister's

arm. "But you must be wiped out. You had a long day with Colin's father."

"It makes no trouble," Lovina said easily. "I was glad to stay until Colin got home. It sounds like he was cooped up with the police for ages, trying to get all the questions answered. He persuaded them not to bother you tonight," she added.

"That was kind of him."

Kind, but then Colin was always kind. That wasn't in question. But she wanted more from him, and that might be impossible.

"YOU SEE, WHAT YOU should have done from the very beginning was come to me. Let the professionals handle it." Chief Burkhalter took another huge bite of Mamm's rhubarb strudel, temporarily stopping his speech.

Rachel couldn't help thinking of Chief Burkhalter's quick dismissal of her concerns each time she had spoken to him, but reminding him wouldn't help now.

"I'm sure you're right," she said diplomatically, and Daad nodded approval at her answer.

The chief had arrived at the farm in midmorning to talk to her and to Benjamin, with Daad sitting in. They'd gone over the whole story, and if Benj skimmed over what Will Esch had really planned that night in the woods, the chief didn't press him on it.

Finally they'd said everything they had to say. Benj had confirmed Mandy's account of how Gene had taken him. Apparently Gene had thrown some pebbles against his bedroom window. Thinking it might be Rachel, he'd come outside looking for her, only to be grabbed by what Mandy had described as a shadow.

"I don't quite understand what happened to the other two boys," she said, hoping to distract Burkhalter from any more talk of what they should have done. "Had Will been in that cellar the whole time?"

She thought of the day she and Colin had been there. How terrible if they'd been so close and not found him.

"No, nothing like that long," Burkhalter assured her. "Seems like Will was more scared than he let on, and he decided to drop out of sight for a while. He'd been hiding in the area."

"So he actually did run away," she murmured.

"Guess so. Sitler didn't find him until Will took Joseph back up to the barn to see if they could figure out what he was doing. He spotted them. Joseph says he kept them in an old hunting cabin back in the woods, but he brought them to the cellar yesterday and left them there with your brother."

"But why put them in the cellar? It was so dangerous." Rachel shuddered, remembering the acrid smell of the chemicals.

The chief studied his coffee mug as if he didn't want to look at their faces. "From what he said to the boys, he was going to leave town as soon as he collected his big payoff from last night's dumping.

He told them he was going to let them go, but I gotta say I wonder. Seems like he might not have wanted them putting the police on his trail that fast. If he left them there until they were found…"

He let that trail off, and Rachel was just as glad he didn't finish the thought. Benj already knew he'd come close to death last night. No need to reinforce it.

"Do you think Gene was the person hanging around my place?" she asked, feeling as if some loose ends had been left dangling.

He shrugged. "Maybe so, but Will had been around, too, trying to talk to Benj where your *daad* wouldn't see him."

"Is Will Esch all right?" Daad asked. "Benjamin says maybe his ankle is broken."

"It's broken. They kept him in the hospital overnight, but he should come home today." The chief shook his head, jowls quivering. "Maybe that cast they put on him will keep him out of trouble for a bit. Serves him right, I say."

"It is God's will," Daad said repressively, and Benj looked down at his hands, probably wishing he were invisible.

"Yes, well, things could have been worse, I guess." The chief pushed his empty plate away with a satisfied air. "The state boys are disappointed not to find a drug ring, but DEP is all over the site, trying to find out how much damage has been done and citing everyone from the drivers to the company owners. They're not inclined to let anyone off lightly, I hear."

"What about Dennis Sitler?" Rachel asked. "I'm sure his cousin's death was an accident. If he hadn't grabbed the gun, I don't know what would have happened." It could have been Colin lying on the ground, bleeding.

"Dennis isn't in any trouble. He was trying to prevent his cousin from firing the gun." The chief rubbed his neck. "Dennis didn't seem to have any idea what Gene was doing. Just heard that your little girl was lost in the woods and went to join the search. Poor guy's pretty broken up about the whole thing, and Franklin—well, I've never seen him like this. At least it's all over now, and you folks can get back to normal."

Normal. She wasn't sure she even knew what that was any longer. Maybe that she could go back to dealing with more routine problems, like trying to make a go of her bed-and-breakfast and providing for her daughter.

At least now Mandy had the family that had been missing in her life up until now. She glanced at Daad, taking comfort from his solid, reassuring presence. No matter what, her family would be sure that Mandy was safe.

She needed to concentrate on being thankful that the breach with her family was healed. Think about that, not about the fact that she hadn't heard anything from Colin since the moment he'd let her go and pushed her toward her father.

CHAPTER TWENTY

THE RECEPTIONIST AT Colin's office looked as if she were bursting with questions when he arrived in midafternoon, but after one look at his face, she just handed him a list of messages. If he looked as bad as he felt, Colin decided, that should be enough to scare anyone off.

He sank into his desk chair, switched on the computer and then rubbed his face with his hands. After spending several hours with Chief Burkhalter last night and several more with the DEP representatives this morning, he had nothing much left for the business, but he thought he should make an appearance, anyway.

He'd talked to everyone, it seemed, but Rachel. He knew from Lovina that she and Mandy were all right. That was the important thing.

But he couldn't kid himself that he was the one who'd protected them. Dennis had done that, at a terrible cost.

Colin clicked onto his email. Unfortunately the messages seemed to form a backdrop for a series of images he'd like to erase from his brain.

Well, maybe all but one. Those moments when he'd held Rachel, thankful that they were both still alive—he wouldn't obliterate that. The words he'd wanted to speak still seemed to linger on his tongue.

I love you, Rachel.

He hadn't said them. His rational mind had been working enough to warn him that it wasn't the moment. And maybe it never would be.

Not wanting to go there, he forced his eyes to focus on the list of messages. Most were routine, but one jumped out at him. It was an answer to the inquiry he'd started days ago about the land Sitler owned on the ridge.

Too late to be of use now, but he clicked on it anyway. He read it once and then, frowning, read it again. Then he picked up the phone. Jeff Morrison, one of his numerous high-school buddies still in the area, now worked for the daily paper and had been doing a series of articles on the recent boom in natural-gas drilling in the area. He might be able to shed some light.

Fortunately Jeff was at his desk. After the usual preliminaries of inquiring about his family and razzing him about his choice of baseball teams, Colin got to the point.

"I'm interested in finding out whether any of the energy companies have been developing leases in the Deer Run area. Any thoughts?" He hoped Jeff's reportorial instincts might encourage him to cooperate if he thought there was a story to be had.

"Would this have anything to do with that illegal-dumping story that's all over the paper this morning?"

"In a way," he said cautiously. "That was done without the knowledge or consent of the landowner. I just wondered what he might have in mind for that piece of property."

"Funny you should ask that." The shuffling of papers sounded through the phone. "You know how hush-hush the energy companies keep their negotiations, but I happen to have come across some inside dope on that. It looks as if the owner might be contracting with a company looking into horizontal drilling for natural gas."

"That surprises me. I wouldn't think Franklin Sitler would even consider that. He's always been so intent on keeping Deer Run the way it was when he was a boy."

"Money can change a lot of people's minds," Jeff said, his tone cynical. "Wait—did you say Franklin Sitler?"

"He's the owner."

"Not according to the report I got. The company is negotiating with one Dennis Sitler."

Colin leaned back, his mind working furiously. "Are you sure of that?"

"Positive. Why? What's up?" Jeff's tone sharpened.

"Not much, except that as far as I know, he doesn't own that land. His grandfather does."

"Maybe the grandfather turned it over to him to negotiate."

"Maybe." But he couldn't see Franklin turning his business over to anyone. "Thanks, Jeff."

"No problem. If there's a story in this, just remember where you heard it."

"I will." He hung up.

Money. Jeff was right about one thing—there was a lot of money involved in those energy leases. There was also a lot of controversy over the drilling's effect on the land and the surrounding area. Would Franklin Sitler embark on a project like that?

He didn't see any way that could connect with what Gene had been doing, but it was odd, all the same. He couldn't ignore it.

Colin shoved back his chair. There was one person who'd know the answer to this—Franklin Sitler himself. Maybe it was time to have a talk with him.

RACHEL CROSSED THE covered bridge, her footsteps echoing hollowly. With Mandy happily occupied at the farm, she might be able to get some much-needed work done. Probably the best thing for both of them would be to stay too busy to dwell on what had happened.

She passed the spot where Mandy had found the note, her footsteps slowing. With everything else that was going on, she'd hardly had time to think of it. Meredith would no doubt want to discuss it again. Their brief conversation wouldn't satisfy her.

How strange it was, that Mandy should find the hiding place they'd searched for all those years ago. Or rather, Princess had found it, apparently.

Had the contents of the note been true, or a malicious lie, designed to cause trouble between Aaron and Laura? Maybe Aaron had never even seen it, and it was totally irrelevant to his accident. She found herself hoping that had been the case. Aaron and Laura had had little enough time to enjoy being in love. She'd hate to think it had degenerated into anger and disappointment.

Like her marriage, beginning with such hope and ending in despair? She pushed that thought away and went up the back stairs to the house.

Mason House was quiet with Mandy and Princess over at the farm. She could take this opportunity to finish up the website questions Meredith had left for her.

In fact, she ought to tell Meredith to go ahead and make the website live. The electrician and the safety inspector were scheduled to come in the next week. If she intended to make a living from Mason House, it was time to take the plunge.

Coffee. She'd need a cup to keep her awake if she planned to get any work done. Too many bad images had crowded her mind last night to let her rest.

The note Mandy had found still lay on the countertop where they'd left it last night. Rachel couldn't stop herself from picking it up again. Who had written it? Someone who knew the hiding place, and that restricted the circle to those who were close to Aaron and Laura, probably. It seemed to her that the possibilities were limited.

The doorbell rang, its tone startling her. She headed to the front hall. If it was Chief Burkhalter with more questions…but she could see who it was through the wavy glass. Dennis Sitler.

Her heart wrenching with pity for him, Rachel dropped the note on the registration table and went quickly to open the door.

"Dennis. How are you?" He looked dreadful, and probably felt worse.

He came into the hall, shrugging. "It's been a ghastly twenty-four hours, hasn't it? I don't suppose any of us will get over what happened very quickly."

"No. I'm so sorry for…well, for your loss. How is your grandfather?"

Again the shrug. Dennis moved aimlessly across the wide hallway and leaned against the table. "Pretty broken up, as you can imagine. He couldn't believe it at first. He kept insisting it was all a mistake, until Chief Burkhalter confirmed what happened. I've been trying to get him to let the doctor take a look at him, but he won't." He grimaced. "You know how he is."

She nodded. Like Amanda Mason, Franklin wouldn't be one to give in to grief or admit he needed help.

"Do you think he'd want to talk to me about it?"

"It's good of you to offer, Rachel. I can imagine

you'd just like to forget the whole thing. Not right now, but maybe in a day or two. I'll let you know."

She nodded, not sure what else there was to say. She had no desire to go over the situation with Franklin, but if it would bring him some peace, she'd have no choice.

"He is thinking about you, though," Dennis said. "He wanted me to come over and make sure you and Mandy are all right."

"We're fine." Well, that wasn't true, but Dennis probably understood that. "Mandy is over at the farm, and that's keeping her distracted."

Dennis nodded. "I'm sure that's—" He stopped, every movement, every breath seeming frozen. He was staring at the note the way she might stare if she encountered a rattlesnake in the laundry.

But how could he know…? Of course. The realization gelled in her mind. Dennis would only know what that note was if he had written it.

"You wrote it, didn't you?" The words came out without volition.

He reached out to touch the paper gingerly. "Imagine this surfacing after all these years. I guess I might have known that if someone found it, it would be you."

His words were even, his emotions hidden.

"I wasn't looking for it. Mandy found it in the bridge." She hesitated. "You intended it for Aaron, obviously. Do you know if he ever saw it?"

He turned from the note to look at her. "Maybe

not, if it was still in their hiding place. I had good intentions, believe it or not. I knew he was going to get hurt when she broke up with him. And he did, obviously."

She stared at Dennis, puzzled. "I don't know what you mean."

"It's obvious, given what he did." When she still didn't react, he smiled. "Poor little Rachel, still idolizing Aaron? Didn't the three of you ever realize? Laura broke up with him, and he killed himself."

Everything in her rebelled at the words. Aaron wouldn't, surely. "I don't believe it."

Dennis tilted his head, seeming a little amused. "Don't you? It's true enough. Sorry if it clashes with your image of him."

She stared at the faint smile on Dennis's face, and suddenly she knew what it was that the shadowy figure in Lainey's drawing hid. Malice—that was it. He hadn't just watched. He had manipulated.

"Maybe it is best to forget it." She did her best to hide her revulsion. "There's no point in dragging up the past. We have enough trouble to deal with in the present."

"That's certainly true. My poor grandfather. It was rough on both of us to discover what Gene was really like. I suppose Grandfather will rely on me even more now."

She opened her lips to give the expected response, to say that Franklin was lucky to have him.

But instead she found she was listening to other voices, sounding in her mind.

Dennis didn't have any idea what his cousin was up to. He just joined the search for Mandy. Chief Burkhalter had said that, and Dennis had just affirmed it, saying he hadn't known what Gene was doing.

But she heard his voice last night, sounding through the rain and the truck motors and the terror. *What are you doing? Let those boys go....*

She shook her head slowly. Dennis had mentioned the boys. She knew it. But if he didn't know what Gene was up to, he couldn't have known the boys were there. None of them was in sight when he'd appeared—Benj was in the woods and the other two still in the cellar.

"What's wrong, Rachel?" Dennis moved away from the table. "You look as if you've seen a ghost." His voice was soft, his mask back in place...the polite, well-meaning friend.

But she knew better, and she knew, as well, that she was in danger.

"Nothing." She tried to force a smile. "I'm just so tired I'm not thinking straight."

"I'd like to believe that." Dennis sounded genuinely regretful. "But unfortunately you're not very good at lying. It must be that solid Amish virtue in you." He sighed, shaking his head, and his hand came out of his jacket pocket. It was holding a gun.

COLIN STOOD BEHIND the swinging door to the kitchen, trying to make out what was happening in the hallway. Maybe nothing, in which case he was going to look like a fool, sneaking in the back door of Rachel's house.

But when Franklin had told him that Dennis had gone to see Rachel, every alarm bell began to sound in his mind. For once he'd followed his instincts, and they'd led him here.

"What are you doing with that gun?" The fear in Rachel's voice told him his instincts had been right, and his fear escalated to match hers. But now what?

"Don't bother trying to lie, Rachel." Dennis sounded amused. "I can see the truth in your face. You know. How did you figure it out?"

"You said you didn't know anything about Gene's activities." Her voice had steadied, as if she'd drawn on some inner well of strength. "You said you'd only come to the barn because you joined the search for Mandy. But when you spoke to Gene, you said something about the boys. You couldn't have seen them. So you had to know already they were there."

"Such a little slip. No one else noticed."

Colin's thoughts worked feverishly. How far was Dennis from the doorway? Not too far, judging by his voice. Rachel had to be farther away. But was he close enough that Colin could reach him before he fired the gun?

"I suppose you found out about Gene's activities

and tried to stop him," Rachel said. "Why didn't you just call the police?"

Rachel was trying to keep Dennis talking, probably. Hoping someone would come. Well, he was here, but what action was safest for her? If he slipped out the back to call for help, Dennis might do something in his absence. He couldn't risk it.

"Rachel, Rachel. You're underestimating me, just as people always do." There was something in Dennis's voice that said he'd decided on his course of action. "I'm the one who put Gene in contact with the company that needed a place to dump unwanted waste. I knew Gene couldn't resist the chance to make a bundle of cash, even if it was illegal."

"But you didn't even like Gene. Why would you help him?"

He'd helped Gene only to expose him and get him kicked out, Colin thought. With Gene out of the way, Dennis would have a clear shot at managing the old man's affairs. Including the lucrative energy lease, and that timbering operation, which he'd bet Dennis had negotiated as well.

"Let's just say I thought I'd give Gene enough rope to hang himself where my grandfather is concerned. Unfortunately the situation turned more deadly than I expected, but that's totally his fault. He was the idiot with the gun. And I'm the tragic hero who killed his own cousin by accident, trying to protect the innocent."

Colin gave a frantic glance around the kitchen for

something he could use as a weapon, but there was nothing—no handy fireplace poker or baseball bat. He'd have to charge at Dennis and pray for the best.

"You did it deliberately." Rachel's voice shook.

"No. But unfortunately taking care of you will be deliberate. You've made that necessary." He must have moved, because Colin heard a step. "Just walk through to the kitchen quietly. I think it will be best if your accident takes place there."

Colin flattened himself against the wall behind the door. Dennis had given him a chance, and he couldn't mess it up. *Last chance.* The words echoed in his head.

The door swung toward him, and he held his breath. Rachel emerged into the kitchen. Colin could see Dennis's movement through the crack between door and wall. He was close behind her, too close, but there was no choice—

He slammed the door into Dennis. Barrel after it, grab him while he was off balance. Reach for the gun.

"Run, Rachel." He grappled, trying to gain control of the gun. Dennis clung to it, it could go off, just as the rifle had, he had to get it—

A sharp crack sounded. Dennis staggered. Colin lunged, the weight of his body carrying them both to the floor. He had to get the gun....

But it had already dropped from Dennis's lax hand. He lay crumpled, moaning. Colin looked up,

understanding. Rachel had hit him with the coffeepot.

"Call 911," he said, settling on top of Dennis, just
in case he wasn't as stunned as he seemed. "Do it."

Rachel, eyes wide in a white face, nodded. She
dropped the pot, splashing coffee everywhere, and
reached for the phone. Now, finally, it was over.

MANDY SNUGGLED next to Rachel as they finished
reading a chapter in *Little House in the Big Woods*
that evening. Rachel had thought she needed something soothing.

"Being Amish is sort of like the way Laura In-
galls and her family lived, isn't it?" Mandy asked,
referring to the character in the book.

"Sort of," Rachel said, not sure she wanted to
get into a discussion of Amish beliefs when Mandy
should be going to sleep. "Maybe that's why Amish
kids love the *Little House* books. I read all of them
when I was about your age."

Mandy nodded, her head against Rachel's shoulder. Was Mandy having a reaction to the horrors of
the past few days? This was one area of parenting
for which Rachel wasn't prepared.

"It must be fun to have lots of brothers and sisters, like you did."

That didn't sound traumatized. More like Mandy
was trolling for information.

"Usually it was fun," she said. "I know you don't
have any brothers or sisters, but you do have your

cousins, and your new friend, and your aunts and uncles and grandparents."

Mandy seemed to study the patches of her quilt. "I wouldn't have if we moved away again."

So that was what was worrying her. "We're not moving away. What gave you that idea?"

"I heard Colin and Benj talking, and Colin said he hoped you wouldn't be so upset you wanted to move away. So I thought maybe you were thinking about it."

She didn't want to look too closely at the comment about Colin. "I'm not." She squeezed Mandy's shoulders. "This is home, right? We're not going anywhere."

Mandy threw her arms around Rachel's neck in a throttling hug. "Good. I'm glad. I like being at home."

"Me, too, sweetheart." She dropped a kiss on Mandy's cheek. "Now I think it's time for sleep. If you're not tired, I am."

"Are you going to bed now?" Mandy slid down under the covers.

"As soon as I take Princess out one last time and clean up a bit. Good night. Sleep tight."

"Don't let the bedbugs bite." Mandy finished the silly rhyme. "See you in the morning."

Rachel blew her a kiss from the doorway and went back down the stairs. Sometimes she thought that Mandy was old enough to relax some of her bedtime rituals, but she still clung to them. And they were a comforting end to Rachel's day, as well.

She could stand a little comfort after this day. She stopped at the bottom of the stairs, for an instant seeing Dennis's face as he stood there, taking the gun from his pocket, still looking like the ordinary, pleasant man everyone thought he was.

At least she could remind herself that she wasn't the only person he'd fooled.

A knock at the door sent her whirling around, heart thudding until it seemed it would jump out of her chest. When Colin opened the door and stepped inside, her heart slipped into a different rhythm altogether.

"This door should be locked." He frowned at her and then flipped the dead bolt.

"I know. I was just going to check it. I guess with all the people in and out this afternoon, it was left open." She couldn't prevent a small shiver at the memory of all the police officers tramping through her house, while the portrait of Amanda Mason looked on disapprovingly.

"I stopped by because I thought you might want to know what's going on with Dennis."

"He's still in jail, isn't he?" Her voice went up despite her best efforts to control it.

"He is. You don't need to worry about that." Colin moved closer, close enough that she could see the lines around his eyes that she didn't think had been there before. "He's never going to be able to threaten you again."

"You look exhausted." She touched his arm lightly, and then drew her hand away. She wouldn't want him to think she expected…well, anything. "Let's go back in the family room to talk."

He nodded, following her. "The scene of our battle giving you the creeps, is it?"

Rachel was relieved that he could speak so lightly, and she tried to respond the same way. "If you can call it a battle when one side isn't armed and the other one is."

"What do you mean, not armed?" He gave her a faint shadow of his old, mocking smile. "You had your trusty coffeepot."

"I think I might have to get a new one." She gestured him to the sofa and took the rocking chair, not sure it was a good idea to sit down next to him. She was too aware of his every movement, every breath right now.

"What's going to happen to Dennis?" She'd better know everything, since she'd committed to staying here, whatever happened. "I suppose he's denying everything."

"Actually, he's gotten an attorney and is not saying a word right now." Colin's frown sent creases between his eyebrows. "I'm not sure whether they'll be able to charge him with anything in relation to Gene's death or not. We might feel it wasn't an accident, but that could be hard to prove. Still, I don't see how he'll get out of his complicity with Gene in the dumping operation. Or with signing contracts with an energy company saying he had his grandfather's power of attorney."

"He actually did that?" It was hard to believe Dennis thought he could get away with tricking that fierce old man.

"He did." His frown deepened. "He may have thought that when Gene's actions came out, Franklin would be so upset he'd turn to Dennis to deal with everything."

She nodded, remembering Dennis's words. "He did imply something like that. Do you think Franklin will go through with this drilling operation?"

"Not a chance," Colin said promptly. "I happened to be present when someone suggested that to Franklin, and he blew his stack. Wherever they're going to be drilling for natural gas, it won't be right above Deer Run if he has anything to say about it."

"That's a relief. I don't think it would help my business any."

Colin focused on her face, and she suspected they'd reached the heart of what they'd been talking around. "You're staying, then?"

"We're staying," she said. Even if nothing was meant to develop with Colin, this place was still home.

"I'm glad." His gaze held hers, so intense that her breath caught in her throat.

She was the first to look away. "I wondered why Amanda left the house to me, given how she felt, but I think I understand now. In the end, what counts is family."

"Yes." A shadow crossed Colin's face, and she knew he was thinking about his parents.

"Poor Franklin. All of his family is gone now, in a way." She'd always thought him lonely. How much worse must it be now?

"Maybe it would have been better if he'd never had to know the truth about his grandsons," Colin said.

She considered that, weighing her own marriage to Ronnie, thinking of the tragic end to Aaron and Laura's love. "No," she said at last. "No matter what, the truth is always best, even if it hurts."

Colin seemed about to speak but he hesitated, making her wonder. Was he going to tell her some truth she'd rather not hear?

"I haven't thanked you yet," she said, giving him time. "For what you did today. If you hadn't tackled Dennis—"

"You'd probably have knocked him out with the coffeepot anyway," he said quickly, turning aside her gratitude. "But I'm glad I could help."

The words seemed needlessly formal. Was he setting up the boundaries between them again?

"You saved my life," she said, leaning toward him. The rocking chair tipped forward, making their knees touch. They were so close she could see every fine line around his eyes, every tiny muscle that twitched near his lips, even the pulse that throbbed at his temples. "At least let me thank you for that, even if you don't want…" She stopped, realizing that she was stumbling into dangerous territory.

"If I don't want what?" His voice was a low rumble, and he grasped her hands in his.

She'd said she'd rather have the truth. That meant she should speak it, as well. "If you don't want... well, anything closer between us."

His fingers tightened on hers so that she seemed to feel their pulses pounding together. "That's just what I do want. But our lives are so complicated, yours with your daughter, mine with my father...." He let his thought fade out, and suddenly his eyes were dancing with the laughter she remembered. "Does that sound as stupid as I think it does?"

Her heart lightened, as if something heavy had suddenly been lifted. "Yes. It does. Burdens shared are burdens halved. That's what my *grossmammi* always said."

"Rachel." He said her name softly. Then he lifted her from the rocker so that she slipped over onto his lap. His arms closed around her, and he pressed his face into the curve of her neck. "I love you. I think I've loved you since the first time I kissed you, all those years ago. But is love going to be enough?"

She put her arms around his shoulders, holding him close, the touch sending her senses into overdrive. She knew the answer to that question, didn't she?

"It's not just enough." She touched his face, her heart full. "It's the only thing."

* * * * *

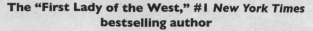

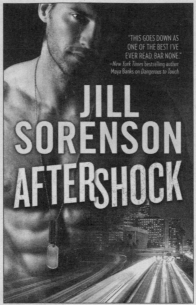

**Two timeless tales of romantic suspense
from award-winning and *New York Times* and
USA TODAY bestselling author**

LINDA HOWARD

The Cutting Edge

Brett Rutland is a bull. As the top troubleshooter at Carter Engineering, he's used to getting his way. When he's tasked with cracking an internal embezzlement case, he meets firm accountant Tessa Conway. She's beautiful and interested, but falling for her will not only test Brett's control, it may also jeopardize the case—especially since she's the prime suspect.

White Lies

Jay Granger is shocked when the FBI shows up on her doorstep, saying her ex-husband has been in a terrible accident. She keeps a bedside vigil, but when Steve Crossfield awakes from his coma, he is nothing like the man Jay married. Ironically, she finds herself more drawn to him than ever. She can't help but wonder who this man really is, and whether the revelation of his true identity will shatter their newly discovered passion.

Available wherever books are sold!

REQUEST YOUR FREE BOOKS!

2 FREE NOVELS
FROM THE SUSPENSE COLLECTION
PLUS 2 FREE GIFTS!

YES! Please send me 2 FREE novels from the Suspense Collection and my 2 FREE gifts (gifts are worth about $10). After receiving them, if I don't wish to receive any more books, I can return the shipping statement marked "cancel." If I don't cancel, I will receive 4 brand-new novels every month and be billed just $5.99 per book in the U.S. or $6.49 per book in Canada. That's a savings of at least 25% off the cover price. It's quite a bargain! Shipping and handling is just 50¢ per book in the U.S. and 75¢ per book in Canada.* I understand that accepting the 2 free books and gifts places me under no obligation to buy anything. I can always return a shipment and cancel at any time. Even if I never buy another book, the two free books and gifts are mine to keep forever.

191/391 MDN FVVK

Name	(PLEASE PRINT)

Address	Apt. #

City	State/Prov.	Zip/Postal Code

Signature (if under 18, a parent or guardian must sign)

Mail to the **Harlequin®** Reader Service:
IN U.S.A.: P.O. Box 1867, Buffalo, NY 14240-1867
IN CANADA: P.O. Box 609, Fort Erie, Ontario L2A 5X3

Want to try two free books from another line?
Call 1-800-873-8635 or visit www.ReaderService.com.

* Terms and prices subject to change without notice. Prices do not include applicable taxes. Sales tax applicable in N.Y. Canadian residents will be charged applicable taxes. Offer not valid in Quebec. This offer is limited to one order per household. Not valid for current subscribers to the Suspense Collection or the Romance/Suspense Collection. All orders subject to credit approval. Credit or debit balances in a customer's account(s) may be offset by any other outstanding balance owed by or to the customer. Please allow 4 to 6 weeks for delivery. Offer available while quantities last.

Your Privacy—The Harlequin® Reader Service is committed to protecting your privacy. Our Privacy Policy is available online at www.ReaderService.com or upon request from the Harlequin Reader Service.

We make a portion of our mailing list available to reputable third parties that offer products we believe may interest you. If you prefer that we not exchange your name with third parties, or if you wish to clarify or modify your communication preferences, please visit us at www.ReaderService.com/consumerchoice or write to us at Harlequin Reader Service Preference Service, P.O. Box 9062, Buffalo, NY 14269. Include your complete name and address.